PLOUGHSHARES

Winter 1994–95 · Vol. 20, No. 4

EXECUTIVE DIRECTOR
DeWitt Henry

EDITOR
Don Lee

POETRY EDITOR
David Daniel

ASSOCIATE EDITOR
Jessica Dineen

EDITORIAL ASSISTANT
Jodee Stanley

FOUNDING PUBLISHER
Peter O'Malley

ADVISORY EDITORS

Russell Banks
Anne Bernays
Frank Bidart
Rosellen Brown
James Carroll
Madeline DeFrees
Rita Dove
Andre Dubus
Carolyn Forché
George Garrett
Lorrie Goldensohn
David Gullette
Marilyn Hacker
Donald Hall
Paul Hannigan
Stratis Haviaras
Fanny Howe

Marie Howe
Justin Kaplan
Bill Knott
Maxine Kumin
Philip Levine
Thomas Lux
Gail Mazur
James Alan McPherson
Leonard Michaels
Sue Miller
Jay Neugeboren
Tim O'Brien
Joyce Peseroff
Jayne Anne Phillips
Robert Pinsky
James Randall
Alberto Alvaro Ríos

M. L. Rosenthal
Lloyd Schwartz
Jane Shore
Charles Simic
Maura Stanton
Gerald Stern
Christopher Tilghman
Richard Tillinghast
Chase Twichell
Fred Viebahn
Ellen Bryant Voigt
Dan Wakefield
Derek Walcott
James Welch
Alan Williamson
Tobias Wolff
Al Young

PLOUGHSHARES, a journal of new writing, is guest-edited serially by prominent writers who explore different and personal visions, aesthetics, and literary circles. PLOUGHSHARES is published in April, August, and December at Emerson College, 100 Beacon Street, Boston, MA 02116-1596. Telephone: (617) 578-8753. Phone-a-Poem: (617) 578-8754.

STAFF ASSISTANTS: Brijit Brown and Matt Jones. FICTION READERS: Billie Lydia Porter, Esther Crain, Michael Rainho, Maryanne O'Hara, Lee Harrington, Karen Wise, Elizabeth Rourke, Stephanie Booth, Jodee Stanley, David Rowell, Barbara Lewis, Phillip Carson, Holly LeCraw Howe, Christine Flanagan, Sara Nielsen Gambrill, Kim Reynolds, Kevin Supples, and Joseph Connolly. POETRY READERS: Bethany Daniel, Jason Rogers, Mary-Margaret Mulligan, Rachel Piccione, Renee Rooks, Tanja Brull, Susan Rich, Tom Laughlin, Karen Voelker, Leslie Haynes, and Rebecca Lavine. PHONE-A-POEM COORDINATOR: Joyce Peseroff.

SUBSCRIPTIONS (ISSN 0048-4474): $19/domestic and $24/international for individuals; $22/domestic and $27/international for institutions. See last page for order form.

UPCOMING: Spring 1995, Vol. 21, No. 1, a fiction and poetry issue edited by Gary Soto, will appear in April 1995. Fall 1995, Vol. 21, Nos. 2&3, a fiction issue edited by Ann Beattie, will appear in August 1995. Winter 1995-96, Vol. 21, No. 4, a fiction and poetry issue edited by Tim O'Brien and Mark Strand, will appear in December 1995.

SUBMISSIONS: Please see back of issue for detailed submission policies.

BACK ISSUES are available from the publisher. Write or call for abstracts and a price list. Microfilms of back issues may be obtained from University Microfilms. PLOUGHSHARES is also available as a full-text product from EBSCO, H.W. Wilson, Information Access, and UMI. INDEXED in M.L.A. Bibliography, American Humanities Index, Index of American Periodical Verse, Book Review Index. Self-index through Volume 6 available from the publisher; annual supplements appear in the fourth number of each subsequent volume. All rights for individual works revert to the authors upon publication.

DISTRIBUTED by Bernhard DeBoer (113 E. Centre St., Nutley, NJ 07110), Fine Print Distributors (500 Pampa Dr., Austin, TX 78752), Ingram Periodicals (1226 Heil Quaker Blvd., La Vergne, TN 37086), and L-S Distributors (436 North Canal St. #7, South San Francisco, CA 94080). PRINTED in the United States of America on recycled paper by Edwards Brothers.

CONTENTS

Winter 1994–95

DON LEE & DAVID DANIEL

Introduction

This issue marks a transition for *Ploughshares*—a small but not insignificant change in editorial policy, one of several that have occurred over twenty-three years of publication.

Originally, *Ploughshares* was edited by a committee of writers who had founded the journal: Harvard graduate students, Irish expatriates, Iowa Workshop refugees, New York School and Bowery veterans, and experimental Black Mountain poets. Predictably, reaching a consensus proved difficult, and the editors eventually agreed to adopt a rotation, with each taking a turn at the helm for an issue. Later, prominent writers outside of the founding circle were invited to serve as guest editors of *Ploughshares,* and these guest editors were then encouraged to structure their issues around explicit themes, topics, or aesthetics—a policy that has been extant for the last five years.

Without question, focusing on different themes, trying to lend some coherence to the work selected for an issue, has made *Ploughshares* a more interesting reading experience. But it has also encumbered the submissions process for writers and editors alike. A wonderful story or poem might arrive, but not be appropriate for the next few issues. Or, even if a piece is thematically relevant, questions about balancing the contents of an issue might come into play—subject, style, tone, gender, diversity. Consequently, we always have a surplus of good work at the end of the year—material we love, but are unable to publish for one reason or another—and the process sometimes breaks everyone's heart.

We knew the focus of the Spring and Fall 1994 issues—the first concentrating on tribes, the second featuring personal essays—would exclude the majority of submissions during our most recent reading period, so we decided to close out the year with this open, staff-edited issue. We established a theme of not having a theme, not being bound by any organizing principle or political agenda other than our judgments of literary quality. We just took the best poems and stories that we received.

This is, we've concluded, the way *Ploughshares* should proceed (although we cannot rule out the occasional exception). We will still appoint guest editors, and no doubt they will unconsciously thread together a motif of some kind. That is, after all, what makes having guest editors appealing—learning about their personal visions and obsessions. But we'll let these motifs evolve on their own, without any preconceptions. Only after the final selection for an issue has been made will we attach a theme, or merely a generic title. In the end, our regular readers will probably not notice a difference. But writers will. No longer asked to conform to announced themes, the door will be open a little wider for those who wish to submit their work to us. And for us, as editors, the process will be more inviting as well. We will simply look forward to what comes in.

*This issue is dedicated to all of our manuscript
readers, past and present. Thanks also
to David Rivard for his assistance
and guidance in selecting
the poems in this issue.*

ALLY ACKER

White Noise at Midnight

They all want me to stop talking to you.
My mother with the face of a television
blaring answers to the game no one ever guesses—
Bill Holden and Deborah Kerr in Bombay making nookie
on the graves. The wind cawing senseless to the Blue Moon.

Even you are tired of my chatter— Smart girl
your ears stuffed with happiness,
lying with your incest victim a year now
you haven't sent me word as you promised, my darling
of second chances.

In the light graves the sheets are so clean.
I gather them up and sheath their silk
for bandages. When the armies arrive, Deborah
and Bill and I all lie and spread
for them. The way you like me: stupid and silent.

We want to please them. We want every
thing absorbed—the liquids taken in like a sponge.
No messes. No white horses running wild at midnight.
Nothing fecund left to the brown fields. The blue

herons lift—their wings wild with applause. The moon turns
creamy. Everyone gets excited. There is nothing to do.
I cannot stop talking to you.

Departure

Thousands of tiny
fists tamping the surface of the lake
flowing like a wide
river gone crazy, southeast, westnorth
letting the wind push
it around in its bed and the boat
hull hugging the shore.
What else can she do? Even the trees
agree, shaking
their crowns, throwing down their leaves as if
she were their only
child. Caught cold-footed in Magnuson
grass, trying to cut
free of the creosote-soaked pilings sunk
deep in the shallow
mud holding the water, holding her
wake for a moment,
furrow folding back over into
confusion. Cascade
gray crosscurrents! Sharp switching eddies!
Unreliable
shoals! Let the cloth argue with itself,
gasping like a child
with the air knocked out and the wind
socking the center.
Let the sail, shot-silk green and white, now
snapping, billowing
slowly draw her away from this beach
marked with broken glass, rocks
as smooth as plovers' eggs, and small

stones splashed iron red
and orange like the sky breaking open.
Let the windows ignite
flickering copper on the other side.
Let the water be
disked with silver from here to there
churning as if roiled
by the flanks of a great, gentle fish.

Armistice

Not far from San Diego

steel ship containers packed with jeeps sit unopened

and someone I know very well
stands on the boulevard, surrounded by the pink
and white stucco walls
outside my window

suspended in this moment between breathing out and
    breathing in

the men and women at Camp Pendleton relax their arms
and listen

to the high tide covering the frayed and jagged edges
disappearing

off the docks, overwhelmed
by waves breaking on the girders, pushing
from the shore into the sea

the street dog trembles for the clear
water in the coffee can

the pigeon's up-bent wings embrace another gust

horses race across the field
legs wrapped in blurs of red, blue, yellow, kelly green

just back from overseas, my love
takes off his olive coat
unclips the holster strap

slips it off
and rests his lovely hands on his hips

fuchsia, hibiscus, bougainvillea, lantana, guava,
mango, bird of paradise

the footsteps on the stairs

dear welcome voice!
dear God, the graceful angles of your face unchanged!

listen

to the sea dissolving into the sky
at the horizon, mist curving
into the lath-moon bay, arced walls
of water encircling the city and its ships.

Where the Long, Lazy Mothers Stroll

with their children running ahead, the shore
is as messy as any other grassy edge
where birds nest, rock spotted,
blotched by gulls, geese, and gadwalls.

Into the flocks, unexpected
outburst of a hundred startled teal,
wingtips all together, thrumming the air
this close! Almost to touch. Wet sand

slopped by my daughter's small hands fast enough
to streak pastel corduroy dark dun.
Into the roll of waves yanked out
to sea by the eggshell china saucer

moon rising in full day. Into the rasp
of branches blurred by shawls of falling
petals. Into the barely perceptible lapping
of the feral cat drinking muddy water

from the run-off ditch, in that moment
just before dusk when everything
quiets—my daughter
seems small, still in sight—I could race to her—

I could yell—at this moment—
mine is the sloth of the hawk
steady in the cottonwood while crows drive
their beaks through the air as close

to my eyes as the wind. Mine is the torpor
of old travelers who have seen shores like this
in Nantes, Rio, Zanzibar, New York. Mine
is the languor of the young who believe even

the eldest can always go back home. Mine
is the lethargy of faith. I remember following
my own mother's journeys on my grandmother's
pre-war porcelain globe that glowed slightly yellow

with the light of its old twenty-watt bulb shining
through the countries, still brightly colored,
red, yellow, green. Can you believe it? After
all these years. I remember reaching up to touch

the glass sphere high on the shelf, following my
mother's flights one day, boats the next, tracing my
mother with my hands as if I were blind,
as if I were still a child, studying my mother's

face with my fingertips, and my mother, without
being asked, stood still for a moment, just for a moment.

Gertrude's Ear

A sow rooting around in a
garden uncovered a silk purse.

"Oh Good Heavens!" she
squealed in horror. "That's
Gertrude's ear!"

Another sow trotted over,
and stared at the soiled object.

"No, no," she concluded,
with a relieved snuffle. "That
can't be Gertie's ear. Gertie's
ear didn't have a clasp."

*Moral: We are sometimes right
in spite of ourselves.*

A Dry Wake for Ex

Mummified by gauzy July heat, my escape
into the library's neutral cool brings me to
the dog-eared, thumbed-through news:
"His failure was his greatest success,"
says "Milestones" in *Time* magazine:
"Died—Frederick Exley."

And then this prick of a hurt born of
the aforementioned fact, and I feel it: Brain-
muddled, maybe, but still functional—pulse flushes
my skin's pigment, damp T-shirt chill to my back.

My tonic of choice? Rationality—with a splash of
discernment. I consult the text. *I lighted a cigarette,*
Exley, the author, wrote more then once, a touchstone
or coda for the testimony he adumbrated, memory
harnessed by the rigor of a syntax he primed
with the sacramental octane of nicotine and booze.
Meanwhile, he perched his narrator on a rickety, jury-
rigged scaffolding: *Frederick Exley,* the character
he suffered as purgative for his purpose:
the practice of a logy sort of art.

He proffered, did Exley, a blurring of genre—
fact and fiction, epic and lyric—your *greatest*
success your *failure,* Frederick, *me lurverly*
lurve. Such excess, and unendurable, finally.
But writ large, how those myth etceteras' spasms
cast an antic sort of shadow play. And upon
such a chthonic movie screen: that vegetable glass
of old Billy Blake, still on time, Ex,
                    still right up to date.

So what have we here, Ex, divined from the rubric
of this obit? I say it's all about attitude. I say give it
a gap-toothed *what the fuck* and go another round.
Once again, may the auctorial match pop and spark
the flame's surge, almost leap off the tip, but catch
hold of the old-fashioned stick and get on with
the business of burning. No two-faced magazine,
no *Time* between us and the library's artifactual calm,
mute runes along book spines, all tomes shelved,
catalogued, accounted for. This is all aswim in my
mind's eye: a vision-humid mull of querulous vintage.
I'll settle for it, allow it "dominion."

So place flame to cigarette. Lungs pull another puff;
the tobacco blooms; embers seethe. Lo and behold,
Ex, how the smoke doth weave a cursive spell:
Dentures gape in a highball of Old Grandad, as
the bourbon, perversely latent, collects those
sunset rays and spangles them a darker sort of gold.
Encaged by milk-white ribs on memory's hard-
scrabble, pock-marked plane, comedy forecloses
on the tragic: father and son still having it out,
still letting it rip—the adored, loathed,
and the loathed, adored: Hero and fool, surrogate.

Above them both and their grappling, Possibility—
that blowsy, titular goddess, and frightful with whom
to parley—she warbles the soundtrack of the scene.
She's as drunk as a lord and as blind as a mirror.
What a flirt: still tickling the edges, still blurring
the borders. That two-faced siren, she coos her
too-sweet syrup, her double-sided mantra:
    What might be... What might have been...

The Oysters

Pat Boone—not *the* Pat Boone but only a graduate student in Agricultural Science—was driving the oysters down to Mulberry to have them irradiated. He was used to being the wrong Pat Boone but was nevertheless miserable, careening down Interstate 75 in the windless predawn, gripping the wheel of the Food Science van with his troubled pink fingers. He thought he might have a fever; he kept sneezing and his own freckles kept getting in his eyes like gnats, reflecting off his pale face and blinding him. He whizzed past lit signs and enticements, antic neon-red coffee cups with legs flashing on and off, simulating dancing, and bold messages in balloons above them urging him to WAKE UP. He was awake but dreaming, dreaming of Maura Malone. He saw bits of her—breast, hand, thigh—but none were what he wanted, or, wanting them, he only wanted more. To be awake at this hour was to be unable to see Maura's marriage as hypothetical.

Keep your mind on the oysters, he told himself. He had two, almost three degrees. He believed the unknown was simply a subset of the known; he expected, logically, the unexpected. The oysters were packed in dry ice in ten bushel cartons, sitting like obedient campers on the long van seats behind him, the first live food items ever to be irradiated. The preservation process was new, not yet commercialized, and on local news programs almost nightly, angry college students and young mothers could be seen protesting, mildly scornful doctors and scientists rebutting. Month-old irradiated strawberries that looked and tasted fresh had just arrived on the market; grocery shoppers were videotaped sampling and appraising them. Farmers both excited and skeptical were shown standing in their groves, making thrilling and dire predictions about their industry. The oysters were the biggest story yet; as a representative of his department, Pat would be a part of history. He had twice been interviewed on the evening news, and *The Tampa Tribune* woman was going to meet him at the plant in Mulberry. In twenty-four hours, people up and down the Florida coast would begin commenting to one another over their English muffins about his funny name.

But Maura, Maura slept beside her husband even now: her large, tropical husband with his flourishing mustache, not the kind you hid behind but the kind you cultivated with cheerful, automatic faith, the way you would plant a vegetable garden or have children. Pat had met the man at bars and buffet tables many times and found him unbearable. "I'm Trinidadian," he'd told Pat once, "and we sing when we talk." The Trinidadian's smile was so open and precious that it made a small sound, breaking out upon his large, honest face. Pat shook the sound out of his head and drove sneezing and invisible down the dark and empty highway.

In a recent *Food Science Newsletter* feature story, Maura had claimed to have known within twenty minutes of meeting the Trinidadian that he was "the one." The photo showed her standing glamorously beside the Gammacell 220 as though it were a sewing machine she was about to demonstrate. She wore her white coat and held a pint of strawberries she was preparing to feed into the irradiator, the hard fluorescent lab lights making her sleek, tightly bound-up hair appear glossy and beautiful. "Professor Malone operates our own modest machine," the caption read.

Pat clenched the vibrating steering wheel with both hands as though it alone could save him. *He* had known within twenty minutes of entering Maura's classroom that *she* was the one. In a year he had thought this a thousand times, and had even known enough not to say it aloud, known that not saying it was the way to sustain it. And surely the eerie, thrilling consummation of his feelings, her finally humming in the familiar hiss of his shower or standing at his range scrambling eggs as casually as a ghost— surely these things were proof of their love's inevitability. He had *known* it. Her words in the interview caused him a shocking, embarrassing kind of pain, as though someone had without warning ripped a Band-Aid off his heart. He could not bear to think of the Trinidadian sashaying around so happily unconscious, the way he himself must have looked before he met her. He could not even remember what he'd spent time thinking about before he met her. His own mind, his own heart, before Maura, were lost to him.

He tried as a game to imagine the oysters as cheerful children in his charge, giddy prodigies eager to take part in such a significant experiment, but this was just fantasy and he couldn't sustain it. Instead, he recalled something he hadn't thought about in years, a childhood vacation on Sanibel Island which he and his brothers had spent feverishly collecting the best whelks and scallops and periwinkles, the rare ones with the live creatures still in them. They took dozens back to their room at the Jolly Roger each afternoon to be boiled on the hot plate, never tiring of watching the mysterious blobs spreading out over the bottom of the pot, the strange sightless animals surrendering in their rubbery, milky puddles. The sexy, velvety smell of the mineral oil they'd used to polish the empty shells came back to him, carrying with it a surge of the old wonder, the nameless thrill of boiling the sea creatures.

But the oysters behind him now were cold and silent and clamped shut, hiding their secrets. His life seemed small and doomed and embarrassing, and the loop of time between his days at the Jolly Roger and the present seemed like someone's, maybe Maura's, idea of a good joke. How Maura could be responsible for the sad loop of his life, he could not explain.

I am not invisible, he told himself, his eyes blurring. *I exist.* He wanted to state these things out loud to someone, someone in a position of authority, but he had only himself to address.

Ebb and flow, stir and settle, bubble and curl. This was what the oysters knew. But now they sensed a change. Something was happening. Of course, they had known everything that would ever happen to them from the moment they had come into existence, from even before they had existed, but they had certainly not bargained for this. Excitement was in the air. A new element hissed around them like a predator. Beneath them rumbled more than the usual uncomfortable earth. They stirred thickly in their shells, uncertain.

The month-old strawberries, for their part, resented that they were not considered to be "live." They understood, in their pungent, opaque way, that life was romance. They had played an important part in more than one courtship. Around them almost always the air harbored human hopes and celebration, or at least appreciation. They knew enjoyment. They knew ceremony. If they were not "live," what was? A machine had once been invented to measure their cries when they were bitten into. Another machine recorded and amplified the sounds of insects eating their way through the strawberries' viscera. Men had gotten rich off these machines, but where were these men now? Strawberries everywhere felt important and, now, cheated.

Pat pulled into the plant's back lot and rolled down a window to clear, expectant tropical air. The sky was yellowing up for morning, and the swampy, froggy smell of north Florida seemed far away. He backed the van up to the loading dock, thinking of Maura's Indian ringneck parakeet, who imitated the backing-up beep of her neighborhood's garbage truck. The bird was retarded, Maura said; all it did was yell nonsense words and sing over and over what it had learned of "Yankee Doodle Dandy": "I'm a doo." Sometimes when the Trinidadian was out, Maura phoned and Pat could hear the bird exclaiming in the background as though it were desperate to speak to him. Once, lying unclothed in Pat's bed, holding him, Maura had told him she loved his apartment because it was as quiet as a graveyard. "Oh, thanks," he said.

"No," she said, "it's wonderful here. You're completely unencumbered."

He remembered watching her get dressed that day, feeling too moody to get up himself and see her out, but the moodiness had seemed only like love, a particularly strong swoon. She kissed him, already wearing her dark sunglasses, and said again, "I wish *I* had a place like this," and then darted out to her minivan and backed out of his driveway using only her rearview mirror, not even turning her head. He remembered watching this from the window over his bed, not wanting to remove himself from the wanton crumble of sheets.

Keep your mind on the oysters! he told himself furiously.

He unloaded all ten cartons by himself, as no one appeared to greet him. Each weighed fifty pounds, and when he was finished, his heart pounded with resentful diligence. If Betsy Murphy had come along, she could have helped. She was a girl in Human Nutrition whose short, strong body he'd often appraised, but he could never quite find time for her. Always Maura was there, surprising him, phoning at odd hours, blocking out more solid individuals. He stood by the locked warehouse doors, puffing in what he pictured as a cloud of his own foolishness.

A bald man in a blue jumpsuit finally threw the doors open and shook Pat's hand in both of his, apologizing steadily for being late. "You're the guest of honor," he told Pat. Pat began to feel better. Together they hoisted the wax-sealed bushels onto dollies and began wheeling them inside. "You must be tired," the man said.

"I'm all right," Pat said. The plant was only weeks old, and the corridor's whitewashed cinder-block walls gleamed with promise on either side of him.

"We'll just get these babies into the holding room, and then get some coffee," the man said.

"Are you Dr. Roland?" Pat said, remembering his instructions.

The man laughed loudly, throwing back his head. "Oh, no, no," he said. "I'm no one."

The oysters furrowed and trembled, wondering. They felt themselves being moved closer to the source, but the source seemed unusual, unfamiliar. This was not the source they remembered. It was not in the oysters' nature to be suspicious, but their milky flesh curled a little. They waited, curling and subsiding. Waiting was the same as existing, for them.

The man who had invented the machine that measured the screams of fruits and vegetables was tired of waiting. He was tired of getting up every day and drinking coffee out of the same cup and waiting for purpose to come back into his life. No one had cared about his machine for years. No one cared if a tree cried when you cut it. This was the kind of thing people had cared about in the seventies. In the seventies, the man had lived in a wood-frame house that sat jauntily on stilts at the edge of the Gulf of Mexico like some happy mantis sunning itself on the beach. His smart, young wife had cooked him simple, whimsical foods, grits with wacky garnishes, while he worked on his important machines. His baby daughter, Deenie, crawled around as if motorized, her strange cries filling the airy rooms with promise and egging him on to new inventions, finer tunings. Clouds flew by overhead, hurrying to their satisfying consummations.

When had it all evaporated? It was impossible to trace. The house had long ago blown down in a brief, peevish storm too small to have been given a name. He lived now in a dusty, buggy walk-up with his daughter, who was now a fat nurse, while his wife studied the classics in some stifling, snowbound state up north. Deenie, who could not seem to get a promotion or a boyfriend, came home from the hospital late each night and sat through one silent, reproachful beer with her father before going to bed. He stayed up later, letting the TV's false light harass his eyes, wondering what was now expected of him. Was he just supposed to sit here, waiting for people to care again, or was his purpose something else? The days rolled by, paying him no attention.

The man who had invented the machine that recorded and amplified the sounds of insects eating the insides of fruits and vegetables rode his stationary bicycle and whistled a happy tune. Agricultural and Food Science departments at universities all over the country were clamoring for his machine, and large corporations had fought one another for purchasing rights to the patent. They had paid for his stationary bike, his limestone patio, his wife's pony, his son's all-terrain vehicle, and some necessary roof repairs on the house. He puffed confidently away on his bicycle, watching through clean glass doors the steam rising off his lawn. Because of his invention, the sky would not fall on him or his family. He rarely thought of his old graduate school colleague, the man who had invented the machine that measured the screams of fruits and vegetables. That story was too sad. His own story had also been one of grief and long struggle, actually, but now that he was a success, no one wanted to hear it. He was expected to shut up and be grateful, and that was what he did.

Dr. Roland was demonstrating for Pat the plywood turntable on which the oysters would ride during their irradiation. He caressed the plywood with absent, tobacco-stained fingers, gazing up at Pat with a salesman's pride and determination. "You'll want to keep an eye on those lids," he told Pat, "but otherwise feel free to circulate during the dosing."

The wax lids on the cartons would gradually yellow as they absorbed the radiation, but there would be no other visible change. A makeshift-looking motor was rigged up under the plywood to spin it, like some child's science project. The oysters, though an important part of history, did not, Pat had learned, merit treatment by the plant's showy and immense automated system. This little approximation, which might as well be a homemade microwave, was going to do the job. Pat tried not to show his disappointment. Other than its larger capacity, it was no more impressive than the Gammacell back in Gainesville. What did they think he was, a Boy Scout? He scribbled figures on his pad, the minutes it would take to dose a carton with x kilograys, the total minutes he would have to keep watch. Dr. Roland stood by with neutral respect, keeping a hand on his machine. "This is quite a load of shells to haul," he said to Pat. "You order them special?"

"Nope," Pat said. "Just garden-variety Apalachicola oysters."

"Oh yes, and your reporter is here," Dr. Roland said. "She's out in the reception area whenever you're ready."

Maura was waking up now beside the Trinidadian; perhaps he sang when he awoke. A weak, sick terror took hold of Pat: What if Maura planned to visit some other student today, someone she had managed to keep secret this whole time? Then he thought of her running her hand through his own thin hair so kindly, so easily—it was impossible. It was impossible that she not love him. "Your body is perfect," she had told him. "Your body has nothing to do with reality."

"If you're wondering about safety," Dr. Roland was saying, "as well you might, let me assure you there is no cause for concern. As you'll see when you take the complete tour, there's a significantly thick concrete wall between us and the source. I just thought we'd best get started right away with these little devils in case there's a hitch. Plenty of time later to go exploring."

"Right," Pat said. He blinked and stamped his feet. "Let's go. Let's load them on."

Silent men in jumpsuits moved at Dr. Roland's command to lift the oysters onto the machine. There was nothing left for Pat to do but watch.

The insects who ate their way through fruits and vegetables did not waste time worrying about what would become of them. They knew they were romanticized by no one, and they lived accordingly, hurling themselves with abandon at mouths and ears, TV screens and light bulbs, suns and caves. If they died, they died. On the wheel of samsara, they had no place to go but up. Life for them held no shame, mystery, or promise, and they did not care who spied or recorded them going about the business of it.

Whatever it was, it was beginning to happen. The sun itself seemed to be rotating. Each oyster sat deep in its own mystery, waiting for the shock. The shock was moments away, already sending waves back in time at them, though the waves were impossible to interpret. The air around the oysters was like music. Ordered currents began to flow. The new earth beneath them began to turn. And then the light cracked into them, and the question mark that was the world snapped itself out straight, dividing them from mystery forever.

"Back in Gainesville," Pat told the reporter, "I'd have to orient each oyster individually. Here we have the advantage of dosing whole bushels at a time. We can study both shelf life and microbiology in one experiment."

The reporter peered at him through grass-green contact lenses, her breath smelling strongly of buttered toast. "How will you be able to tell if the oysters are dead?" she asked.

"We know they won't be dead," he said impatiently.

"But just hypothetically," she said, grinning.

He didn't see the joke, but he explained to her that any looseness in the shell was an indicator. There could be no slippage between the halves, none.

"Wow," she said.

He glanced over her shoulder at a carpeted vestibule in which was set up a courtesy telephone for guests of the plant. The phone had drawn his eyes throughout the interview, like a bomb or an unlocked safe. It shone blackly on a small table on which also sat a plate of crullers.

"What's next?" the reporter said.

"I beg your pardon?" Pat said.

"What other foods will you be working on?"

"Oh, dead chickens," Pat said, sighing.

"I can see I'm wearing you out," the reporter said, finally. She went away looking a little annoyed, her eyes somewhat dimmed.

Pat, when she was gone, went and sat by the phone. He removed the pocket dosimeter from his belt loop and set it on the table beside the crullers. It was a small instrument that resembled a Sharpie pen, only with a lens at one end. Zero, it had read when he commenced the tour of the plant, and zero it read now. He had absorbed no radiation. He had penetrated wall after wall within the warehouse-sized building, moving ever closer to the source. At every new level, Dr. Roland had pointed out more buttons, more controls, more men. There were earthquake buttons and flood buttons, hurricane buttons and buttons for if someone fell asleep. There were men whose job it was to watch buttons, and men who watched only other men. The whole thing reminded Pat of some giant child's ant farm. He had gone as close as one could go to the great source, and his dosimeter still registered zero.

He looked again at the little instrument and felt his frustration well back up. That's me, he thought. A big zero, coming and going. Nothing will ever change—I *am* invisible. He grabbed at the phone's receiver and punched the buttons in a fury. *I've had it with this secret life,* he would tell her. *Keep your deceptions, your illusions, your stupid, hopeful Trinidadian. Without you, my life will open up like a wonderful picture book, what people know of me will be the truth.* The phone was ringing blankly in his ear. It went on, ringing and stopping, ringing and stopping. He let his head fall for a moment and felt the pink blood rushing to his face like a child's hot tears. He felt like a child planning to run away from home. His courage was already dissolving, he could not sustain it. *Fine, I'll call her later,* he told himself. *From the hotel, let the university pay for it.* But even as he thought this, it was already passing out of him, going out of reach like a helium balloon. It was passing out of him and it was gone. He lifted up his head and landed back in the sweet hopelessness of his life. The oysters awaited him.

The oysters felt different, but it was difficult for them to say how. They felt as though something had been added or something taken away. They felt vaguely the urge to produce pearls, but they could not produce them. Clearly, they were leaving something behind, moving with smooth speed away from something of great importance, but what this thing was they could not remember. They felt frustrated, distracted. Where were they going? they wondered. What would happen to them? What were they supposed to do? Oh, they were only oysters! Who was there to tell their story, and who was there to listen?

BRUCE COHEN

The Whispering Campaign

Hazy Friday afternoon, traffic slugs.
I get off a strange exit miles before mine
hoping for the shortcut home. Between tenements,
the sun's intuition peeks through a pink
bowling shirt on a clothesline.

I project the night. After a shower,
my evening peck—the click of plastic glasses—
kids' muted voices of cocktail hour—
I never glue any more photographs in the album:
instead: stash my family in ice cube trays.

I'm Lost. Literally. I just want back
on the congested highway. A male = reluctant
to ask directions, I orbit. No one anymore
speaks English anyway, I say to myself.
The things one never says out loud . . .

Eavesdropping phone operators?
At coffee breaks they swap gossip,
play the intimate tapes, tap codes on the trafficky
wires that electrocute pigeons during thunderstorms.
The thing one never utters

is we're all quickies. Eternal Life's a con
to keep us in check. Listen, chaos would have too much
kick without sugar and milk. The tea kettle might whistle
itself blue-dry. I find the freeway by luck.
A fantasy: What if every car simultaneously runs out of gas?

All the crazed drivers slam doors
of stalled vehicles mumbling *What the fuck?*

Even passengers get a little nervous.
And so begins the whispering campaign.
Commuters, who otherwise change lanes without signals,

make delicate joint decisions: whether to hike for help
or remain with their cars, a polite chaos
because the world has lost its ability to move.
Those with car phones are paranoid
and choose not to call, at least anyone they know.

Good people, though strangers,
start kissing and screwing on the still hot hoods.
This stalled religion of amoral traffic,
where even operators know as little as we,
permits us to say out loud what we usually whisper.

A song on the radio brings me back in the nick
to be tempted to violate the yellow and black
detour posted on my exit ramp.
But I'm a lawful citizen.
I drive beyond where I live.

Original Sin

My mother waited till now
to hand down this gold razor
her father let slip
in the washbowl.
In a hurry to teamster the horses,
soap in his earlobe and nostril,
he climbed into the fire wagon.
When she poured the wash water
onto pebbles, hard gold
sluiced at the bottom
with the whiskers.
A gold razor, small for travel,
beside the soap,
I wipe a circle in the foggy mirror,
my face doughy and wet,
the age I always am,
burrs sprung on my cheek,
chin, under my lip.
Sister Josephine chalked dots, sins
born inside the circle, the soul.
Death camps originated in Eden.
Abel, the shepherd, was murdered.
I scrape my chin.
Already our baby sees me
as a dot, translucent
on the slippery wall,
shadow on the fetal eyelash,
and in the next century a whisper,
"shit," like my father, not often
but when he nicked his jaw.
My parents met
packaging Blue Blades

at Gillette's plant on a river,
for workers to smooth
their Hellenic chins in the war,
for prisoners and jailers to swap,
for cold fingers sawing the wrist.
I was afraid too.
For me it was sex.
Not the delicate way
I unbutton your dress,
and huddle over the body
inside the body, but once
I saw my parents. On their lunch break,
having merely opened the blouse and pants
like secret lovers, they kept laughing,
and then they whispered when they came.
They went back to work. That was my sin.
Shadow in shadow, riding the dark water.
Not till now have I known
my father and mother were in love,
young, happy, skinny like me.

STUART DISCHELL

The Talking Cure

He had done what he promised himself he would do—
Kept his mouth shut in the bar—but now driving
The miles to her house he felt the talk rising
Inside him like ardor, the heat of self-love.
But he swore to himself that tonight he would talk
Mostly with his shoulders and eyes, let his best
Features do the work and answer her questions
With phrases like "It happens" or "That's the way
It is sometimes," constructions that would confirm
By the set of his jaw both the knowledge and sorrow
Of human behavior, as though life had tested him
And taught him that saying little says the most.
He kept his promise and let her do the talking:
Ex-husband, ex-boyfriend, parents who thought her wild,
That last word clinching for him the certainty
They would go home together, that tonight he could trade
His talking for sex. He understood that much
About himself, knew the way women looked at him
Funny whenever he told the versions of his life,
How the light that was passion turned to caution
In their eyes, how between them opened an intersection
That should be avoided—tire skids be damned!
Now driving back to her place, he would not slip
Or even sing along with the music on the radio.
He would refrain from telling her she was beautiful
Beside him in the green glow of the dash. Later,
After their seat belts were unbuckled and reeled back,
Jeans unzipped, the patterned sheets turned back,
After kiss and nuzzle and thrust and the many changed
Positions till she rocking on top, palms pressed
Against the cage of his chest and she gasping,
And folding her flesh upon him, would his moaning

Her name, his calling her both baby and momma,
And his fluid of tears and come and sweat and spit
Soak them both with the high tide of his loneliness,
Then she would hear him and he would turn away and dress.

So I Guess You Know What I Told Him

Floyd Beefus was picking a tick off one of the springers when the gas man slipped on a cracked dinner plate on the cellar stairs and went bump, bump, bump, right to the bottom. "Yow!" went the gas man. The springer jumped but Floyd kept gripping him tight between his knees until he had cracked the tick between his forefinger and thumb, then he limped slowly to the cellar door.

The gas man lay in a heap at the bottom. He was a well-fed-looking fellow in a green shirt, green pants, and a little green cap. He was moaning and rubbing his leg.

"You hurt yourself?" called Floyd Beefus.

The gas man stared up the stairs at him with a confused look, as if his eyes had gone loose in his head. He was about forty, maybe twenty years younger than Floyd himself. "I think I broke my leg. I need an ambulance. You got a phone?"

"Nope," said Floyd. "No phone." He limped back to the springer and let him into the pen in the backyard before he peed on the rug. The springer had picked up the tick when they had been out hunting pheasants that morning. Floyd had thought the frost would have killed the ticks. It was early September and Floyd had a small farm outside of Montville, about twenty miles from Belfast. As he put the springer into his pen, he glanced around at the maples just beginning to turn color under the bright blue sky. Soon it would be hunting season and Floyd might get himself a nice buck. Frieda would appreciate that if she was still with them. After a moment, he went back inside to check on the gas man.

"You want an aspirin or maybe a Coca-Cola?" he called. He understood that the gas man posed a problem but he wasn't yet sure how to deal with it.

"Jesus, I'm in pain. You got to call a doctor." The gas man had stretched himself out a little with his head on the bottom step. He had a thick, red face. Floyd Beefus thought the man looked excitable and it made Floyd suck his teeth.

"I already told you I don't have no phone." Floyd had had a phone but he lost track of the bill and the phone had been temporarily disconnected. Frieda used to take care of all that. Floyd Beefus lowered himself onto the top step and gazed down at the gas man. He guessed he'd have to step over him if he went into the basement to fetch any of his tools.

"Then use a neighbor's phone. This is an emergency!"

"The nearest neighbor's two miles," said Floyd. "That'd be Harriet Malcomb in the mobile unit. Course I just call it a trailer. I'd be surprised if she had a phone. She don't even have a car. If you'd done this a week ago, then you would have caught some summer people, but the last of them left on Tuesday: Mike Prescott, a lawyer from Boston. Sometimes he has parties. I'd hate to tell you what goes on."

"You can use my car."

"I can't drive no more on account of the Dewey."

"Dewey?"

"DWI."

The gas man was staring at him in a way that Floyd Beefus thought bordered on the uncivil. "You sure you don't want that aspirin?" added Floyd. "Or maybe a pillow?"

"I can't just lie here," said the gas man, letting the whine grow in his voice. "I could be bleeding internally!"

Floyd scratched the back of his neck. He saw cobwebs on the stairs that would never have been allowed to settle before his wife got sick. "I don't like to leave Frieda. She's up in bed." He started to say more, then didn't.

"Jesus," said the gas man, "don't you see this is a crisis situation? I'm a supervisor. I can't just lie here in your cellar. I could die here."

"Oh, you won't die," said Floyd. He considered the gas man's excitability. "If you're a supervisor, how come you're reading my meter?"

"We're understaffed. You got to get a doctor!"

Floyd pulled his pocket watch out of the pocket of his dungarees and opened the lid. It was shortly past ten-thirty.

"The visiting nurse should be here in a while. She usually shows up a little after lunchtime. Billy, that's my son, he took the

Ford down to Rockland this morning. He said he'd be back by late afternoon. Had to go to the pharmacy down there. I don't see why they don't sell the damn stuff in Belfast. You'd think bedsores'd be the same in both places."

"After lunchtime?" said the gas man.

"Around one, one-thirty. Loretta likes to stop for the blue plate special out at the Ten-Four Diner. And if they have blueberry pie, she generally takes a slice. She's a fat old thing. She'll fix you right up."

"That could be three hours," said the gas man.

"Just about. You want to think again about that aspirin?"

"It upsets my stomach. You have any Tylenol?"

"Nope," said Floyd. "Course Frieda's got some morphine. I could give you a shot if you like. I've become practiced at it."

The gas man had big blue eyes and Floyd found himself thinking: Googly eyes.

"Morphine?"

"The visiting nurse brings it. A month ago Frieda only needed two shots a day. Now she needs four. Loretta, that's the nurse, she said she's seen patients taking six and even eight shots before their time's up. You sure you don't want a little shot? Loretta will be giving us some more."

The gas man shut his eyes. "I don't take morphine. Perhaps you could get me a glass of water. And I'll have some aspirin after all. God, it'd be just my luck to start puking."

The aspirin was above the bathroom sink. Before getting it, Floyd looked in on Frieda. She was sleeping. Her gray hair was spread out on the pillow around her face. Floyd thought of the tumor in her stomach. It didn't sleep; it just got bigger. The bedroom was full of medicines and an oxygen tank. It had a sweet hospital smell. Floyd himself had been sleeping in the spare room for six weeks and he still couldn't get used to it. He got the aspirin, then went downstairs for the water. One of the springers was barking but he was just being conversational.

Floyd had to wash out a glass. Since Frieda had been sick, he and Billy had been doing the cooking and cleaning up but it didn't come easy. A pot on the stove was still crusted with spaghetti sauce from two nights earlier.

Floyd descended the cellar stairs, watching out for the stuff that was on the steps: newspapers and empty Ball jars. He sat down above the gas man and handed him the water and bottle of aspirin. "You married?" he asked.

The gas man pried the top off the bottle of aspirin. "I got a wife," he said.

"Kids?"

"Two."

"I been married forty years," said Floyd. "We done it right after Frieda finished high school. I didn't graduate myself. Didn't need it back then."

The gas man didn't say anything. He took two aspirin, then took two more. There was sweat on his forehead. Floyd thought his face looked unhealthy but maybe it was the pain. The gas man drank some water, then shut his eyes.

"You like your wife?" asked Floyd.

The gas man opened his eyes. "Sure, I mean, she's my wife."

"How'd you feel if you didn't have her anymore?"

"What do you mean?"

"Well, if she died or went away."

"She wouldn't do that. Go away, I mean." The gas man's voice had an impatient edge.

"But what if she died?"

"I guess I'd be surprised."

"Is that all? Just surprised?"

"Well, she's thirty-eight. There's nothing wrong with her." The man took off his green cap and pushed a hand through his hair. It was dark brown with some gray at the temples.

"A car could hit her," said Floyd. "She could be struck down when crossing the street. It happens all the time."

"She pays attention. She looks both ways."

"It could still happen."

The gas man thought a moment, then got angry. "Can't you see I don't want to talk! I hurt and you won't even get help!"

Floyd pursed his lips. He sat above the gas man and looked down on his bald spot. "I already explained about that." He thought how the gas man's bald spot would get bigger and bigger till it ate up his whole head. "You live around here?" he asked.

"I live in Augusta."

"They got a lot of dangerous streets in Augusta," said Floyd. "I seen them."

The gas man sighed.

"Wouldn't you mind if your wife was hit by a car?"

"Mind, of course I'd mind! Jesus, what are you saying?"

"I'm just trying to get the picture," said Floyd.

"We got two kids, like I say. They're both still in school. Who'd take care of them?"

"My two oldest are grown up," said Floyd. "A daughter in Boston and my older boy in Portland. But they'd be here in a minute if Frieda got took worse. You sleep with your wife?"

"Of course I sleep with my wife. What are you getting at?" The gas man turned his head but it was hard to see Floyd seated behind him. Floyd had his arms folded across his knees and was resting his chin on his wrist.

"Me and Frieda, we can't sleep together no more. At first without her there I could hardly sleep at all. The bed seemed hollow, like it was no more than an empty shoe. She'd move around a lot in the night and she'd cry. She's scared but she won't say anything. I would've stayed right there in the old double bed but the visiting nurse said it would be better if I moved. At first I sat up in a chair with her but I couldn't do that for too many nights. Sleeping in the spare room feels like I done something wrong."

The gas man didn't speak for a moment. Then he said, "Can you get me a pillow for my head?"

Floyd got a pillow upstairs from Billy's room. His knee hurt from walking around the fields that morning and he moved slowly. Frieda was still asleep. He stood a moment in the doorway and watched her breathe. After she exhaled there was a pause that seemed to stretch on and on. Then she would breathe again and Floyd would relax a little. Her skin was the color of old egg cartons. He took the pillow back down to the gas man, who was rubbing his leg below the knee.

"I can feel the bone pressing against the skin," said the gas man. "It's sure to be bleeding inside. I could lose my whole leg." He had pulled up the green pant leg and showed Floyd the red bump in his skin where the bone was pressing.

Floyd put the pillow behind the gas man's head. "I broke my leg falling off the tractor once. I lay in the field for two hours and no harm was done except for the pain. It's not like cancer. The body can take a lot."

"It hurts," said the gas man.

"That's just your body telling you there's something wrong. You want me to haul you upstairs and put you on the couch?"

The gas man considered that. When he thought, he moved his tongue around in his mouth. "I think I better stay right here until the rescue squad shows up."

Floyd wasn't sure he could get the gas man up the stairs in any case. "You pray?" he asked.

"I'm not much for church," said the gas man.

"Me neither, but there's a Bible around somewheres if you need it. Frieda likes to look at it. Right up to last March she'd never been took sick. Never complained, always kept us going with her jokes. You ever been unfaithful to your wife?"

The gas man's head jerked on his pillow.

"Jesus, what kind of question is that?"

"I just wanted to know."

"My affairs are none of your business, absolutely none of your business."

Floyd settled himself more comfortably on the step. He was sorry that the gas man was so unforthcoming. "You know Belfast?"

"I been there."

"You know how it used to have those two chicken processing plants? Penobscot Poultry and the other one. I forget its name. A guy named Mendelsohn run it. Every summer Belfast used to have a poultry festival with rides and activities in the city park. It used to be something special and high school bands would come from all over. And the Shriners, too."

The gas man didn't speak. He began rubbing his leg again. There was a bend in it that Floyd didn't think looked right.

"There was a woman who worked upstairs at Penobscot. She had a job putting the little piece of paper between the chicken parts and Styrofoam. Her name was Betsy. My, she liked to make trouble. She was never buttoned clear to the neck. About twelve years ago me and Frieda went to that poultry fair. The kids were young enough to still like it. I was drinking beer. That's always a mistake with me. After dark I got Betsy back on a tree stump. I was just unbuttoning myself when Frieda found me. Jesus, I already had Betsy's shorts off under her dancing skirt."

"Why are you telling me this?" The gas man stretched his neck to get a glimpse of Floyd.

"I was just thinking about it, that's all," said Floyd.

"Don't you see I don't care what you've done?"

"Then what do you want to talk about?" asked Floyd.

"I don't want to talk at all."

Floyd sat for a moment. The gas man had a fat gold wedding ring, then another ring with a blue stone on his right pinkie finger. He had shiny teeth and Floyd thought it was the kind of mouth that was used to eating a lot, the kind of mouth that enjoyed itself.

"How's your leg?" asked Floyd.

"It hurts."

"That aspirin help any?"

"It makes my stomach queasy."

"You sure you don't want a Coke?"

"I just want to get out of here. You got to take my car."

"The Dewey'd get me for sure," said Floyd, "and then there's Frieda. If she woke up, you couldn't do anything."

Floyd leaned back with his elbows on a step. The cellar was filled with evidence of forty years in this house: broken chairs, old bikes, tools, canning equipment, a dog bed for Bouncer, who had been dead fifteen years. The cellar had a musty smell. He wondered what he would do with this stuff when Frieda died. The thought of her death was like a pain in his body.

"You ever think," said Floyd, "that a bad thing happens to you because of some bad thing you've done?"

"What do you mean?" asked the gas man suspiciously.

"Well, that time I fell off the tractor and broke my leg was right after I'd been with Betsy at the poultry festival. Even when I fell I had the sense that something was giving me a shove. If I'd had two more seconds I'd've stuck it into her . . ."

"I don't want to hear about this," said the gas man.

"What I was wondering is maybe you've been doing something you shouldn't. You always play straight with your wife?"

"This is none of your business."

"You never felt temptation?"

"I only wanted to read your meter," said the gas man. "That's all, just your meter."

"You're a better man than I am. I felt temptation. I felt it every time I went into town. It wasn't that I don't love my wife. I was just exercising myself, so to speak. I'd go into Barbara's Lunch and just breathe heavily. Going into houses like you do, you must of felt temptation a whole lot."

"I don't want to talk about it. I'm a supervisor."

"But younger, when you were a plain gas man. Didn't some woman look at you and smile?"

"Why are you saying this?" asked the gas man. He spoke so forcefully that little drops of spit exploded from his lips. He tried to turn but couldn't quite see Floyd sitting behind him.

"You know," said Floyd, "after Frieda caught me behind the beer tent with Betsy McCollough, she'd look at me with such... disappointment. I don't mean right at the time. Then she was just angry. But later, at dinner or just walking across the room, she'd look up at me and I could see the wounding in her face. She still loved me and I loved her, too. It was eleven, almost twelve years later the cancer took hold of her, but I find myself thinking that my time with Betsy had opened the cancer to her. It made a little door for the cancer to enter."

The gas man had his face in his hands. He didn't say anything. The tips of his ears were all red.

"We were married right in Montville," said Floyd. "All our families were there, most of them dead now. We planned to be so happy. Even now, lying in bed, Frieda will look at me with that look of disappointment. Maybe that's too strong a word. She doesn't regret her marriage or regret having met me. It's like she thought I was a certain size and then she found out I was a little smaller. And I can never say she's wrong. I can't make myself bigger. When she was first sick, I used to make her dinners and bring her stuff and she appreciated it but it never made me as big a person as she used to think I was. And soon, you know, she'll be gone, and then I won't be able to explain anything or fix anything. All our time will be over."

The gas man didn't say anything.

"What d'you think about that?" asked Floyd.

"I just want a doctor," said the gas man.

"If you're so good," said Floyd, "then why won't you talk to me about it?"

"About what?"

"About what I done."

"Because I don't care," said the gas man. "Don't you understand it? I don't care."

"Fine gas man you are," said Floyd. He sat without speaking. He rubbed his knee and the gas man rubbed his leg.

"I don't mean to hurt your feelings," said the gas man.

"That's okay," said Floyd, "I'm not worth much."

"It's not what you're worth," said the gas man. "My leg's broken. I hurt. I'm preoccupied."

"You think I'm not preoccupied?" said Floyd. "My wife's dying upstairs and I can't do anything about it. I look in her face and I see the memories there. I see how I hurt her and how I said the wrong things and how I got angry and how I wasn't the man she hoped I'd be. I see that in her face and I see she's going to die with that. You think I'm not preoccupied?"

The gas man put his cap back on his head and pulled down the brim. "I don't know what to say. I come into this place. All I want is to read your meter. Why the hell can't you keep that stuff off the stairs? You think it's nice to be a gas man going into strange basements all the time? All I want is to get in and get out. Then I go home, eat dinner, watch some TV, and go to bed. Is that too much to ask? Instead, I slip on a dinner plate and you say I must've deserved it. I must've been cheating on my wife. All I want is to get my leg fixed. I'm sorry your wife's dying. I can't do anything about it. I'm just a gas man."

Floyd leaned back and sighed. He heard one of the springers howling. Frieda had a buzzer that sounded off in the kitchen if she needed anything. Apart from the springer, the house was silent except for the gas man's heavy breathing. Floyd felt dissatisfied somehow, like finishing a big meal and still being hungry. He looked at his watch. It was almost eleven-thirty.

"Old Loretta should be reaching the Ten-Four Diner in another hour," he said. "My, she loves to eat. I've known her even to have two pieces of pie with ice cream. If they got blueberry and if they got rhubarb, then I bet she'll have both."

"What's the latest she's gotten here?"

"Three o'clock."

The gas man groaned. "I hurt, I hurt a lot."

"There's still that morphine," said Floyd.

"No morphine," said the gas man.

"Anything else you want? Maybe a tuna fish sandwich?"

"You got any whiskey?"

"There might be some White Horse somewheres."

"Maybe a shot of that, maybe a double."

Floyd made his way back upstairs. He was sorry the gas man didn't want a tuna fish sandwich. He wanted to feed him, to have the gas man think well of him. Looking in on Frieda, he saw she had turned her head but that was all. She said the morphine gave her bright-colored dreams. She dreamt about being a kid or going to school or having children again. Rich, vigorous dreams and Floyd Beefus envied her for them. When he went to bed he was just grinding and grinding all night long like a tractor motor.

He poured the gas man half a glass of whiskey, then poured himself some as well. Floyd made his way back down the cellar stairs. He handed the gas man the bigger glass.

"Here you go," he said.

The gas man gripped it with both hands and took a drink, then he coughed. He had fingers like little sausages.

"You like being a supervisor?" asked Floyd.

"Sure."

"What do you like about it?"

"It commands respect."

"You ever fired anybody?"

"Well, sometimes you have to let somebody go."

"You feel bad about that?"

"I feel my duty is to the company and to the trust they put in me." The gas man took another drink.

Floyd couldn't imagine being a gas man or what it would be

like going into people's houses. He had been a farmer all his life. "You ever stole anything from them?"

The gas man cranked his head around. The whiskey had brought a little color to his nose. "Of course not!"

"Not even a ball-point pen or a couple of paper clips?"

"They trust me."

"How long you worked for the company?"

"Almost twenty-three years."

"That's a big chunk of time. You must've done a lot of stuff for them."

"I've had a wide variety of experience." The gas man talked about the sort of things he had done: office work, field work, repairing broken equipment. He finished his whiskey and Floyd gave him another. The gas man took two more aspirins. It was just after twelve o'clock.

"You won't change your mind about that sandwich?"

"I don't like tuna fish," said the gas man. "Maybe some toast with a little butter. Not too brown."

Floyd went back up to the kitchen. The bread had a little mold but he cut it off. He checked the toaster to make sure no mice had gotten electrocuted. Sometimes they crept inside and got caught like lobsters in a trap. Floyd wiped a plate off on his pant leg, then he buttered the toast using a clean knife. Through the kitchen window he saw four cows moseying in a line across the field. He and Billy had milked all thirty before sunup. Floyd took the toast back down to the gas man.

"How many houses can you go into in a single day as a gas man?" asked Floyd.

"Maybe sixty out in the country, double that in the city." He had his mouth full of toast and he wiped his lips with the back of his hand.

"And nothing strange ever happens?"

"In and out, that's all I want. Sometimes a dog gives you some trouble. I'm like a shadow in people's lives."

"And you've never felt temptation?"

The gas man drank some whiskey. "Absolutely never."

"No women give you the eye?"

"Their lives don't concern me. It's their meters I'm after." The gas man put the empty plate on the step. He was still chewing slowly, getting a few last crumbs, running his tongue along the gap between his teeth and his lower lip. "It's my duty not to get involved."

"But people must talk to you. A woman must give you a friendly look."

"Oh, it's there all right," said the gas man. "I could be bad if I wanted."

"You seen things."

"I seen a lot."

"It must be a burden sometimes."

"My duty's to the gas company, like I say. That's why they made me supervisor, because I make the right decisions, or try to. They appreciate my loyalty."

"What kind of things have you seen?" asked Floyd.

The gas man drank some more whiskey, then rested the glass on his thigh. "There was a woman in Augusta, a divorcée, who had it in mind to make trouble. I seen that."

"Good-looking?"

"A little thick, but good-looking. This was ten years ago."

"What'd she do?"

The gas man took off his cap again and wiped his brow. He set his cap carefully on the step beside him. "Well, the first time I went by her house she offered me a cup of coffee. I know that doesn't sound like much but it was just the beginning. She asked if I wanted a cup of coffee and if I wanted to sit down and rest a little. She was wearing a bathrobe, a cream-colored bathrobe. She had thick brown hair past her shoulders and it was nicely brushed."

"You take the coffee?"

"I always make a point of never taking anything."

"Then what happened?"

"A month later, I went by her house again. She was waiting for me. She followed me down to the basement when I went to read her meter. I turned around and she was standing right in front of me, still in her bathrobe, like she'd been wearing it for the entire month. I said howdy and she asked if I'd like to rest a little and I said I had to keep moving. Then she asked if I liked to dance and I said I didn't, that I hadn't danced since high school. So I walked around her and left."

"You think she wanted to dance right then?" asked Floyd. He liked dancing but he hadn't had much occasion in his life. When he was younger, there had been barn dances during the summer and sometimes he still recalled the smell of perfume and hay.

"I don't know if she wanted to dance," said the gas man. "I didn't think about it. I was in a hurry."

"She must have been lonely."

"A gas man doesn't socialize. It's like being a priest but you deal with meters instead. One time a man asked me for five dollars so he could feed his family. I didn't even answer him. I don't even like it when people ask me the time of day or what the weather is like outside. In and out, that's my motto."

"So what happened with the woman?" asked Floyd.

"So the third month I check her meter she doesn't follow me down to the basement. She was still wearing her robe and I thought she'd been drinking a little. She greeted me heartily, like I was an old friend. People have done that before trying to get around me. I just nodded. I go down in the basement and check her meter. When I start back up the basement stairs, she's standing at the top. She's taken off her bathrobe and she's wearing only this pink underwear, pink panties. Her titties are completely bare and she's pushing them up at me. Big, pink titties. She was blocking the door so I couldn't get through. 'Take me,' she says, like she thinks she's a cab or something."

"What did you do?" asked Floyd.

"I asked her to get out of my way, that I was in a hurry. She still didn't move. So I yelled at her. I told her I was a busy man and I didn't have time to waste. She took her hands away from her titties pretty quick, I can tell you. I said her behavior was awful and she should be ashamed."

"Then what happened?"

"She stepped aside and I left."

"And the next month?"

"The next month she was gone and the house was shut up. I didn't think much of it but a month later I asked one of her neighbors if she'd moved. I don't know why I asked but I kept thinking of her. Maybe it was because the woman seemed crazy. Anyway, the neighbor told me the woman was dead. One morning she just hadn't woken up. The neighbor said it was pills. She just took all the pills she could find. It was the neighbor who told me that the woman was a divorcée. She said the husband had gotten the kids and married someone else. I don't know when she died, just sometime during the month."

Floyd finished his whiskey. One of the springers was barking again. Floyd thought that no woman in his entire life had ever looked at him and said, "Take me," not even his wife. "You could have kept her alive," he said.

"What d'you mean?"

"You could have talked to her. She might still be around."

"She wanted sex. She was crazy."

"But you could have talked to her. She probably only wanted a little conversation."

"That's not my job. To me, she was only a person with a gas meter. In and out, like I say."

"What if you'd found her bleeding on the floor?"

"I would have called the cops."

"But the stuff she told you, it was like she was bleeding." Floyd regretted he had given the gas man any of his White Horse.

"It's not my job to deal with bleeding."

"You should've danced with her," said Floyd. "I would've danced with her. I would've danced till my feet fell off."

"We already know about you," said the gas man. "You and that woman behind the beer tent."

"You as good as killed her," said Floyd. He felt angry but he knew that only a piece of his anger was connected to the gas man. The rest seemed a blanket over everything else. He didn't like the whole setup: people coming into and going out of this life and none of it being by choice.

Floyd heard Frieda's buzzer and he got to his feet. He felt dizzy from the whiskey. He made his way upstairs holding onto the bannister. The gas man kept saying something but Floyd didn't pay any mind.

Frieda's eyes were only half-open. "I would like some more water." Her voice was very soft.

Floyd got the water from the kitchen and put in a couple of cubes of ice. When he handed it to Frieda, he said, "There's a real jerk in the basement."

"Tell him to go away."

"I can't. He's broken his leg."

Frieda nodded solemnly. The morphine and her approaching death made her more accepting of the world's peculiarities. "Then give him something to eat."

"I already did."

"Then just bear with it," she said.

When Floyd looked back down the basement stairs, he saw the gas man was holding his head in his hands. "More aspirin?" He found it hard to be polite.

"Leave me alone."

"Any food? Maybe a blanket?" It was approaching one o'clock. Loretta could be arriving in as little as half an hour.

"I don't want anything from you," said the gas man.

Floyd was about to turn away and fix himself some lunch, then he changed his mind. "That's why you fell," he said. "Because of that woman who wanted to dance. That's the punishment you got, busting your dancing leg. Ten years ago, you said. That punishment's been coming after you for a long time, just creeping along waiting for its chance."

"Shut up!" said the gas man. "Shut up, shut up!"

Floyd told Billy about the gas man that night at dinner. Billy was a thin, heavily freckled youngster in his late teens who wore old dungarees and a gray University of Maine sweatshirt. His mother's illness was like an awful noise in his ears.

"So the rescue squad is carrying this fellow out of the house," said Floyd. "His hands were over his face but you could tell he was crying. I was standing there holding the dog. The guy sees me. 'Damn you,' he says, 'Goddamn you to hell!'"

"After you'd been taking care of him and fed him?" asked Billy. They were eating beans and franks.

"Some people have no sense of how to behave," said Floyd. "Some people would act bad even in front of St. Peter. 'Damn you,' he kept saying. Well, I wasn't going to take that in front of the rescue squad. A man can be provoked only so far."

"I can't believe you kept your trap shut," said Billy.

"I don't like being messed with." Floyd paused with his fork halfway to his mouth. "I guess you know what I told him."

"I bet you gave him the very devil."

"That's just the least of it," said Floyd.

JAMES DUFFY

Fat Tuesday

I sit on the porch tonight,
smoking my last cigarette, savoring it
the way a crow at the edge of the highway feeds
until the last second,
hopping a little dance on the carcass.
The trees are stark, the branches hover,
ready to sprout in this warm feast of air.
I would like to feast with good friends,
get drunk and build a fire down by the lakeside,
dive into the water and rise with
gathered stones, leaving them in our places.

I stub the butt out, move my hand
to my jacket pocket. Nothing left.
An alcoholic once told me she slept with her bottle
the night before she went to her first AA meeting.
She prayed her fingers could drink right through the glass,
so I am wary of my promise
to keep the smoke from my lungs.

Last night we filled the kitchen with gas
trying to start the oven. I almost pushed you
outside into the rain, extended an umbrella
like my cry, "Marcia! The baby!"
Tonight, before you went into the shower,
you told me your dream:
our child was two inches long, perfectly formed
in the palm of your hand.
You put her on the bookshelf and fed her applesauce,
and I can see how your body loves the life
we have made in you.

Tomorrow you want to get ashes
from the priest across the lake, put them on your forehead.
You could get ashes here, ashes from the logs
I lugged in last weekend
when the lake suddenly froze;
ashes from the driftwood I gathered,
and kept for as long as ten years.
I used to place them on the windowsill
of every room I lived in, wanting to feel
protection, to be connected.
Let me take you to bed and knead your back,
your legs; let me hold your feet.
I don't know if tomorrow will be good or not.

A Different Kind of Birth

—from the Inuit tale The Man Who Was a Mother

A man and a woman couldn't have any children.
No one knew whose fault it was. This couple was unhappy
and the butt of jokes. The man sucked on his wife's breasts.
The woman cradled her husband in her arms.
But pretending about babies wasn't enough.
So the man headed south where a woman shaman,
who had gained her powers in being struck by lightning,
was sometimes able to help the barren.
The shaman handed the husband two dried fish.
If you want a boy, give your wife this boy fish.
If you want a girl, give her the fish that is a girl.
The hopeful husband jumped into his kayak
anxious to get the fertile fish home. But it wasn't long
until the husband grew hungry, and weighing
the fish in both of his palms, decided that it wouldn't be
    that bad
to eat the fish that was a girl, since it was a boy child he
    really wanted.
So he ate the female fish, the soft bones scraping his throat.
Soon a cramp, then a bout of nausea that wasn't seasickness.
By the time he arrived home, he could barely squeeze himself
out of his boat. His belly stretched far ahead of him
as though it wanted to leave and walk away on its own.
His wife recognized the signs and tended to her husband
day and night. When he gave birth to a little baby girl,
she slipped through him like a fish and flopped
into the cold air. What did it matter
if one of her mothers was also her father?

Grief

I am ashamed as I try to sleep,
counting the wounded and the dead
in this old day's news,

the grieving ones they leave behind.
Counting stones and bullets, averted needs,
the pretty breaths of my family beside me,
counting on a world that I don't trust
to keep my children safe.

What was I thinking? Did I forget those others,
the rubble of their troubled worlds
and mine? Does it fill their days—

their remembering? Or do they remember too
to choose their favorite breakfast bowls,
that red dress, the time to step out of doors?
When I lean my body over the fragile forms
of my husband and children, I am afraid

I am not strong enough to bear
the grief of so much loving, the burden
of our survival from day to day,

or of what we can't live without, but will.
How each of us fends off despair—
that is what we are made of
when all else is dust or luck.
Each stranger's grief is not my grief

but it lies under everything, like ice.
Sometimes I fall through it.
Sometimes I walk achingly.

I am not saying their voices rise
above the hum of comfort here and now.
I'm saying I believe that even sweet blue skies
will break away, leaving nothing
between my eyes and the face of a god

who says, Look down into that dark place,
meet your own shadow there.
Go on, take it, take it on. Grieve:

Go down into the dirt.
I want to have already known its taste.
I want to have swallowed it alive.
If I fall asleep tonight,
if I do not die before I wake,

what will have lifted me back to perfect
that other thing that we call hope
is more love: The leaven of all sorrow.

Beholden

Still I am not sure which is most vivid—
the love now risen from its previous absence,
or the future loss it rides like a shadow,
the eye's after-image of a bright light gone.
In any case, with its harrowing blades,
this fertile line of love already
draws through me a beautiful symmetry:
The invisible, downward reaching of dark and buried roots,
and the opening, airing branches that they mimic.
Always, love is something coming to an end,
something that could die before its time
and so you live in it, a world, a frame,
the borders that define. You memorize it,
day by day, like the lines of the earth's face
mapped and changing, mapped again and again
changing, over centuries, the impossible
becoming true before you. And like that,
you look for the shapes of things now being
that once were not: No matter
how you hold a day, it sets into the year,
buried, lost. In memory its sheen
is another branch. We see that coming.
It is precisely that passage, that change, that tunneling
through the soil of time—that dread—
that makes love what it is: So rich, so far
beside itself with beauty, beholden to it,
because it can never be held.
It's just that love is the highest point, the lightning rod
that draws to it the crooked path of sorrow—
which it waits for, depends upon, uses in advance,
not the way that we use air—of necessity, for life—
but, instead, the way that birds use air:
For balance, unbalancing, uplift.

The Swim Team

The elevator is full of the swim team.
The swim team knows

How many goldfish
Will fit in a phone booth.

The window and its attendant shadows
Are not wise. They are an insult

To the swim team,
Which has God on its side.

The swim team knows
How to pull a knife on the swim team.

From time immemorial, ages of hapless freaks
Have attended and will attend

The swim team, from the grass surrounding
The great glass of the pool.

Is the outsider better off
Staying outside?

Is there an outside,
Considering the window is not wise?

Ask the swim team. Lead by Carol,
Who works in the hospital.

They keep a watch on all windows.
They are featured on the video billboard

In the pharmacy that reads you back to you
And knows your dirty little desire for a cigarette.

She leads them in song,
And in prayer on the sunny side

Of the stained glass. Nothing means much to them,
And the everything they can touch.

ELIZABETH GILBERT

The Names of Flowers and Girls

At the time of Babette, my grandfather was not yet twenty. Although today, and perhaps even then, such youth is not necessarily married to innocence, in his case it was. There were boys his age who had already served in the war and returned, but he was not among them for the unromantic reason that one of his feet was several sizes larger than the other. Outfitting him with boots would have inconvenienced the United States Army enough that he was not selected, and he passed the war years, as before, in the company of his elderly great-aunt.

On this particular Wednesday night, he chose not to tell his aunt where he was going. This was not out of deviousness, for he was not by nature a liar. Rather, he believed that she would not have understood or even heard him in the advanced stage of her senility. He did ask the neighbor, a widow with bad knees, to look in on his aunt throughout the evening, and she agreed to. He had already been to a boxing match the month before, and had briefly, late one Saturday, stood in the doorway of a loud and dangerous local bar, so this was not his first attempt to observe a seediness he had never known. He learned little out of those first two experiences, however, except that the smell of tobacco smoke clings stubbornly to hair and clothing. He had higher hopes for this evening.

The nightclub he found was considerably darker inside than the street outside had been. It was an early show, a weekday show, but the place had already filled with a shifting, smoking audience of men. The few lights around the orchestra dimmed just as he entered, and he was forced to feel his way to a seat, stepping over feet and knees in the aisle. He tried not to actually touch people, but brushed nonetheless against wool and skin with every move until he found an empty seat and took it.

"Time?" a voice beside him demanded. My grandfather tensed, but did not answer.

"The time?" the voice questioned again. My grandfather asked quietly, "Are you talking to me?"

There was a sudden spotlight on the stage, and the question was forgotten. Babette began to sing, although at that time, of course, he did not know her name. When his eyes adjusted to the glaring white light, it was only the color of her dress that he saw—a vivid green that today we call lime. It is a color decidedly not found in nature, but is manufactured now artificially for the dying of paint, clothing, and food. It cannot shock us anymore, we are too familiar with it. In 1919, however, there were not yet cars to be found in that shade, or small houses in the suburbs, or, one would suspect, fabric.

Nonetheless, Babette wore it, sleeveless and short. My grandfather did not at first even notice that she was singing on account of that vivid lime-green dress. She was not a gifted singer, but it is almost petty to say so, as musical ability was clearly not required for her job. What she did, and did well, was move in swaying, dancing steps on very pleasant legs. Novelists writing only a decade before that night still referred to beautiful women as having "rounded, well-shaped arms." By the end of World War I, however, fashion had changed such that other features were now visible, and arms got considerably less attention than they once had. This was unfortunate, for Babette's arms were lovely, perhaps even her best feature. My grandfather, however, was not very modern, even as a young man, and he noticed Babette's arms appreciatively.

The lights at the back of the stage had risen, and there were several dancing couples now behind Babette. They were adequate, efficient dancers—the men slender and dark, the women in short, swinging dresses. The nature of the lighting muted the shades of their clothing into uniform browns and grays, and my grandfather could do little more than note their presence and then resume staring at Babette.

He was not familiar enough with show business to know that what he was watching was the insignificant opening act of what would be a long, bawdy night of performance. This particular number was no more than an excuse to open the curtain on something other than an empty stage, to warm up the small orchestra, and to alert the audience that the evening was commencing. There was nothing risqué about Babette except the length of her hemline, and it is likely that my grandfather was the only member of the audience who felt any excitement at what he was watching. It is almost certain that none of the other men around him were clutching at their trousers with damp hands, or moving their lips, silently searching for words to describe that dress, those arms, that startling red hair and lipstick. Most of the audience had already heard the song on a recording made by a prettier, more talented girl than Babette, but my grandfather knew very little of popular music or of pretty girls.

When the performers bowed and the lights dimmed, he jumped from his seat, and moved quickly back over the men in his row, stepping on feet, stumbling, apologizing for his clumsiness in a low, constant murmur. He felt his way up the center aisle and to the heavy doors that threw quick triangles of light onto the floor behind him as he pushed them open. He ran into the lobby and caught an usher by the arm.

"I need to speak with the singer," he said.

The usher, my grandfather's age, but a veteran of the war in France, asked, "Who?"

"The singer. The one with the red, the red—" He pulled at his own hair in frustration.

"The redhead," the usher finished.

"Yes."

"She's with the visiting troupe."

"Yes, good, good," my grandfather said, nodding foolishly. "Wonderful!"

"What do you need with her?"

"I need to speak with her," he repeated.

Perhaps the usher, seeing that my grandfather was sober and young, thought that he was a messenger boy, or perhaps he only wanted to be left alone. In any case, he led him to Babette's room, which was under the stage in a dark, door-lined hall.

"Someone here to see you, miss," he said, knocking twice and then leaving before she answered.

Babette opened the door and looked down the hall to the departing usher, and then to my grandfather. She wore a slip, and had a large pink towel wrapped around her shoulders like a shawl.

"Yes?" she asked, lifting her high, arched eyebrows even higher.

"I need to speak with you," my grandfather said.

She looked him over. He was tall and pale, in a clean, inexpensive suit, and he carried his folded overcoat under one arm as if it were a football. He had a bad habit of stooping, but now, out of nervousness, was standing perfectly straight. This posture helped his appearance somewhat, forcing his chin out and lending his shoulders a width they did not generally seem to have. There was nothing about him which would have compelled Babette to shut the door in his face, so she remained there before him in her slip and towel.

"Yes?" she asked again.

"I want to paint you," he said, and she frowned and took a step back. My grandfather thought with alarm that she had misunderstood him to mean that he wanted to apply paint to her bodily, as one would paint a house or a wall, and horrified, he explained, "I meant that I would like to paint a picture of you, a portrait of you!"

"Right now?" she asked, and he answered quickly, "No, no, not now. But I would like to, you see. I would love to."

"You're a painter?" she asked.

"Oh, I'm terrible," my grandfather said. "I'm a terrible painter, I'm ghastly."

She laughed at him. "I've already had my picture painted by several artists," she lied.

"Certainly you have," he said.

"You saw me sing?" she asked, and he said that he had indeed.

"You aren't staying for the rest of the show?" she asked, and he paused before answering, realizing only then that there was a show other than what he had seen.

"No," he said. "I didn't want to miss you. I was afraid you might leave right away."

She shrugged. "I don't let men into my dressing room."

"Of course you don't!" he said, hoping he had not insinuated that he expected an invitation. "I had no intention of that."

"But I'm not going to stand in this hallway and talk to you," she continued.

My grandfather said, "I'm sorry that I disturbed you," and unfolded his overcoat to put it on.

"What I mean is that if you want to talk to me, you're just going to have to come inside," Babette explained.

"I couldn't, I didn't mean to—"

But she had already stepped back into the small, poorly lit room, and was holding the door open for him to enter. He followed her in, and when she shut the door, he leaned up against it, anxious to intrude as little as possible. Babette pulled an old piano stool over to the sink, and looked at herself in a silver hand mirror. She ran the water until it was hot, dampened two fingers, and pressed a curl just behind her ear back into shape. Then she looked at my grandfather over her shoulder.

"Now why don't you tell me just what it was that you wanted."

"I wanted to draw you, to paint you."

"But you say you're no good."

"Yes."

"You shouldn't say that," Babette said. "If you're going to be something, if you're going to be someone, you've got to start telling people that you're good."

"I can't," he said. "I'm not."

"Well, it's easy enough to say that you are. Go on, say it. Say, 'I am a good artist.' Go on."

"I can't," he repeated. "I'm not one."

She picked an eyebrow pencil off the edge of the sink and tossed it to him.

"Draw something," she said.

"Where?"

"Anywhere. On this wall, on that wall, anywhere. Doesn't matter to me."

He hesitated.

"Go on," she said. "It's not as if you could make this room look any worse, if that's what you're worried about."

He found a spot next to the sink where the paint wasn't too badly chipped or marked with graffiti. Slowly, he began to draw a hand holding a fork. Babette stood behind him, leaning forward, watching over his shoulder.

"It's not a good angle for me," he said, but she did not answer, so he continued. He added a man's forearm and wristwatch.

"It's smudging like that because the pencil is so soft," he apologized, and she said, "Stop talking about it. Just finish it."

"It is finished." He stepped back. "It's already finished."

She looked at him, and then at the sketch. "But that's just a hand. There's no person, no face."

"See, I'm no good. I told you I was no good."

"No." Babette said. "I think you're very good. I think this is an excellent hand and fork. From just this I'd let you paint my portrait. It's just that it's a queer thing to draw on a wall, don't you think?"

"I don't know," he said. "I never drew on a wall before."

"Well, it's a nice drawing," Babette decided. "I think you're a good artist."

"Thank you."

"You should tell me that I'm a good singer now."

"But you are!" he said. "You're wonderful."

"Aren't you sweet to say so," Babette smiled graciously. "But I'm really not. There are no good singers in places like this. There are some fine dancers, and I'm not a bad dancer, but I'm a terrible singer."

He didn't know what to say to this, but she was looking at him as if it was his turn to speak, so he asked, "What's your name?"

"Babette," she said. "And when a girl criticizes herself, you really should crawl to the ends of the earth to contradict her, you know."

"I'm sorry," he said. "I didn't know."

She looked at herself in the mirror again. "So do you want to only paint my hand?" she asked. "I haven't got a fork with me."

"No," he said. "I want to paint you, all of you, surrounded by black, surrounded by a whole crowd of black. But then there will be a white light, and you in the center"—he lifted his hands to show placement in an imaginary frame—"in the center in green and red." He dropped his hands. "You should've seen that green and that red."

"Well, it's just the dress you like, then," she said. "Just the dress and the hair."

And your arms, he thought, but only nodded.

"None of that is really me, though," Babette said. "Even my hair is fake."

"Fake?"

"Yes. Fake. Dyed. Please don't look so shocked. Really, you can't have ever seen this color hair before."

"No!" my grandfather almost shouted. "I never had. I think that's exciting, that you can make it that way if you like. I wondered about it, but I didn't think, of course, that it had been dyed. I think that there are so many colors I've never seen—could I touch it?"

"No," Babette said. She reached for a comb from the sink and pulled a single red hair from its teeth. She handed it to him. "You can have this one piece. I'm sure that I don't know you well enough to let you drag your hands all over my head."

He carried the strand to the lamp and stretched it taut under the bulb, frowning in concentration.

"It's brown at one end," he said.

"That's the new growth," she explained.

"Your real hair?"

"The whole thing is my real hair. That brown is my real color."

"Just like mine," he said in surprise. "But you'd never know it to see you onstage. I tell you, you'd never imagine we two would have the same sort of hair. Isn't that remarkable?"

Babette shrugged. "I wouldn't say it was remarkable. But I suppose I'm used to my hair."

"Yes, I suppose you are."

"You're not from New York City, are you?" she asked.

"Yes, I am. I've always lived here."

"Well, you don't act like it. You act just like a little boy from the country. Don't be put off by that, now. It's not a bad thing."

"I think it is. I think it's awful. It comes of not talking to enough people."

"What do you do all day, then?"

"I work in the back of a print shop sometimes. And I live with my great-aunt."

"And she's very old," Babette said.

"Yes. And senile. All she can remember anymore are the names of flowers and girls."

"What?"

"The names of flowers and girls. I don't know why, but that's how it's become. If I ask her a question, she thinks and thinks, but then finally she'll say something like, 'Queen Anne's Lace, Daisy, Emily, Iris, Violet...'"

"No!" Babette said. "I think *that's* remarkable. She must be very pretty to listen to."

"Sometimes. Sometimes it's just sad, because I can see how frustrated she is. Other times she just lets herself talk and strings them altogether: 'Ivy-Buttercup-Catherine-Pearl-Morning Glory-Poppy-Lily-Rose.' Then it's pretty to listen to."

"I'm sure that it is," Babette said. "You forget how many flower's names are girl's names, too."

"Yes," my grandfather nodded. "I've noticed that, also."

"She used to take care of you, didn't she?"

"Yes," he said. "When I was young."

"You still are young," Babette laughed. "I'm even young, and I think I'm much older than you."

"I couldn't imagine how old you are. I hadn't even thought about it."

"I can see why you wouldn't." Babette lifted her mirror again and looked at herself. "All this makeup covers everything. It's hard to tell what I look like at all. I think I am pretty, anyway, but I only realized this week that I'm not going to age well. Some women I know look like girls their whole lives, and I suspect that it's on account of their skin. From a distance I still look fine, and onstage I'll look wonderful for years, but if you come close to me, you'll see the change already."

She jumped up and ran in two steps to the opposite corner of the room from my grandfather.

"You see, I'm just heavenly from here," she said, and then leapt right up to him so that their noses almost touched. "But now look at me. See the little lines here, and here?" She pointed to the corners of each of her eyes. My grandfather saw nothing like lines, only quickly blinking lashes and makeup. He noticed that her breath smelled of cigarettes and oranges, and then he stopped breathing, afraid that he might touch her somehow, or do something wrong. She took a step back, and he exhaled.

"But it's like that with everything you look at too closely," Babette continued. The green dress that she had worn earlier was hanging over a low ceiling pipe. She pulled the dress down, and backed into the far corner again, holding it up against herself. "Just look at this lovely green thing," she said. "Onstage it'll turn a man's head, won't it? And I looked so swish in it, didn't you think?"

My grandfather said that he had thought just that. She approached him again, although, to his relief, did not stand so close this time.

"But you can see what a cheap thing it really is," she said, turning the dress inside out. "It looks just like a child sewed those seams, and it's all kept together with pins. And feel it. Go on."

My grandfather lifted a bit of the skirt in one hand, although he did not really feel the material as he had been told to.

"You can tell right away that it's not really silk, that there isn't actually anything nice about it at all. If I wore this to someone's home, I would look just like some kind of street girl. It's pathetic." She turned from him, and then, over her shoulder, she added, "I will spare you the smell of the thing. I'm certain that you can imagine it."

Actually, he couldn't begin to imagine what it smelled like. Cigarettes and oranges, he suspected, but he had no way of knowing. Babette let her pink towel slide to the floor, and then turned and faced my grandfather in only her slip and stockings.

"I would guess that I look very nice this way," she said, "although I don't have a large mirror, so I'm not sure. But if I were to take this slip off, and if you were to come over here next to me, you'd see that I have all sorts of bumps and hairs and freckles, and you might be very disappointed. You've never seen a naked woman, have you?"

"Yes, I have," he said, and Babette looked at him in quick surprise.

"You have never," she said sharply. "You have never in your life."

"I have. It's been three years now that my aunt can't care for herself. I keep her clean, change her clothes, give her baths."

Babette grimaced. "I think that must be disgusting." She picked up the towel from the floor and wrapped it around her shoulders again. "She probably can't even control herself anymore. She's probably all covered with nasty messes."

"I keep her very clean," he said. "I make sure that she—"

"No." Babette held up her hands. "I can't listen to that, any of that. I'll be sick, really I will."

"I'm sorry," my grandfather said. "I didn't mean—"

"That doesn't disgust you? To do those things?" she interrupted.

"No," he said honestly. "I think it must be just like taking care of a baby, don't you?"

"No. Absolutely not. Isn't that funny, though, that I would be so disgusted by what you just told me? I'm sure there are things in my life that would shock you, but I didn't think that you could shock me."

"I didn't mean to shock you," he apologized. "I was only answering your question."

"Now I'll tell you something shocking," she said. "When I was a little girl in Elmira, we lived next to a very old man, a Civil War veteran. He had his arm amputated during a battle, but he wouldn't let the surgeon throw it away. Instead, he kept it, let all the skin rot off, dried it in the sun, and took it home. A souvenir. He kept it until he died. He used to chase his grandchildren around the yard with it, and then beat them with his own arm bone. And one time he sat me down and showed me the tiny crack from where he'd broken it when he was a boy. So do you think that's disgusting?"

"No," my grandfather said. "It's interesting. I never met anyone from the Civil War."

"Now that's funny," Babette said, "because everyone I ever told that to was shocked, but it never shocked me. So why can't I listen to you talk about cleaning up your old aunt?"

"I don't know," he said. "Except that your story was a lot more interesting."

"I didn't think I still could be disgusted," she said. "I'll tell you another story. The church in my hometown used to have ice cream socials for the children, and we would eat so much that we would get sick. But it was such a treat that we wanted more, so we used to go outside, vomit what we'd eaten, then run back in for more. Pretty soon all the dogs in town would be at the church, eating up that melting ice cream as fast as we could throw it up. Do you think that's disgusting?"

"No," my grandfather said. "I think that's funny."

"So do I. I did then, and I still do." She was quiet for a moment, and then she continued. "Still, there are things that I have seen in the last few years that would make you sick to hear. I could shock you. I've done things that are so awful I wouldn't tell you about them if you begged me to."

"I wouldn't do that. I don't want to know," he said, although when he had left his home that evening, he had wanted to know just that sort of information, desperately.

"It's not important, anyhow. We won't talk about it at all. You're a funny one, though, aren't you? I feel just like an old whore saying that. There are so many old whores in this business, and they all look at young men and say, 'You're a funny one, aren't you?' It's true, though, with you. Most men get a sniff of a girl's past, and want to know every single thing she's ever done. And you keep looking at me, but not like I'm used to."

My grandfather blushed. "I'm sorry if I stared," he said.

"But not just at me! You've been staring at the whole room. I'll bet you've memorized every crack on these walls, the rungs on the bed frame, and what I've got in the bottom of my suitcases, too."

"No."

"Yes you have. And you've been memorizing me. I'm sure of it."

He did not answer her, because, of course, she was absolutely right. Instead, he nervously shifted his weight back and forth, suddenly acutely aware of the different sizes of his feet. Not for the first time in his life, he felt unbalanced from the ground up because of this deformity, almost dizzy from it.

"Now I've made you flustered," Babette said. "I think that's easy enough to do, so I won't be proud." After a pause, she added, "I believe you really are an artist because of how you've been staring. You're a watcher, not a listener, am I right?"

"I don't know what you mean," he said.

"Hum me a bar from my song tonight, or even tell me a line from the chorus. Go on."

He thought back quickly, and at first could only come up with the sound of the faceless man beside him demanding the time. Then he said, "You sang something about being blue because someone left, a man, I think..." He trailed off, then added weakly, "It was a pretty song. You sang it well."

She laughed. "It's just as well that you didn't listen. It's a stupid song. But tell me, how many couples were dancing behind me?"

"Four," he answered without hesitation.

"And who was the smallest girl on stage?"

"You were."

"And how big was the orchestra?"

"I couldn't see, except the conductor, and the bass player, of course, because he was standing."

"Yes, of course." Babette walked to the sink, and spent a few moments doing something with the toiletries there. Then she turned and approached him with one arm outstretched. She had striped the white underside of her forearm with five short strokes of lipstick, each shade only slightly different than the one before it. She covered her mouth with her other hand and asked, "Which color do I have on my lips right now?"

My grandfather looked down at her arm, unexpectedly alarmed at the slashes of red across white skin. He paused before answering because something else had caught his eye, a faint, bluish vein that ran diagonally across the inside bend of her elbow. Then he pointed to the second lipstick stripe from her wrist and said assuredly, almost absently, "This one."

He looked up at her face only after she had let her arm drop, and the intriguing blue vein vanished from view. She was still holding her other hand to her mouth, and staring at him with eyes so wide and spooked that it seemed as if the hand belonged to a stranger, an attacker. He slowly pulled her arm down away from her face, and looked at her in silence. He looked at her lips and confirmed that he had chosen correctly. Without thinking about what he was beginning to do, he lifted her chin so that her face was out of shadow, and studied the shape of her forehead, nose, and jaw. Babette watched him.

"Look," she said. "If you're going to kiss me, just—"

She stopped talking as he released her chin and took hold of her wrist, turning it over and exposing where she had marked herself with the lipsticks. He stared for a long while, and she finally began to rub at the smearing red lines with the corner of her towel, as if embarrassed now by what she had done. But my grandfather wasn't looking at that. He was studying that faint blue vein again, examining its short path across its cradle, the soft fold of her arm. After some time, he lifted her other arm and compared the twin vein there, holding her wrists gently, but with a thorough self-absorption that negated the lightness of his touch. She pulled away, and he released his hold without speaking.

He crossed the room and looked once more at the dress, carefully noting the alarming green again, frowning. Then he returned to Babette to confirm the color of her hair. He reached up to touch it, but she caught his arm.

"Please," she said. "That's enough."

My grandfather blinked, and stared at her blankly, as if she had just woken him from a nap, or delivered a piece of unexpected bad news. He glanced around the room as though searching for someone else, someone more familiar, and then frowned, and looked back at Babette.

"You should know that there are ways to act," she said evenly. "There are things to say so that a girl doesn't have to feel so used." Her face was empty of expression, but she had lifted the hand mirror, and was holding it tightly, as one might hold a tennis racket, or a weapon.

He blushed then, realizing. "I'm sorry," he stammered. "I didn't mean . . . I get that way sometimes, looking, staring like that—"

Babette cut him off with a sharp, irritated glance that crossed her face as fast and dark as a shadow.

"You can't do that to people," she said. He started to apologize, but she shook her head. Finally she continued, "It's going to be a very good painting, but not very flattering to me. Which is fine," she added, shrugging cavalierly, "because I'll never see it."

"I'm sorry," he repeated, feeling and sounding like a stranger again, as if he was once more standing outside her door in the dark, cobwebbed hall beneath the stage.

She shrugged once more, and lifted a hand to touch a red curl that was already in place. My grandfather watched, silent.

"Don't you think you should leave now?" Babette asked at last.

He nodded grimly, disgusted by the futility of apology, and left. He found his way through the dark hall and out of the nightclub alone, not needing, or even remembering, the young usher who had led him to Babette. Outside it had stopped raining. His overcoat had dried in her room, and he had already forgotten that it had ever been wet.

The widow with the bad knees was waiting for him when he got home. She did not question where he had been, but said only that his aunt was asleep in her chair, and had been quiet all night.

"I gave her some soup," she whispered as he unlocked the door.

"Thank you," he said. "You're very kind."

My grandfather closed the door quietly behind him and took off his shoes so that he wouldn't wake his aunt when he passed through the sitting room. In his own bedroom, he began working on what would be the first important painting of his career. He filled several pages with the charcoal-smudged, faceless crowd of the nightclub audience, leaving a glaringly empty white space in each sketch, always in the same spot. After several hours, he examined his work, irritated to see that all of the pictures were identical: uniformly solid and dark with a gaping opening in the center for a singer he didn't know how to begin to draw.

He laid his head down on his sleeve and shut his eyes. He breathed in the tobacco smell of his shirt, at first inadvertently, and then with great purpose, as if his skill would be enhanced by deeply inhaling that dank, reminiscent odor. After some time, he opened his small box of oil paints and began to try mixing the green of Babette's dress. Although later in his life his mastery of color would be considered unrivaled, that night, as a young man with a limited collection of oils, he was overwhelmed by the task of precisely recalling that shade. He worked carefully, and several times felt that he was close to success, but found that, as the paint dried, the effect was lost, the color dulled. He was struck by the inevitability of his own limitations.

His desk was covered already with torn pieces of paper and patches of sticky, inadequate green. He looked at the charcoal sketches again, and thought about what Babette had said. She was correct to say that it would be a good painting, but wrong to think that it would not flatter her. My grandfather visualized the figure that he knew would eventually fill the empty white space, and he was certain that it would be a very appealing character. Nonetheless, the painting was destined, in his eyes, to always be a clumsy rendition of a transient, fantastic moment. It was he, ultimately, who would not be flattered by this work. It was his misfortune to realize this so young, and so completely.

He heard a sound, and set his sketchbook quietly down on the floor. His aunt was talking, and he wondered how long she had been awake. He went into the sitting room, where he turned on a small reading lamp. She was rocking slowly, and he listened for a while to her mumbling.

"Black-eyed Susan," she said, "Grace, Anna, Marigold, Pansy, Sarah..."

She had become smaller with age. In this lighting, however, with dark blankets over her legs and embroidered pillows around her, she appeared stately, if not strong. My grandfather sat at her feet like a child waiting for a story.

"Lady's-slipper, Rosehip, Faith, Zinnia, Cowbell," she said.

He rested his head on her knee, and she stopped talking. She laid her hand on his head and kept it there, where it trembled with the constant palsy of old age. He began to fall asleep, and, in fact, had dozed off when she woke him by saying, "Baby." He half-opened his eyes without lifting his head, not sure what he had heard.

She repeated the word, and then again and again, in the same low tone as her strange, rambling lists.

"Baby, baby, baby," she said, and in his distracted exhaustion, he misunderstood her. He believed that she was saying "Babette," over and over. Of all the flowers and girls, he thought, it was this rich, painful name that she had finally settled on to repeat and repeat and repeat.

He closed his eyes again. Even shut, they ached, as if somehow they had been forced to look on himself in sixty years: elderly and dying, calling to his daughters and his granddaughters, calling them all to him, calling them all Babette.

Real Life #2: Scraps

Althea kept a list of the things she could live without—
perfumed soaps, clean rugs, cats. It was a long list. She added to
it from scraps she wrote on when she thought of them.
Every fortnight or so she gathered up the scraps and in her
ancient and exquisite longhand added them to her bound list.
Love wasn't on it but a list of the people she might have expected
it from was. Who did he think she was? The shiny sleeve he
wiped his mouth on? *Sit down,* her husband said on the
telephone one afternoon after she got home. The possibility
of slow transformation strains the modern sensibility, but change
occurs, the reef's meticulous accrual, the iceberg melts
and floods ensue. Even a rise of one degree in temperature and
slowly, slowly. People rise in trees. *Sit down. I have something
to tell you.* So then he said, *I've got something good to tell you.*
Out the window the sky is flat as an old cheek. There is no
end to it. Althea takes out a clean page and draws a line down
the middle. Column A, she titles *The Ones I Love;* Column B is
The Ones Who Love Me. The sky is flat and she can touch it.

She blushes. Not the fine weather of inevitability. Not desire,
that fringed purse, but she feels just fine. What's left? And does
she bless the pressed flowers of occasion? Outside,

the sky. *"My visibility is greatly enhanced,"* she writes,
"by the flatness of the terrain."

The Spindle Turns on the Knees of Necessity

—Plato, Republic

The cold call of the cold to the cold
Follows itself to the moon,
To the edge of the storm, to the fold in the fold
In the shrouds of the fallen-too-soon.
The call of the cold to the never-held,
The sung-over, the one-by-one
Follows the moon to the world where the world
Pulls always, pulls all, and pulls down.
From high to higher, from sharp to celeste,
From already over to barely begun,
From once to after, from east to east,
The call's cold turnings find what cold cannot turn:
The knees of the knees of the must
And the breasts of the never again.

What One Would See If One Did Not

—*Wittgenstein,* Remarks on Colour

A chair,
A nuthatch on the trunk of a walnut tree,
The bloated belly of a dead deer,
A man of seventy
Grunting at toenails he struggles to pare.
A woman
In a straw hat over straw-textured hair
Kneeling in a garden.
What is not now departure will be.
Foam on the shore of a lake,
An indigo butterfly,
A cloud in a long orange-tinged lavender arc,
The last tiny gasps of a room long empty,
A silver forest growing dark, dark, dark.

This Morally Neutralized Domain of Intercourse

—*Habermas,* Communication and the Evolution of Society

The man with the crooked dick strikes a match.
The woman with one arm breaks into flame.
The man finds a bird's skull and wants to play catch.
The woman hears the skull calling her name.
He looks out the window. She looks in the door.
He crushes a spider onto the pane.
Her sun is the ceiling. His stars are the floor.
She bites her knuckles until he feels pain.
She knows his thoughts while he still has to guess.
He knows when she knows what he has to learn.
His favorite word is now. Her word is yes.
Apart, each is only radiant stone,
But one touch brings them to critical mass.
He likes to burn things and she likes to burn.

Jet

Sometimes I wish that I was still out
on the back porch, drinking jet fuel
with the boys, getting louder and louder
as the empty cans drop out of our paws
like booster rockets falling back to earth

and we soar up into the summer stars.
Summer. The big sky river rushes overhead,
bearing asteroids and mist, blind fish
and old space suits with skeletons inside.
On earth, men celebrate their hairiness

and it is good, a way of letting life
out of the box, uncapping the bottle
to let the effervescence gush
through the narrow, usually constricted neck.

And now the crickets plug in their appliances
in unison, and then the fireflies flash
dots and dashes in their grass, like punctuation
for the labyrinthine, untrue tales of sex
someone is telling in the dark, though

no one really hears. We gaze into the night
as if remembering the bright unbroken planet
we have come from, to which we will never
be permitted to return.
We are amazed how hurt we are.
We would give anything for what we have.

Self-Improvement

Just before she flew off like a swan
to her wealthy parents' summer home,
Bruce's college girlfriend asked him to
improve his expertise at oral sex,
and offered him some technical advice:

use nothing but his tongue tip
to flick the light switch in his room
on and off a hundred times a day
until he grew fluent at the nuances
of force and latitude.

Imagine him at practice every evening,
more inspired than he ever was by algebra,
beads of sweat sprouting on his brow,
thinking, *thirty-seven, thirty-eight,*
seeing, in the tunnel vision of his mind's eye,
the quadratic equation of her climax
yield to the logic
of his simple math.

Maybe he unscrewed
the bulb from his apartment ceiling
so that the passersby would not believe
a giant firefly was pulsing
its electric abdomen in 3B.

Maybe, as he stood
two inches from the wall,
in darkness, fogging the old plaster
with his breath, he visualized the future
as a mansion rising from the hillside
of the shore that he was rowing to
with his tongue's exhausted oar.

Of course the girlfriend dumped him:
met someone, après-ski, who,
using nothing but his nose,
could identify the vintage of a Cabernet.
Sometimes we are asked
to get good at something we have
no talent for,

or we excel at something we will never
have the opportunity to prove.
Often we ask ourselves
to make absolute sense
out of what just happens
and in this way, what we are practicing

is suffering,
which everybody practices,
but strangely few of us
grow graceful in.

The climaxes of suffering are complex,
costly, beautiful, but secret.
Bruce never played the light switch again.

So the avenues we walk down,
full of bodies wearing faces,
are full of hidden talent:
enough to make pianos moan,
sidewalks split,
streetlights deliriously flicker.

CHRISTINE HUME

Flush

Not sure what to leave in,
I begin with Jenny, her sister
and me at the anchor of our great mall,
Sears: We stuff cassettes
down her crooked spine's brace,
and stroll through
our mother's aisle (lifting douches),
into the store ladies' room
where we fill the drooping bags
at taps that keep running.
Past the vinyl fainting couch,
inside the pink stalls
we open our legs
to the plastic finger hollow—
before tampons, wine bottle necks,
diaphragms—our dry dark straddles
vinegar-drenched cool and for the sake
of endurance, we hold it, clenching
the delicate lie: One of us would be
a bitter mother, wedding band around
a bloated finger; a bad wife,
mirroring any man's need;
and someone's body would fail.
So bracing ourselves
against dizzy appetite
and the awful hush—
as all summer I've slummed
in your drug-ragged body,
the woods dogging the windows

around our bed which is anyone's
at night like the shapeless wet
between my legs or a hand
tucked there in sleep.

Birthmates

This was what responsibility meant in a dinosaur industry, toward the end of yet another quarter of bad-to-worse news: You called the travel agent back, and even though there was indeed an economy room in the hotel where the conference was being held, a room overlooking the cooling towers, you asked if there wasn't something still cheaper. And when Marie the new girl came back with something amazingly cheap, you took it— only to discover, as Art Woo was discovering now, that the doors were locked after nine o'clock. The neighborhood had looked not great but not bad, and the building itself, regular enough. Brick, four stories, a rolled-up awning. A bright-lit hotel logo, with a raised-plastic, smiling sun. But there was a kind of crossbar rigged across the inside of the glass door, and that was not at all regular. A two-by-four, it appeared, wrapped in rust-colored carpet. Above this, inside the glass, hung a small gray sign. If the taxi had not left, Art might not have rung the buzzer, as per the instructions.

But the taxi had indeed left, and the longer Art huddled on the stoop in the clumpy December snow, the emptier and more poorly lit the street appeared. His buzz was answered by an enormous black man wearing a neck brace. The shoulder seams of the man's blue waffle-weave jacket were visibly straining; around the brace was tied a necktie, which reached only a third of the way down his chest. All the same, it was neatly fastened together with a hotel-logo tie tack about two inches from the bottom. The tie tack was smiling; the man was not. He held his smooth, round face perfectly expressionless, and he lowered his gaze at every opportunity— not so that it was rude, but so that it was clear he wasn't selling anything to anybody. Regulation tie, thought Art, regulation jacket. He wondered if the man would turn surly soon enough.

For Art had come to few conclusions about life in his thirty-eight years, but this was one of them—that men turned surly when their clothes didn't fit them. This man, though, belied the rule. He was courteous, almost formal in demeanor; and if the lobby seemed not only too small for him, like his jacket, but also too much like a bus station, what with its smoked mirror wall, and its linoleum, and its fake wood, and its vending machines, what did that matter to Art? The sitting area looked as though it was in the process of being cleaned—the sixties Scandinavian chairs and couch and coffee table were pulled every which way, as if by someone hellbent on the dust balls. Still, Art proceeded with his check-in. He was going with his gut here. Here, as in any business situation, he was looking foremost at the personnel; and the man with the neck brace had put him at some ease. It wasn't until after Art had taken his credit card back that he noticed, above the check-out desk, a wooden plaque from a neighborhood association. He squinted at its brass face plate: FEWEST CUSTOMER INJURIES, 1972–73.

What about the years since '73? Had the hotel gotten more dangerous since then, or had other hotels gotten safer? Maybe neither. For all he knew, the neighborhood association had dissolved and was no longer distributing plaques. Art reminded himself that in life, some signs were no signs. It's what he used to tell his ex-wife, Lisa—Lisa who loved to read everything into everything; Lisa who was attuned. She left him on a day when she saw a tree get split by lightning. Of course, that was an extraordinary thing to see. An event of a lifetime. Lisa said the tree had sizzled. He wished he had seen it, too. But what did it mean, except that the tree had been the tallest in the neighborhood, and was no longer? It meant nothing; ditto with the plaque. Art made his decision, which perhaps was not the right decision. Perhaps he should have looked for another hotel.

But it was late—on the way out, his plane had sat on the runway, just sat and sat, as if it were never going to take off—and god only knew what he would have ended up paying if he had relied on a cabbie to simply bring him somewhere else. Forget twice—it could have been three, four times what he would have paid for that room with the view of the cooling towers, easy. At this hour, after all, and that was a conference rate.

So he double-locked his door instead. He checked behind the

hollowcore doors of the closet, and under the steel-frame bed, and also in the swirly green shower stall unit. He checked behind the seascapes, to be sure there weren't any peepholes. That *Psycho*—how he wished he'd never seen that movie. Why hadn't anyone ever told him that movies could come back to haunt you? No one had warned him. The window opened onto a fire escape; not much he could do about that except check the window locks, big help that those were—a sure deterrent for the subset of all burglars that was burglars too skittish to break glass. Which was what percent of intruders, probably? Ten percent? Fifteen? He closed the drapes, then decided he would be more comfortable with the drapes open. He wanted to be able to see what approached, if anything did. He unplugged the handset of his phone from the rest, a calculated risk. On the one hand, he wouldn't be able to call the police if there was an intruder. On the other, he would be armed. He had read somewhere a story about a woman who threw the handset of her phone at an attacker, and killed him. Needless to say, there had been some luck involved in that eventuality. Still, Art thought a) surely he could throw as hard as that woman, and b) even without the luck, his throw would most likely be hard enough to at least slow up an intruder. Especially since this was an old handset, the hefty kind that made you feel the seriousness of human communication. In a newer hotel, he probably would have had a new phone, with lots of buttons he would never use but which would make him feel he had many resources at his disposal. In the hotel where the conference was, there were probably buttons for the health club, and for the concierge, and for the three restaurants, and for room service. He tried not to think about this as he went to sleep, clutching the handset.

He did not sleep well.

In the morning he debated whether to take the handset with him into the elevator. Again he wished he hadn't seen so many movies. It was movies that made him think, that made him imagine things like *what if in the elevator*. Of course, a handset was an awkward thing to hide. It wasn't like a knife, say, that could be whipped out of nowhere. Even a pistol at least fit in a guy's pocket. Whereas a telephone handset did not. All the same, he brought it with him. He tried to carry it casually, as if he were going out for a run and using it for a hand weight, or as if he were in the telephone business.

He strode down the hall. Victims shuffled; that's what everybody said. A lot of mugging had to do with nonverbal cues, which is why Lisa used to walk tall after dark, sending vibes. For this he used to tease her. If she was so worried, she should lift weights and run, the way he did; that, he maintained, was the substantive way of helping oneself. She had agreed. For a while they had met after work at the gym. That was before she dropped a weight on her toe and decided she preferred to sip piña coladas and watch. Naturally, he grunted on. But to what avail? Who could appreciate his pectorals through his suit and overcoat? Pectorals had no deterrent value, that was what he was thinking now. And he was, though not short, not tall. He continued striding. Sending vibes. He was definitely going to eat in the dining room of the hotel where the conference was being held, he decided. What's more, he was going to have a full American breakfast, with bacon and eggs, none of this continental breakfast bullshit.

In truth, he had always considered the sight of men eating croissants slightly ridiculous, especially at the beginning, when for the first bite they had to maneuver the point of the crescent into their mouths. No matter what a person did, he ended up with an asymmetrical mouthful of pastry, which he then had to relocate with his tongue to a more central location, and this made him look less purposive than he might. Also, croissants were more apt than other breakfast foods to spray little flakes all over one's clean dark suit. Art himself had accordingly never ordered a croissant in any working situation, and he believed that attention to this sort of detail was how it was that he had not lost his job like so many of his colleagues.

This was, in other words, how it was that he was still working in his fitfully dying industry, and was now carrying a telephone handset with him into the elevator. Art braced himself as the elevator doors opened slowly, jerkily, in the low-gear manner of elevator doors in the Third World. He strode in, and was surrounded by, of all things, children. Down in the lobby, too, there were children, and here and there, women he knew to be mothers by their looks of dogged exasperation. A welfare hotel! He laughed out loud. Almost everyone was black, the white children stood out like little missed opportunities of the type that made Art's boss throw his tennis racket across the room. Of course, the racket was always in its padded protective cover and not in much danger of getting injured, though the person in whose vicinity it was aimed sometimes was. Art once suffered what he rather hoped would turn out to be a broken nose, but was only a bone bruise with so little skin discoloration that people had a hard time believing the incident had actually taken place. Yet it had. *Don't talk to me about fault, bottom line it's you Japs who are responsible for this whole fucking mess,* his boss had said—this though what was the matter with minicomputers, really, was personal computers. A wholly American phenomenon. And of course, Art could have sued over this incident if he could have proved that it had happened. Some people, most notably Lisa, thought he certainly ought to have at least quit.

But he didn't sue and he didn't quit. He took his tennis racket on the nose, so to speak, and when the next day his boss apologized for losing control, Art said he understood. And when his boss said that Art shouldn't take what he said personally, in fact he knew Art was not a Jap, but a chink, plus he had called someone else a lazy wop just that morning, it was just his style, Art said again that he understood. And then Art said that he hoped his boss would remember Art's great understanding come promotion time. Which his boss did, to Art's satisfaction. In Art's view, this was a victory. In Art's view, he had perceived leverage where others would only perceive affront. He had maintained a certain perspective.

But this certain perspective was, in addition to the tree, why Lisa left him. He thought of that now, the children underfoot, his handset in hand. So many children. It was as if he were seeing before him all the children he would never have. He stood a moment, paralyzed; his heart lost its muscle. A child in a red running suit ran by, almost grabbed the handset out of Art's grasp; then another, in a brown jacket with a hood. He looked up to see a group of grade school boys arrayed about the seating area, watching. Already he had become the object of a dare, apparently—there was so little else in the way of diversion in the lobby—and realizing this, he felt renewed enough to want to laugh again. When a particularly small child swung by in his turn—a child of maybe five or six, small enough to be wearing snowpants—Art almost tossed the handset to him, but thought better of the idea. Who wanted to be charged for a missing phone?

As it was, Art wondered if he shouldn't put the handset back in his room rather than carry it around all day. For what was he going to do at the hotel where the conference was, check it? He imagined himself running into Billy Shore—that was his counterpart at Info-Edge, his competitor in the insurance market. A man with no management ability, and no technical background either. But he could offer customers a personal computer option, which Art could not; and what's more, Billy had been a quarterback in college. This meant he strutted around as though it still mattered that he had connected with his tight end in the final minutes of what Art could not help but think of as the Wilde-Beastie game. And it meant that Billy was sure to ask him, *What are you doing with a phone in your hand? Talking to yourself again?* Making everyone around them laugh.

Billy was that kind of guy. He had come up through sales, and was always cracking a certain type of joke—about drinking, or sex, or how much the wife shopped. Of course, he never used those words. He never called things by their plain names. He always talked in terms of knocking back some brewskis, or running the triple option, or doing some damage. He made assumptions as though it were a basic bodily function: Of course his knowledge was the common knowledge. Of course people understood what it was that he was referring to so delicately. *Listen, champ,* he said, putting his arm around you. If he was smug, it was in an affable kind of way. *So what do you think the poor people are doing tonight?* Billy not only spoke what Art called Mainstreamese, he spoke such a pure dialect of it that Art once asked him if he realized that he was a pollster's delight. He spoke the thoughts of thousands, Art told him, he breathed their very words. Naturally, Billy did not respond, except to say, *What's that?* and turn away. He rubbed his torso as he turned, as if ruffling his chest hairs through the long-staple cotton. Primate behavior, Lisa used to call this. It was her belief that neckties evolved in order to check this very motion, uncivilized as it was. She also believed that this was the sort of thing you never saw Asian men do—at least not if they were brought up properly.

Was that true? Art wasn't so sure. Lisa had grown up on the West Coast, she was full of Asian consciousness; whereas all he knew was that no one had so much as smiled politely at his poll-ster remark. On the other hand, the first time Art was introduced to Billy, and Billy said, *Art Woo, how's that for a nice Pole-ack name,* everyone broke right up in great rolling guffaws. Of course, they laughed the way people laughed at conferences, which was not because something was really funny, but because it was part of being a good guy, and because they didn't want to appear to have missed their cue.

The phone, the phone. If only Art could fit it in his briefcase! But his briefcase was overstuffed; it was always overstuffed; really, it was too bad he had the slim silhouette type, and hard-side besides. Italian. That was Lisa's doing, she thought the fatter kind made him look like a salesman. Not that there was really anything the matter with that, in his view. Billy Shore notwithstanding, sales were important. But she was the liberal arts type, Lisa was, the type who did not like to think about money, but only about her feelings. Money was not money to her, but support, and then a means of support much inferior to hand-holding or other forms of finger play. She did not believe in a modern-day econo-my, in which everyone played a part in a large and complex whole that introduced efficiencies that at least theoretically raised every-one's standard of living. She believed in expressing herself. Also in taking classes, and in knitting. There was nothing, she believed, like taking a walk in the autumn woods wearing a hand-knit sweater. Of course, she did look beautiful in them, especially the violet ones. That was her color—Asians are winters, she always said—and sometimes she liked to wear the smallest smidgeon of matching violet eyeliner, even though it was, as she put it, less than organic to wear eyeliner on a hike.

Little Snowpants ran at Art again, going for the knees—*a tack-le,* thought Art, as he went down; Red Running Suit snatched away the handset and went sprinting off, triumphant. Teamwork! The children chortled together; how could Art not smile a little, even if they had gotten his overcoat dirty? He brushed himself off, ambled over.

"Hey, guys," he said. "That was some move back there."

"Ching chang polly wolly wing wong," said Little Snowpants.

"Now, now, that's no way to talk," said Art.

"Go to hell!" Brown Jacket pulled at the corners of his eyes to make them slanty.

"Listen up," said Art. "I'll make you a deal." Really he only meant to get the handset back, so as to avoid getting charged for it.

But the next thing he knew, something had hit his head with a crack, and he was out.

Lisa had left in a more or less amicable way. She had not called a lawyer, or a mover; she had simply pressed his hands with both of hers and, in her most California voice, said, *Let's be nice.* And then she had asked him if he wouldn't help her move her boxes, at least the heavy ones that really were too much for her. He had helped. He had carried the heavy boxes, and also the less heavy ones. Being a weight lifter, after all. He had sorted books and rolled glasses into pieces of newspaper, feeling all the while like a statistic. A member of the modern age, a story for their friends to rake over, and all because he had not gone with Lisa to her grieving group. Or at least that was the official beginning of the trouble; probably the real beginning had been when Lisa—no, *they*—had trouble getting pregnant. When they decided to, as the saying went, do infertility. Or had he done the deciding, as Lisa later maintained? He had thought it was a joint decision, though it was true that he had done the analysis that led to the joint decision. He had been the one to figure the odds, to do the projections. He had drawn the decision tree, according to whose branches they had nothing to lose by going ahead.

Neither one of them had realized then how much would be involved—the tests, the procedures, the drugs, the ultrasounds. Lisa's arms were black and blue from having her blood drawn every day, and before long he was giving practice shots to an orange, that he might prick her some more. He was telling her to take a breath so that on the exhale he could poke her in the buttocks. This was no longer practice, and neither was it like poking an orange. The first time, he broke out in such a sweat that his vision blurred and he had to blink, with the result that he pulled the needle out slowly and crookedly, occasioning a most un-orange-like cry. The second time, he wore a sweatband. Later he jabbed her like nothing; her ovaries swelled to the point where he could feel them through her jeans.

He still had the used syringes—snapped in half and stored, as per their doctor's recommendation, in plastic soda bottles. She had left him those. Bottles of medical waste, to be disposed of responsibly, meaning that he was probably stuck with them, ha ha, for the rest of his life. A little souvenir of this stage of their marriage, his equivalent of the pile of knit goods she had to show for the ordeal; for through it all, she had knit, as if to gently demonstrate an alternative use of needles. Sweaters, sweaters, but also baby blankets, mostly to give away, only one or two to keep. She couldn't help herself. There was anesthesia, and egg harvesting, and anesthesia and implanting, until she finally did get pregnant, twice, and then a third time she went to four and a half months before they found a problem. On the amnio, it showed up, brittle bone disease—a genetic abnormality such as could happen to anyone.

He steeled himself for another attempt; she grieved. And this was the difference between them, that he saw hope still, some feeble, skeletal hope, where she saw loss. She called the fetus her baby, though it was not a baby, just a baby-to-be, as he tried to say; as even the grieving-group facilitator tried to say. She said he didn't understand, couldn't possibly understand, it was something you understood with your body, and it was not his body but hers that knew the baby, loved the baby, lost the baby. In the grieving class the women agreed. They commiserated. They bonded, subtly affirming their common biology by doing eighty-five percent of the talking. The room was painted mauve—a feminine color that seemed to support them in their process. At times it seemed that the potted palms were female, too, nodding, nodding, though really their sympathy was just rising air from the heating vents. Other husbands started missing sessions—they never talked, anyway, you hardly noticed their absence—and finally he missed some also. One, maybe two, for real reasons, nothing cooked up. But the truth was, as Lisa sensed, that he thought she had lost perspective. They could try again, after all. What did it help to despair? Look, they knew they could get pregnant and, what's more, sustain the pregnancy. That was progress. But she was like an island in her grief, a retreating island, if there was such a thing, receding to the horizon of their marriage, and then to its vanishing point.

Of course, he had missed her terribly at first; now he missed her still, but more sporadically. At odd moments, for example now, waking up in a strange room with ice on his head. He was lying on an unmade bed just like the bed in his room, except that everywhere around it were heaps of what looked to be blankets and clothes. The only clothes on a hanger were his jacket and overcoat; these hung neatly, side by side, in the otherwise empty closet. There was also an extra table in this room, with a two-burner hot plate, a pan on top of that, and a pile of dishes. A brown cube refrigerator. The drapes were closed; a chair had been pulled up close to him; the bedside light was on. A woman was leaning into its circle, mopping his brow. *Don't you move, now.* She was the shade of black Lisa used to call mochaccino, and she was wearing a blue flowered apron. Kind eyes, and a long face—the kind of face where you could see the muscles of the jaw working alongside the cheekbone. An upper lip like an archery bow, and a graying afro, shortish. She smelled of smoke. Nothing unusual except that she was so very thin, about the thinnest person he had ever seen, and yet she was cooking something—burning something, it smelled like, though maybe it was just a hair fallen onto the heating element. She stood up to tend the pan. The acrid smell faded. He saw powder on the table. It was white, a plastic bagful. His eyes widened. He sank back, trying to figure out what to do. His head pulsed. Tylenol, he needed, two. Lisa always took one because she was convinced the dosages recommended were based on large male specimens; and though she had never said that she thought he ought to keep it to one also, not being so tall, he was adamant about taking two. Two, two, two. He wanted his drugs, he wanted them now. And his own drugs, that was, not somebody else's.

"Those kids kind of rough," said the woman. "They getting to that age. I told them one of these days somebody gonna get hurt, and sure enough, they knocked you right out. You might as well been hit with a bowling ball. I never saw anything like it. We called the man, but they got other things on their mind besides to come see about trouble here. Nobody shot, so they went on down to the Dunkin' Donuts. They know they can count on a ruckus there." She winked. "How you feeling? That egg hurt?"

He felt his head. A lump sat right on top of it, incongruous as something left by a glacier. What were those called, those stray boulders you saw perched in hair-raising positions? On cliffs?

"I feel like I died and came back to life head-first," he said.

"I'm going make you something nice. Make you feel a whole lot better."

"Uh," said Art. "If you don't mind, I'd rather just have a Tylenol. You got any Tylenol? I had some in my briefcase. If I still have my briefcase."

"You what?"

"My briefcase," said Art again, with a panicky feeling. "Do you know what happened to my briefcase?"

"Oh, it's right by the door. I'll get it, don't move."

And then there it was, his briefcase, its familiar hard-sided, Italian slenderness resting right on his stomach. He clutched it. "Thank you," he whispered.

"You need help with that thing?"

"No," said Art, but when he opened the case, it slid, and everything spilled out—his notes, his files, his papers. All that figuring—how strange his concerns looked here, on this brown shag carpet.

"Here," said the woman, and again—"I'll get it, don't move"— as gently, beautifully, she gathered up all the folders and put them in the case. There was an odd, almost practiced finesse to her movements; the files could have been cards in a card dealer's hands. "I used to be a nurse," she explained, as if reading his mind. "I picked up a few folders in my time. Here's the Tylenol."

"I'll have two."

"Course you will," she said. "Two Tylenol and some hot milk with honey. Hope you don't mind the powdered, we just got moved here, we don't have no supplies. I used to be a nurse, but I don't got no milk and I don't got no Tylenol, my guests got to bring their own. How you like that."

Art laughed as much as he could. "You got honey, though, how's that?"

"I don't know, it got left here by somebody," said the nurse. "Hope there's nothing growing in it."

Art laughed again, then let her help him sit up to take his pills. The nurse—her name was Cindy—plumped his pillows. She administered his milk. Then she sat—very close to him, it seemed—and chatted amiably about this and that. How she wasn't going to be staying at the hotel for too long, how her kids had had to switch schools, how she wasn't afraid to take in a strange, injured man. After all, she grew up in the projects, she could take care of herself. She showed him her switchblade, which had somebody's initials carved on it, she didn't know whose. She had never used it, she said, somebody gave it to her. And that somebody didn't know whose initials those were, either, she said, at least so far as she knew. Then she lit a cigarette and smoked while he told her first about his conference and then about how he had ended up at the hotel by mistake. He told her the latter with some hesitation, hoping he wasn't offending her. But she wasn't offended. She laughed with a cough, emitting a series of smoke puffs.

"Sure must've been a shock," she said. "Land up in a place like this. This no place for a nice boy like you."

That stung a little. *Boy!* But more than the stinging, he felt something else. "What about you? It's no place for you, either, you and your kids."

"Maybe so," she said. "But that's how the Almighty planned it, right? You folk rise up while we set and watch." She said this with so little rancor, with something so like intimacy, that it almost seemed an invitation of sorts.

But maybe he was kidding himself. Maybe he was assuming things, just like Billy Shore, just like men throughout the ages. Projecting desire where there was none, assigning and imagining, and in juicy detail. Being Asian didn't exempt him from that. *You folk.* Art was late, but it didn't much matter. This conference was being held in conjunction with a much larger conference, the real draw; the idea being that maybe between workshops and on breaks, the conferees would drift down and see what minicomputers could do for them. That mostly meant lunch.

In the meantime, things were totally dead, allowing Art to appreciate just how much the trade show floor had shrunk—down to a fraction of what it had been in previous years, and the booths were not what they had been, either. It used to be that the floor was crammed with the fanciest booths on the market; Art's used to be twenty by twenty. It took days to put together. Now you saw blank spots on the floor where exhibitors didn't even bother to show up, and those weren't even as demoralizing as some of the makeshift jobbies—exhibit booths that looked like high school science fair projects. They might as well have been made out of cardboard and Magic Marker. Art himself had a booth you could buy from an airplane catalog, the kind that rolled up into cordura bags. And people were stingy with brochures now, too. Gone were the twelve-page, four-color affairs; now the pamphlets were four-page, two-color, with extra bold graphics for attempted pizazz, and not everybody got one, only people who were serious.

Art set up. Then, even though he should have been manning his spot, he drifted from booth to booth, saying hello to people he should have seen at breakfast. They were happy to see him, to talk shop, to pop some grapes off the old grapevine. Really, if he weren't staying in a welfare hotel, he would have felt downright respected. *You folk.* What folk did Cindy mean? Maybe she was just being matter-of-fact, keeping her perspective. Although how could anyone be so matter-of-fact about something so bitter? He wondered this even as he took his imaginative liberties with her. These began with a knock on her door and coursed through some hot times but ended (what a good boy he was) with him rescuing her and her children (he wondered how many there were) from their dead-end life. What was the matter with him, that he could not imagine mating without legal sanction? His libido was not what it should be, clearly, or at least it was not what Billy Shore's was. Art tried to think *game plan,* but in truth he could not even identify what a triple option would be in this case. All he knew was that, assuming, to begin with, that she was willing, he couldn't sleep with a woman like Cindy and then leave her flat. She could *you folk* him, he could never *us folk* her.

He played with some software at a neighboring booth; it appeared interesting enough but kept crashing so he couldn't tell too much. Then he dutifully returned to his own booth, where he was visited by a number of people he knew, people with whom he was friendly enough. The sort of people to whom he might have shown pictures of his children. He considered telling one or two of them about the events of the morning. Not about the invitation that might not have been an invitation, but about finding himself in a welfare hotel and being beaned with his own telephone. Phrases drifted through his head. *Not so bad as you'd think. You'd be surprised how friendly the people are. Unpretentious. Though, of course, no health club.* But in the end the subject simply did not come up and did not come up until he realized that he was keeping it to himself, and that he was committing more resources to this task than he had readily available. He felt invaded—as if he had been infected by a self-replicating bug. Something that was iterating and iterating, growing and growing, crowding out everything else in the CPU. The secret was intolerable; it was bound to spill out of him sooner or later. He just hoped it wouldn't be sooner.

He just hoped it wouldn't be to Billy Shore, for whom he began to search, so as to be certain to avoid him.

Art had asked about Billy at the various booths, but no one had seen him; his absence was weird. It spooked Art. When finally some real live conferees stopped by to see his wares, he had trouble concentrating; everywhere in the conversation he was missing opportunities, he knew it. And all because his CPU was full of iterating nonsense. Not too long ago, in looking over some database software in which was loaded certain fun facts about people in the industry, Art had looked up Billy, and discovered that he had been born the same day Art was, only four years later. It just figured that Billy would be younger. That was irritating. But Art was happy for the information, too. He had made a note of it, so that when he ran into Billy at this conference, he would remember to kid him about their birthdays. Now, he rehearsed. *Have I got a surprise for you. I always knew you were a Leo. I believe this makes us birthmates.* Anything not to mention the welfare hotel and all that had happened to him there.

In the end, he did not run into Billy at all. In the end, he wondered about Billy all day, only to finally learn that Billy had moved on to a new job in the Valley, with a start-up. In personal computers, naturally. A good move, no matter what kind of beating he took on his house.

"Life is about the long term," said Ernie Ford, the informant. "And let's face it, there is no long term here."

Art agreed as warmly as he could. In one way, he was delighted that his competitor had left—if nothing else, that would mean a certain amount of disarray at Info-Edge. The insurance market was, unfortunately, some forty-percent of his business, and he could use any advantage he could get. Another bonus was that Art was never going to have to see Billy again. Billy his birthmate, with his jokes and his Mainstreamese. Still, Art felt depressed.

"We should all have gotten out before this," he said.

"Truer words were never spoke," said Ernie. Ernie had never been a particular friend of Art's, but somehow, talking about Billy was making him chummier. It was as if Billy were a force even in his absence. "I tell you, I'd have packed my bags by now if it weren't for the wife, the kids—they don't want to leave their friends, you know? Plus the oldest is a junior in high school, we can't afford for him to move now, he's got to stay put and make those nice grades so he can make a nice college. Meaning I've got to stay, if it means pushing McMuffins for Ronald McDonald. But now you..."

"Maybe I should go," said Art.

"Definitely, you should go," said Ernie. "What's keeping you?"

"Nothing," said Art. "I'm divorced now. And that's that, right? Sometimes people get undivorced, but you can't exactly count on it."

"Go," said Ernie. "Take my advice. If I hear of anything, I'll send it your way."

"Thanks," said Art.

But of course, he did not expect that Ernie would really turn anything up. It had been a long time since anyone had called him or anybody else he knew of; too many people had gotten stranded, and they were too desperate. Everybody knew it. Also, the survivors were looked upon with suspicion. Anybody who was any good had jumped ship early, that was the conventional wisdom. There was Art, struggling to hold on to his job, only to discover that there were times you didn't want to hold on to your job, times to maneuver for the golden parachute and jump. That was another thing no one had told him, that sometimes it spoke well of you to be fired. Who would have figured that? Sometimes it seemed to Art that he knew nothing at all, that he had dug his own grave and didn't even know to lie down in it, he was still trying to stand up.

A few more warm-blooded conferees at the end of the day—at least they were polite. Then, as he was packing up to go back to the hotel, a mega-surprise. A headhunter approached him, a friend of Ernest's, he said.

"Ernest?" said Art. "Oh, Ernie! Ford! Of course!"

The headhunter was a round, ruddy man with a ring of hair like St. Francis of Assisi, and sure enough, a handful of bread crumbs: A great opportunity, he said. Right now he had to run, but he knew just the guy Art had to meet, a guy who was coming in that evening. For something else, it happened, but he also needed someone like Art. Needed him yesterday, really. Should've been a priority, the guy realized that now, had said so the other day. It might just be a match. Maybe a quick breakfast in the a.m.? Could he call in an hour or so? Art said, *Of course.* And when St. Francis asked his room number, Art hesitated, but then gave the name of the welfare hotel. How would St. Francis know what kind of hotel it was? Art gave the name out confidently, making his manner count. He almost didn't make it to the conference at all, he said. Being so busy. It was only at the last minute that he realized he could do it—things moved around, he found an opening and figured what the hell. But it was too late to book the conference hotel, he explained. That was why he was staying elsewhere.

Success. All day Art's mind had been churning; suddenly it seemed to empty. He might as well have been Billy, born on the same day as Art was, but in another year, under different stars. How much simpler things seemed. He did not labor on two, three, six tasks at once, multi-processing. He knew one thing at a time, and that thing just now was that the day was a victory. And all because he had kept his mouth shut. He had said nothing; he had kept his cool. He walked briskly back to the hotel. He crossed the lobby in a no-nonsense manner. An impervious man. He did not knock on Cindy's door. He was moving on, moving west. There would be a good job there, and a new life. Perhaps he would take up tennis. Perhaps he would own a Jacuzzi. Perhaps he would learn to like all those peculiar foods they ate out there, like jicama, and seaweed. Perhaps he would go macrobiotic.

It wasn't until he got to his room that he remembered that his telephone had no handset.

He sat on his bed. There was a noise at his window, followed, sure enough, by someone's shadow. He wasn't even surprised. Anyway, the fellow wasn't stopping at his room, at least not on this trip. That was luck. *You folk,* Cindy had said, taking back the ice bag. Art could see her perspective; she was right. He was luckier than she, by far. But just now, as the shadow crossed his window again, he thought mostly about how unarmed he was. If he had a telephone, he would probably call Lisa—that was how big a pool seemed to be forming around him, all of a sudden; an ocean, it seemed. Also, he would call the police. But first he would call Lisa, and see how she felt about his possibly moving west. *Quite possibly,* he would say, not wanting to make it sound as though he was calling her for nothing, not wanting to make it sound as though he was awash, at sea, perhaps drowning. He would not want to sound like a haunted man; he would not want to sound as though he was calling from a welfare hotel, years too late, to say, *Yes, that was a baby, it would have been a baby.* For he could not help now but recall the doctor explaining about that child, a boy, who had appeared so mysteriously perfect in the ultrasound. Transparent, he had looked, and gelatinous, all soft head and quick heart; but he would have, in being born, broken every bone in his body.

Brazil

It is my birthday, my twentieth birthday, and I'm in the bar of one of the Art Deco hotels on the beach when I meet her. They are always using this hotel on *Miami Vice,* although they are careful to take tight shots of the pink front and not show the bums and junkies down the street, not until later in the episode, so it seems like they are miles away, in another Miami.

The bar is beautiful—*exquisite,* that's the word that comes to me—black and white and chrome. I feel odd here, like I'm watching myself on TV. I am with a guy, Roberto, who I met at Florida State before my student loan money ran out. After I left FSU, I went back to working as a bellboy at the same hotel, the Royale Palms, where my mom and I used to live, where I worked in high school, a big fifties not thirties kind of place, not too far from the Fontainebleau but not nearly as nice. Roberto went on with pre-law, while I got moved up from bellboy to parking attendant. That's how I ran into him again. I parked his BMW and I asked him about Maddy, who used to be my girlfriend before she decided to be Roberto's. He said she was fine, just fine, which is good because while I'm not mad at Roberto, I worry about Maddy. When he heard it was my birthday, he insisted, really insisted, we go out for a drink. So that's how I happen to be in this bar, which is very expensive, because Roberto brought me.

Roberto is Cuban, which I'm not, although everyone always says I look it. When I want to, I claim to be Brazilian, because my father is or was. I never met him, but we share the same name, *Paulo,* Paulo Silvas. Roberto is not only Cuban, he's Batista's grandson or great-nephew or something, and probably he will be the Republican governor of Florida someday. As soon as we sit down, some general disguised as a lawyer comes up and begins to talk the old politics. Even in a place like this, full of Yankee tourists, Roberto can't get away from Little Havana. When the white hair starts talking, Roberto shrugs, pats my shoulder. He buys a drink for me and I go sit at the bar, which is made of glass bricks and underlit so that all the people sitting at it look ghastly or exciting, depending on your mood.

She sits next to me. In the mirror, she looks thin, rich, a woman with dark hair and eyes as brown as mine, although hers are rac-cooned with mascara. She is wearing a black dress so simple it has to be expensive and silver earrings like needles. Pretty good, but pretty old, in her forties somewhere. Almost as old as my mother. She looks me over in the mirror, too, steadily, as if the mirror is where I really am. I am wearing one of the silk shirts Kirov, the old Jew who owns Royale Palms, gave me. He lives in one of the oceanside suites, and when you do something for him—nothing illegal, just something nice like bringing him breakfast and a bot-tle of vitamin C when you know he's been drinking too long to remember about eating—he goes to his closet and gives you one of his shirts. He has them in all sizes, because his weight is always yo-yoing up and down, and they are really beautiful shirts, hand-made.

On top of Kirov's shirt, I am wearing a Giorgio Armani jacket that Freddie, the bell captain, took out of the room of some Colombian who got shot in Hialeah. I felt bad about the jacket for a while. In Brazil there are probably all kinds of taboos against wearing the clothes of the dead.

The woman sitting next to me leans close to say something—they have the music up loud to make this sort of thing neces-sary—and I notice for the first time that they are playing "Brazil," which has been pretty popular since the movie. *Where the songs are passionate. And the smile has flash in it.* She keeps her eyes on the mirror, but I feel her breath warm on my ear. She says, "I want you to treat me like a war."

At first I don't understand. Then I realize she has pronounced the *w* in *whore*. She has an odd accent, not Cuban, not any kind of Spanish. I look at her in the mirror again, and she looks back at me, perfectly expressionless. "I don't have any money," I say. She smiles for the first time, showing teeth.

"I said *like*, yes?" She touches a fingernail to the collar of my jacket. "Not *am*." Her nails are painted dark red but are different lengths, like maybe she bites them. "You don't have to pay."

"Well," I say, "I *am* a whore and you *do* have to pay." I don't know
why I say this. It's a lie, and as soon as the words leave my mouth,
I feel my heart jump. It just seems like the right sort of thing to say
in this bar. The woman takes her eyes off the mirror and puts them
on my flesh for the first time. She shakes her head no.

"But I do need a driver," she says. "You can drive?" Now the
only place people have chauffeurs, I mean not just rented limos, is
on *Dynasty,* so I decide she may be one of those people who are
unable to keep life and TV on different sides of their brains. But it
is my birthday, and I have tomorrow off.

"Sure," I say, "who can't?" even though I only learned to drive
this year, practicing on cars the guests leave in my care at the
hotel. When Kirov offered to move me up from bellboy to parking attendant, I told him I didn't know how to drive, but he just
shrugged and said, "This is America. Learn." Which I did, more
or less.

"My car is outside," the woman says and stands to leave. I nod
and stand, too, and when I do, I notice we are the same height,
five nine or so. A height which feels tall on Miami Beach, where
the parking meters are taller than a lot of the old people. I go over
to the table where Roberto is sitting and explain I have to leave.
The white-haired man frowns.

"Go ahead," Roberto says, very smooth, "take your aunt home.
You wouldn't want her to get into trouble." I feel the woman
watching from the door.

When I join her, she takes my arm and we go out into the pink
lobby. She is shaking her head. "Whore, no," she says. "You are a"—
she makes a little shoving motion with her hand—"a pusher, yes?"
Her accent is suddenly thick, breathless. She glances back at Roberto and the old lawyer, imagining God knows what but certainly not
the usual bitter denunciation of Kennedy's treachery at the Bay of
Pigs. "Yes?" she says again, her head bobbing.

I think about telling the woman the truth, that I am not a
whore or a player, but a college dropout, a parking attendant at a
turquoise-colored, not-so-good hotel. But she puts her hand on
my lapel and says, "You can call me Claudia. What shall I call
you?"

"Paulo," I say, telling the truth, which she doesn't recognize.

"Paulo," Claudia says, and again, "Paulo," as if tasting it. I frown. "Don't worry. It will do. So," she says, "you are not American?"

I give up. "Brazil," I say. "I was born in Brazil."

"I was born in Hungary," she says. "Buda."

"Budapest?"

She shakes her head. "Buda," she says. "The other side of the river, that is Pest."

"Like Miami and Miami Beach," I say, but she doesn't know about that.

We step out of the hotel, and the hot August night air hits us. Claudia puts her hand around mine, and I notice that both our palms are sweating. We go for the car, which turns out to be a black BMW with Palm Beach County plates. BMWs are ugly cars, really, very boxy-looking, for all their expense. Their owners are crazy about them, though. I backed one into a concrete piling in the parking garage, and the owner was really pissed. Luckily, the hotel garage has a big sign that says it doesn't take responsibility. Claudia gives me her keys, and I open the passenger door for her.

As soon as we are in the car, Claudia gets some coke out of the glove compartment—not a very safe place to keep it, any parking attendant could tell you—and hands it to me. In high school when I thought I'd be a lawyer someday, have to pass the bar and all, I practiced a lot of self-restraint. I was known for it, really. But since I went to FSU and came back the same year, it's been hard to see the point. Still, since I'm known for saying no, hardly any-one offers, and I am nervous as Claudia hands me a rolled bill, watches me set up, afraid of not getting it right. Then I do a line, get that chlorine feeling, like pool water up my nose. Immediately I feel a lot better, more cheerful. I do another. I can definitely see the appeal. I offer Claudia the last one, but she shakes her head, so I do that one, too. It is my birthday.

"What now?" I ask. Since Claudia didn't touch the coke, I am guessing she usually does not do this sort of thing, either. Maybe she thinks she is being the perfect hostess.

"I want you to drive," Claudia says. She unrolls the bill, holds it out, and I see it's a hundred, the kind of tip no one at the Royale Palms ever gives. I should be having doubts, I know, but by now I am feeling so cheerful I can't imagine what they could be. I take the money. I'll drive her around, catch a bus home.

"Yes, ma'am," I say. If nothing else, working at a hotel teaches you to be polite. "Where?"

She shrugs. "All night."

I think about it a minute. Since we are on the beach, everything farther east is water. West of Miami is the Everglades, and south is a dead end at Key West, with no ferries to Cuba likely this century. So I head north, following the route the Greyhound bus took to get me to FSU. Claudia turns the AC on high and puts a tape in the Blaupunkt, something African with a lot of drums. She turns it up until I can feel it like a fist in my chest. "To keep you awake, yes?" she says.

Claudia curls up on the seat, her head against the armrest, her stocking feet in my lap. For a while she moves her feet back and forth against the erection I can't help getting, but then she falls asleep. The headlights catch a turnoff, a green road sign, *Lantana—38 miles,* the road I would take in the somewhat unlikely event that this were a trip to visit my mother. As soon as I pass it, I know I have driven farther than I ever have before. I think of my mother in her trailer surrounded by Spanish bayonets. Until my sixteenth birthday, my father sent two checks every month, one to my mother, one to Kirov for the suite. Even after the checks stopped coming, my mother waited three months, just in case, before she announced over breakfast that she was going to take a job assembling B-1 bomber sights in Lantana. An old friend from high school had put her name in for it. "And me?" I asked.

"Kirov will give you a job," she said. "After all these years, he owes us that."

I pop out the tape and put on the radio. The Blaupunkt has shortwave. I turn off the AC, roll down the window a crack, and listen to Radio Havana. It's what drives the Cubans so crazy, makes them all stay in Miami. Humidity just like home and Havana close enough to hear, never touch. When Radio Havana fades out, I twist the dial around and hear all kinds of things, Chinese, Russian, maybe German. I try finding Radio Brazil, if there is such a thing, but I am not sure I would recognize Portuguese if I heard it.

After midnight, when it is no longer my birthday, I start noticing these odd signs on the side of the road, wooden letters mounted on cypress branches that say things like *The World's Oldest Tourist Trap* and *Lady, If He Won't Stop, Hit Him!* Ten minutes later, I spot a low concrete building off to the left, catch a larger sign: *Cypress Knee Museum.* I wonder who stops at such places. Is this what people with cars do, people on vacation, people, say, on their way to the Royale Palms? Then the signs disappear from my side of the road, but a few minutes later I see one lit up by the headlights of a southbound car. From behind, the letters on the dead branch look like hieroglyphics: *!miH tiH, potS t'noW eH fI.*

By dawn, we are outside Orlando. Claudia sits up. She gazes out the window, yawning, though she is the one who has slept most of the night. I pull into a rest stop and get out, stretch. Claudia hands me a bottle with some foreign—French?—writing on it. "Vitamins," she says. The pills inside are blue and look too tiny to be seriously harmful. I take one. Claudia takes three. I ask to borrow some change for the phone, and she says to get some out of her purse which is on the back seat. Inside, there is a regular rat's nest of bills. I find a whole roll of quarters, hold it up to show her what I'm taking. She shakes her head like she's disappointed. "Take more," she says. "Buy some…" She pauses so I know what's coming—American slang. "Some snow"—she closes her eyes—"or is it blow?" I take a couple of fifties.

Claudia goes off in search of tourist information. I call the Royale Palms long-distance, ask for Freddie. *"Hola,"* he says, picking up the phone on the first ring even though it is six in the morning. Like me, he has been up all night. I tell him I may not be in tomorrow, that my grandmother is sick. He laughs at this. When Dagoberto, the night desk clerk, wants time off, he always calls in and says his grandmother died. But I say *sick* and not *dead* because I may, after all, have a living grandmother in Brazil, a superstitious sort of country, and I wouldn't want to wish anything too bad on her. "Okay," Freddie says, still laughing. "I'll cover for you." August is the off-season, and he can afford to be easy. I tell him that if he needs my bed—I am living in one of the spare rooms—to lock my stuff in the linen closet.

"Thanks," I say.

"*De nada.*" Freddie says. "Enjoy."

Inside, at the information desk, the clerk is recommending some fancy mall to Claudia, a place where she says there is serious shopping. The girl and Claudia share a moment of bonding. "Rive Gauche?" Claudia asks.

"No shit," says the girl.

So we go shopping. There is a store full of Giorgio Armani. I feel the French amphetamine take hold and maybe Claudia does, too. She trails her hand down a rack of suits. "For you, yes?" she says in loud voice. After that, the saleswoman, a short Italian woman dressed in shades of gray, sticks to Claudia like mildew on a shower curtain. Together, they pull things from the racks, from the stockroom, even off the male mannequin in the window who has only half a head and that as empty as a bowl. Claudia makes me try on everything, model it for her. The saleswoman hands the clothes over the dressing-room door, then stands behind Claudia and watches me, too. She and Claudia bend their heads together, talking very low, their accents melting into a general for-eignness. Claudia makes no attempt to say that I am her son or anything, and I think the saleswoman is very excited by the idea that I may be Claudia's lover. She is older than Claudia, fifty or so, but I can see she is thinking *Why not?* Thinking maybe she'll find herself a pretty boy, someone who wants one of her suits and can no way afford one.

I turn my back on Claudia and look in the mirror. Each time I see myself, in black silk, in white linen, I keep having the same pair of thoughts. I think, *This guy looks great* and *Who is he?* But each time the thoughts surprise me, like I am very stoned or dreaming. Claudia picks out a white linen suit, a pair of black jeans, two shirts, underwear, socks, a pair of shoes, and a suitcase to put it all in. More clothes than I own, worth more than every-thing I have ever owned, maybe, in my whole life. At least I'm get-ting a wardrobe out of this—the word *trousseau* pops into my mind. I decide to wear the white Armani suit over a yellow eighty-dollar T-shirt out of the store. I wonder what Maddy would think if she saw me.

"Come," Claudia says and pulls me down the mall and into a jewelry store. She points to a display of ear studs. "For you, yes?"

"For me, no," I say. Most of the guys who work at the Palms have gone through this. I mean, the whole question of which ear to get pierced. Does right mean you're gay and left straight, or will you move to Australia, find out that there you've got it backwards and get butt-fucked? A salesgirl appears. She grins at me.

"We can do the piercing here," she says and shows Claudia what looks like one of those things that punches holes in paper. I keep shaking my head. Claudia moves toward me. I back up until I hit the glass counter. She moves in very close, rakes her fingers through my hair, pulling it back from my forehead. It is the first time she has really touched me, and I would jump if I weren't squeezed against the counter. Out of the corner of my eye, I see the girl behind the counter blush, look away.

"Paulo, Paulo," Claudia whispers. She pinches my right earlobe between her fingertips. "A diamond?" Her eyes glitter as she says this.

"Okay," I say. "If it's a diamond."

Before I can move, the salesgirl lifts her punch to my right earlobe, and I close my eyes. I hear her breathing in my ear, and I think she is going to say something to relax me, like *This hurts me more than it does you,* but she doesn't. She just staples my ear. The pain makes my eyes water, and it occurs to me that this is something more permanent than a change of clothes. I take a deep breath, then with a click it is over. I imagine that Claudia is watching, but when I open my eyes, she is inspecting her fingernails as if she is afraid she has broken one off in my hair. She pays cash for the hole and the diamond stud, and at the last minute she buys me a red Swatch watch, which is much too young for me. As we are leaving, the salesgirl says, "Remember to bathe that ear with alcohol. When it comes to your health"—she glances sideways at Claudia—"you can't be too careful."

My ear throbs. As soon as we are out of there, Claudia puts her hand on the back of my neck. "Your head hurts, yes?"

"Yes."

"Poor Paulo," Claudia says, rubbing my neck. She sends me to the men's room to make a buy. I go, but I think she is crazy. This is Orlando. Home of Disney World, of M-I-C-K-E-Y M-O-U-S-E. But there is a tall black guy in a mall maintenance jumpsuit cleaning the urinal, and as soon as he sees me, he's selling. I give the guy what he asks for, not quibbling about the price, which even I know is tourist-high. "Have a good one," he says, stuffing the bills down the front of his coveralls.

Out in the parking lot, the car is like an oven, but Claudia gets in, anyway, kicks off her shoes, twists her feet up under her on the seat. "America," she says. I touch the hot steering wheel of the BMW, tap one of my new Italian shoes on the gas pedal.

"America?" I say, kidding. "Where?"

"You don't know, Paulo?" she says, serious. "Then we must find out." She waves her hand at the heat waves rising from the parking lot. "Is this America?"

"Malls are very American," I say, thinking maybe she is angling to take back my clothes.

"Malls, yes? And what else?" I rack my brain but can't think of anything.

She reaches under the seat and pulls out about fifty tourist brochures she must have gotten at the rest stop. She shows me one with a parrot peddling a bird-size unicycle on the cover. "America?" she says for the third time in less than a minute.

"Looks like it," I say, thinking maybe I should have woken her up for the Cypress Knee Museum.

"Paulo." Claudia touches a finger to my pocket, to the cocaine. The car is so hot now I can smell myself, like I'm in a sauna where what they throw on the rocks is sweat. I crouch down behind the wheel and do the coke while she reads names to me from the pamphlets. *Bible Land USA, Elvis-A-Rama, Confederama.* As soon as I finish, she pokes me hard, lays two pamphlets open on my lap. "We go to this one." She points to *Weeki Wachee, Spring of the Living Mermaids,* which a map on the back shows as somewhere near Tampa. "And this one." She points to a picture of a ceiling hung with department-store mannequins to which someone has carefully added angelic wings and large erect nipples. This is at *House on the Rock,* which is somewhere in Wisconsin.

"Why?" I say.

"Why not?" Claudia asks, and whether it is because of the coke or because I have slept so little, I cannot think of an answer.

Instead I ask, "How far is it?"

"To Weeki Wachee?"

"To Wisconsin."

She goes back under the seat and comes up with a road atlas. She checks the chart in the back. "Twenty-four hours driving." She pauses, reaching for the right word. "Max."

"Max?" I say.

"Max, yes?"

"Max, yes," I echo. I imagine this going on and on, leaving us frozen in the doorway like those cartoon chipmunks—*After you. No, after you*—so I stop. I take the atlas from her, turn to the map of the whole United States. My heart is pounding so hard from the coke that the blue lines that are the interstates jump like veins. I know I should get on a bus and go back to Miami, but the longer I think about it, the less I can see myself back at the Royale Palms, breathing carbon monoxide for two-dollar tips. Not yet. I think: *I am twenty years old and have never been out of Florida.*

I rub my hands over my face. Twenty-four hours. One day. I start the car. "Okay," I say, "first stop, Weeki Wachee," and as I pull out of the parking lot into traffic, it strikes me suddenly just how good it feels to be driving a BMW, like it is something I've missed for a long time without even knowing it.

By five, my usual dinner-break time, we are sitting side by side in a mildewy auditorium while on the other side of a plate-glass window girls wearing fishtails drink RC Colas underwater. The mermaids take occasional breaths from air hoses that bubble away like aquarium filters, and the water is so cold, their lips look blue in spite of their waterproof lipstick. The theme of the show is Carnival in Rio, and Claudia squeezes my hand as if she is afraid the sound of the samba is going to make me cry. At the end of the show, the mermaids wave a fond farewell, flippers flapping, as the PA system blares "We've Got the Whole World by the Tail." I lift Claudia's hand from mine and wave back.

Claudia pays to have a Polaroid taken of me with one of the mermaids, a blond, freckled girl named Cindy from Fort Walton Beach, who is perched on a stool in the lobby for this purpose. Cindy smells so much like strawberry shampoo that my mouth waters. I am tempted to ask her if she goes to FSU, see if she knows Maddy. But I am aware of Claudia watching me. She holds out the Polaroid for me to see, and an old man with a camcorder takes my place beside Cindy. I watch as two white blobs darken into smiling faces, and when I see mine, I am glad that I didn't say anything to Cindy. She looks wholesome in her green tail and modest bathing-suit top, while the circles under my eyes are so deep and dark they look like anuses. My earring gleams.

Claudia takes my hair in both of her hands, pulls it back. "You should show off your cheekbones," she says. She borrows a rubber band from the girl at the ticket counter, fastens my hair in the shortest of ponytails. "Yes?" Claudia asks the girl at the ticket counter.

"Hot," the girl says, smiling at me. "Really."

A couple of hours later we pass the *Welcome to Georgia* sign, but even though I am watching carefully, the only change I see is the color of the pavement. By ten we are in Macon. Claudia insists we stop at a drive-in, where, perhaps because it is so American, she actually eats a barbecue sandwich, the first non-pharmaceutical thing I have seen her put in her mouth. I am careful not to get any of the sticky red sauce on my Armani suit. After we eat, I go to the men's room to wash my hands. A guy, skinny and white this time, is upset because I don't want crack. He offers to trade me some for my watch. This is all beginning to strike me as funny, but when I laugh he gets nervous. So I buy some coke, do it in one of the stalls.

When I come out of the rest room, Claudia is bent over the atlas. "Seventeen hours," she says, without looking up.

"Max," I manage to say. It is twenty-four hours since we left Miami, and I haven't slept in maybe thirty-six. Out in the parking lot, Claudia takes a close look at me and offers to drive, but the coke has kicked in and I feel fine, ready to drive straight into the night, which we do, stopping only for gas near Nashville. I tell Claudia when we cross the border into Kentucky, but she doesn't seem interested. Her eyes are closed, and her lips are set in a line, a little gray. "Why don't you lie down?" I say finally, and she does, this time with her head in my lap. This gives me an erection so hard it hurts, but she goes right to sleep.

I stay on I-65, and I don't stop, not even to piss, because although my bladder is full, Claudia is sleeping on that, too, snoring slightly. Besides, there is something about the way my hands have locked onto the steering wheel, the fact that I cannot feel my toes or fingertips, that tells me to make time while I can before I come down, that the crash waiting for me will be worse than bad, unimaginable.

Claudia sleeps and sleeps. I make it to Indianapolis sometime after dawn, follow the interstate downtown. Downtown Indianapolis is dismal, hot, rain coming down, passing steam going up. The buildings look rusty, vacant. We pass a convention center, windows dark, marquee empty, and I pull into the curved drive of the hotel attached to it. "I'm stopping," I announce to Claudia, but then I can't seem to get my foot off the gas and onto the brake in time. I end up back on the street, have to circle the block and try again. When I turn off the car, I just sit there, afraid I won't be able to stand. I'm so tired I could cry. Claudia sits up, yawns so wide, her jaws crack. I tell her we are in Indiana, and she gives me this surprised look, as if maybe this whole trip is a joke one of us has taken too far. Then she shrugs, puts on lipstick. She leans across the seat and kisses me, slips her tongue between my lips. Surprised, I kiss back, and then I realize there is something bitter and hard in my mouth—one of her pills. I swallow, feel it burn all the way down. Claudia laughs.

A bellboy knocks on the window. "Sir?" he says, although not with any conviction. I give him the keys, watch as he gets the luggage out of the trunk, opens Claudia's door. He is blond, has no chin. Inside, Claudia registers for two rooms, like I am just her driver, just someone along for the ride. I don't know what to think, but mostly I am surprised by this. What about treating her like a war? Claudia yawns, stands closer to the bellboy than to me. So I let the bellboy carry the suitcases upstairs. Claudia slips him a twenty, but the bellboy shoots me a look behind her back. I think I know what is coming. He waits until he has opened her door and she has gone in, then he covers his mouth with his hand, whispers, "Want to buy some pot? It's good shit, man." I almost laugh, start to say no, but then I stop. My hands are shaking, and I can feel Claudia's little blue pill. I need help coming down.

"Sure," I say. "Take my watch for it?" He throws in some papers. But after I've got it, I can't imagine smoking it. I lie down on my bed and wait for time to pass. I hear the TV come on in Claudia's room, the bathroom fan. I think about my father. The last time he came around I was two, and sometimes I think I can almost remember that. I have this memory of something white, like a terry-cloth bathrobe, moving back and forth in front of the bars of my crib, sort of like the way they used to show Jesus in the old movies, all hem and no face.

After a while, it stops raining on Indianapolis. The sun comes out. I can see that much from where I'm lying on the bed. I think about getting up, but somehow I don't. Then it is dark, and I'm confused because I don't think I've been asleep. I call down to the desk and ask what time it is. "Eight-thirty," the girl says. "Probably you thought it was nine-thirty. Lots of people make that mistake because Indiana doesn't go on Daylight Savings. So in the summer, it's like we're on Central Time, and in the winter, like we're on Eastern. Really, we're on Indiana Time."

"Eight-thirty *p.m.*?" I ask, and there's a pause at the end of the line as she realizes just how confused I am.

"Yes," she says. I give up trying to sound normal.

"And it's what day of the week?"

"Friday."

"Thanks," I say. "You've been a big help. Really."

I get up, and after I wash my face I knock on Claudia's door. "Claudia?"

"It's open, Paulo," she says. "I wouldn't lock you out." She is lying on the bed with her shoes off, drinking a Diet Coke and watching TV. I show her the pot. She looks in her purse. She pulls out a fistful of bills, the Polaroid of me at Weeki Wachee. "Maybe a lighter, yes?" she says and keeps digging. "Here"—she pulls out another handful of stuff and hands me a gun—"hold this."

It's a small automatic. I know that much, even though this is the first gun I've touched in my life. I'm surprised how heavy it is, as if Claudia has handed me a Bic Flic that weighs as much as a pipe wrench. I check to see that the safety is on. It's amazing what I've learned from watching TV all these years. I sight down the barrel at a lighted office I can see through the window. If I fired, would I hit someone? I look up to see Claudia smiling at me, a silver lighter open, flaming, in her hand. I can tell she is thinking how good I look with her gun, how experienced. "A nice toy for your line of work, yes?" she says, her excitement as strong as her accent. I remember who she thinks I am. "Was expensive."

I give her back the gun, sorry I know it exists. She puts it in her purse. I pick through the pot, roll a couple of lumpy joints, light one. We smoke half the dope, taking increasingly lopsided turns, two hits for me to her one. Then Claudia is standing by the door, her purse in her hand. "Come," she says. "I'm ravenous, yes?" We find an all-night Zippy Mart, but before we go in, I make Claudia leave her gun in the glove compartment. Claudia wanders dazed down the aisle as if she has forgotten what is edible and what is not. I find this rack of health food munchies and in a fit of homesickness pick out a dozen little bags of dried papaya. We are obviously high, but the checker, a women who must weigh three hundred pounds, barely glances at us, and we make it back to the hotel, Claudia's room, undetected. I rip open the bags, dump them out on the bed. But it is Claudia who hunts down and eats every pinkish orange cube, even the ones that are a little fuzzy from the bedspread, slapping my hand when I go for one.

We smoke the rest of the dope. While Claudia fills her lungs, I flip through the stations on the TV. We seem to be staying in the only major hotel in a major city that doesn't have cable. Indianapolis, my kinda town. I stumble across the opening credits of *Miami Vice*. Just seeing the blue shallows of Biscayne Bay makes me homesick. I groan. On TV, Miami looks better than real. Claudia pulls me back to the bed, puts the joint to my lips. "Shhh," she says, "shhh," kissing my shoulder, my neck. I think we are going to do something more, but the bright colors of Miami pull us into the TV, and we watch hardly blinking as the boat Sonny is on undercover blows up. "Oooh," Claudia says as the black smoke and orange flames roll over the calm aqua water. When Sonny comes to, he's lost his memory, forgotten he's a cop. Everyone tells him he's a dealer, so he goes out to do a deal and ends up shooting a guy who is out to rip him off. He shoots him in the back, then once he has fallen, again in the head. Just like that, like pointing a finger. Claudia lets the joint go out. I relight it, burn my hand.

The show seems different stoned. The fast cutting, the coked-out pacing, is slowed way down so the whole thing just flows, as if when the boat blew up, Sonny went to the bottom of the bay and discovered some other liquid Miami. Sonny makes love to a woman, shoots a man at close range in a car. He's ordered to shoot Tubbs, his black partner, the only person—it seems obvious to me in that moment—that Sonny really loves. And he does shoot him, walks right by him without recognizing him and fires off two shots without flinching. I almost cry out, but luckily Tubbs is wearing a bullet-proof vest and so is not dead.

Sonny sleeps with someone else, shoots someone else—another cop—but it seems to me that he is getting tired, as if this being someone else is losing its thrill. I want to tell him, *Hey, compadre, I know how you feel.* But suddenly the show is over—*To be continued.*

Claudia unzips my fly. On the TV, a woman is dressing exotic birds in costumes fastened in the back by tiny Velcro tabs. I watch as she changes a green parrot into the Incredible Hulk, tiny padded muscles and all. Claudia has her mouth on my cock. I look down at her. I don't feel anything. Maybe it is the coke or the pot or maybe it is Claudia. Maddy used to do all right. Claudia is just sort of mouthing my penis, biting at it with her lips. Claudia lifts my hand and puts it between her legs, closes her thighs on my fingers. I rub Claudia's nylon crotch, but now that it has come down to it, I don't know how to treat her like a whore. I find myself thinking of my mother, so I close my eyes and try thinking of Maddy instead, of this certain smooth spot on her back, right at the base of her spine, where I always held on to her. I start to get hard. But then I remember that Maddy is with Roberto, who at this very moment may be touching her there. "Don't," I say before I think not to say it.

Claudia raises her head. She looks at my limp, wrinkled cock, then at me. Her eyes widen. She smiles, a strange knowing smile as if she is seeing me, really seeing me, for the first time.

"Claudia," I start, reaching for her. Her upper lip curls. Whatever she is seeing fills her with disgust. I don't know what is going on with her, but I don't like it. It is like she has switched channels in her head. One minute I'm a coke dealer and then...

"You do like women," she says slowly. "Yes?" I shake my head *yes, yes.* Then suddenly I remember the time Roberto and I got very drunk at his apartment and how he tried to choke me. I think by way of starting to have sex with me. But I didn't get hard then, either. Really. Not at all. I threw up. I feel Claudia's eyes changing me into something I'm not. I am on my feet, backing across the room. "Stop it," I say. Her lips are pursed. Whatever she is about to say, I don't want to hear it. I reach for the doorknob, wrench the door open.

"Faggot!" she says, spitting. "Brazilian faggot."

I am in the lobby, and then in the car. I drive without thinking, hit the bypass around the city, spin west. I enter a town, am out of it before I think to slow down. I think instead about stealing the BMW, driving south to see Maddy. What would Maddy say if I told her about Roberto? Probably, she wouldn't believe me. *Brazilian faggot.*

My headlights flash on a road sign: *Brazil 3 miles.* For a second I feel like I have entered the Twilight Zone, then I realize it is just an Indiana town. Still, I start looking for a place to make a U-turn, but before I know it I am in Brazil. Storefronts close in on both sides. I hit the gas, trying to get through as quickly as possible, fast-forward through this particular town. The downtown opens up, and a car lot blurs by. Then, a second too late, I see the cruiser sitting in the corner of the lot, nose on the edge of the road. The cop turns on his light. I hit the brake the same second he hits the siren.

I pull over on the edge of town, behind the *Welcome to Brazil* sign. The cruiser pulls up behind me. The officer comes to the window, motions me out of the car. "Up early or out late?" he says. He takes my Florida driver's license without comment, calls that and the BMW in. Standing between the two cars, I can see he's not a highway patrolman but a Brazil cop, probably *the* Brazil cop. He comes back with my license. He is frowning, tapping a big silver flashlight against one leg. I feel totally straight now, as clearheaded as an Olympic diver about to go off the high board. I volunteer that the car belongs to my aunt. "We'll know all that soon enough, son. In the meantime, why don't you just stretch your legs." He shines his long silver flashlight down the edge of the road, along the white line he wants me to walk.

I can and I do. Just for good measure, the cop has me touch my index fingers to my nose with my eyes shut. "Fine, son," the officer says. His radio squeals, and he goes to answer it. When he comes back, he is frowning, tapping the flashlight against one leg. "Why don't you show me the registration for this car, son." I blink, start to shrug. "The glove compartment," he suggests. He turns on his flashlight. I get in the car, reach across the seat, and just as my fingers touch the latch, I remember with a flash of fear that goes through every cell of my body like some cocaine anti-high that the glove box is where I made Claudia put her gun. This is it, I think, the moment when amnesia turns serious, Sonny shoots Tubbs, this cop shoots me, but it is too late to stop. I open the glove box.

No gun. For a second I think I am going to be sick. Claudia must have put it back in her purse before we went up to the room. I grab the papers that are in the glove box, give them to the officer. "Your aunt..."

"Claudia," I say.

"Claudia Vanderhagen?" he asks. He shows me the registration. *William Vanderhagen.*

"Yes," I say. "But she's divorcing Uncle Bill. He drinks." The cop nods. "I'm not sure he knows that she's..."

"Listen," he says. "You're a DePauw kid, right?" He sees me hesitate, holds up his hand. "You're scared because one call to Dean Bunche and your butt is on the line." DePauw. A college or a prep school? "But I know how you boys are. Get your hands on a car— say your aunt brings you up to school, turns in early—and you just gotta blow off steam. No harm done, but listen"—he puts his hand on my shoulder—"if you'd been drinking, I would have to call Dean Bunche, and she'd have to suspend you. Then what would you do? Where would you be if you weren't in college?" He gives my shoulder a squeeze. "Think about it." I nod, my mouth too dry to talk. He gives back my license, writes me a sixty-dollar speeding ticket. "You drive nice and slow back to the frat house," he says, "and tell the other boys all about this. Tell 'em I said to watch out when they drive through Brazil." He pronounces it *Braise-L.*

I watch as the cruiser makes a careful U-turn, heads back into town, leaving me standing somewhere in the middle of America. *America.* A place where parking attendants from Miami and frat boys in Indiana dress just like Columbian coke dealers who all dress like an actor on TV who used to date Barbra Streisand. I rest my head on the hood of Claudia's car.

I drive back to Indianapolis. This is where I am if I am not in college—nowhere. When I hit the bypass I think again about heading south, stealing the BMW, and driving straight to Florida State, not to see Maddy but to register for the fall term, but I don't. I can see in my mind's eye how many police there are between Indianapolis and Florida, and I know in my heart they will not be like the cop in Brazil. I feel a profound awareness of having used up my luck. I will take a bus.

The sun is coming up behind the convention center when I pull into the hotel parking lot, and it occurs to me that since I have been with Claudia, I have seen the sun rise more days than not, maybe more times than I have seen it in my life. The lobby is empty, no one behind the desk, but when I step out of the elevator on my floor, I see the bellboy coming out of Claudia's room. His shirt is untucked, his sneakers untied. He sees me, and for a moment he starts the other way, but we can both see that there is nothing at the end of the corridor but a fire escape. He decides to brave it out, walks toward me smiling. He really has no chin. I hold the elevator door with one hand, then when he is inside, let it go. He opens his mouth to say something, but the closing door cuts him off.

I let myself into my room. The bed is still made, one pillow a little wrinkled where I slept through the afternoon. I hear the shower next door shut off, the toilet flush. The phone rings. "You have my keys," Claudia says. She sounds cool.

"I'll meet you in the lobby, Mrs. Vanderhagen," I say.

"Paulo?" she says.

"Yes?"

"I let him fuck me in the ass."

I take my time, shower and brush my teeth before I get in the elevator with the keys in one hand. All the clothes Claudia bought me, I leave behind in the room. But when I get to the lobby no Claudia, just a group of senior citizens standing looking out through the double glass doors. I come up behind them. There is an ambulance in the parking lot. A white-haired woman in a purple pantsuit turns to me. "Heart attack," she says, sounding excited. As we watch, a paramedic slams the rear doors, and the ambulance pulls away, red light flashing.

The bellboy comes up behind me. "Wanna know which hospital?" he says. He grins. And then it hits me. It was Claudia, Claudia in the ambulance.

I listen as he tells me how to get to the hospital, but then I ask him where the Greyhound station is. The bellboy looks at me, then snorts, as if I have let him in on a joke. The bus station is nearby, closer than the hospital, but in spite of my intentions, I drive past it. I can't leave without a word. I am not my father.

In the emergency room I have to tell them I am Claudia's son before they will send me up to cardiac care. "Five minutes," the doctor there says, holding up that many fingers. Claudia is in one of several glass cubicles watched by a nurse near the door. She is resting with her eyes closed, one tube up her nose, another running liquid into her arm, and she is wired to one of those machines that makes each heartbeat into a game of follow-the-bouncing-ball.

I sit carefully on the edge of the bed. The heart monitor beeps softly. She opens her eyes. She doesn't look rich or exotic now, she looks old and tired, more than ever like my mother. She gives me her hand, and I am surprised to find I am crying.

"They called my husband," she says. "Is he going to be surprised to see you." Then she is crying, too, stiff sobs that hurt, make her monitor jump, the nurse start from her desk toward our glass room.

Lurch, Whose Story Doesn't End

It's as though you're snowed in at the airport forever.
    Or you're sent to purgatory, say:
you spend all this time learning the story of your own life
    and then you don't get to tell it.
This one begins with me and the other guys
    carrying stuff into our half of the house
we had rented for spring break,
    while Whit Little takes his clothes off on the beach,
folds them carefully, and walks into the waves.
    A few minutes later, the girls pull up in their car.
They have their swimsuits on under their blouses and shorts,
    so they take off their clothes, too,
and run down to the water as Whit smiles
    and greets them, his hands on his hips.

Whit, Whit! they scream. How's the water?
    Great, you'll love it, he replies.
Just then the tide goes out with a great sucking roar,
    and Whit is left in water up to his ankles,
his nuts tight from the chill
    and his big, floppy, half-hard penis
sticking out like an elephant's trunk.
    Sondra Broussard, who is in front, digs in her heels;
the other girls scream and crash into her and fall
    in a big heap on the sand. Then they run back up
the beach again, still screaming but laughing now,
    and put their girl stuff into their half of the house
we'd all rented together in Grayton Beach,
    half a day's drive from Baton Rouge.

That night there is a poker game in the kitchen.
    Maybe Lurch is one of the card players;

if that were the case, his story would begin here,
    but I can't remember where he first comes in.
The girls spin records and dance in the living room,
    except for Kathey Smiley, who sits and watches the
      poker game,
not saying anything. Kathey doesn't look so great;
    she'd been on the beach all day in her two-piece,
refusing everyone's offer of lotion because,
    as she kept saying, she was going to get
the "basis" of a tan first and then
    start smearing on the Coppertone later.
She'd been light pink at supper
    and by now she is a deep red, bordering on purple.

Around one, most of the girls have gone to bed,
    and the guys are tired of the beer and the cards,
so we get up to go to our rooms, everybody but Kathey,
    who just sits there. Come on, Kathey, bedtime,
say the guys. See you tomorrow, come on, get up, get up.
    I can't, says Kathey, and everybody stops,
and the guys who have left the room come back.
    What? says someone. I can't get up, says Kathey,
I can't move, and she begins to cry.
    There is a quick discussion, and then the Wilkersons,
two pairs of brothers who are also cousins
    and who played football together in high school,
get on the four corners of Kathey Smiley's chair.
    One, two, three, says somebody,

and the four Wilkersons lift Kathey Smiley up,
    chair and all, and take her out
to Robby Wilkerson's truck, the bed of which
    had been filled that morning with cans of tomato soup
and boxes of evaporated milk and jars of peanut butter
    and loaves of white bread and case after case of beer
but which is now empty.
    And so we take Kathey Smiley
to the Okaloosa County Regional Medical Center,

where she spends the next ten days
on painkillers. Kathey finally comes around,
    but it's long after we'd all driven back to Baton Rouge
and returned to classes at LSU
    and our regular boy- and girlfriends.

And that could be the end of a story,
    though not the story of Lurch,
since he hasn't even appeared yet,
    except perhaps as one of the nameless guys,
the one who says What? to Kathey Smiley, for example,
    or who signals for the Wilkersons to pick her up.
Surely there's enough for a story already:
    there's Whit Little and his big semi-hard dick,
then the serious matter of Kathey Smiley's burns,
    and, finally, Kathey's eventual recovery.
Lots of stories work this way:
    with the joke (Whit), the big scare
(Kathey gets severely burned) and then
    the brow-wiping moment of relief (Kathey gets better).

It would be the story of a day
    in the life of some nice middle-class kids,
half of whose names I've long since forgotten.
    I don't think anyone married anyone else in the group,
although most of them did marry and have children,
    and a good many divorced and probably drank too much
on occasion and fudged on their taxes
    but otherwise had lives much like the day
we had all just passed together,
    lives with some ups and downs, too,
some levity and some pain, yet nothing
    nobody couldn't get over.
The story so far is their story,
    and it's probably *the* story for most people.

But it wouldn't be Lurch's story if it ended here.
    Lurch hasn't even appeared yet, and it would've been better

if he hadn't appeared at all, if he'd been one
  of the ones whose names I can't remember.
In fact, Lurch got into and then out of the story
  without me knowing it. I'd gone to the hospital
with Kathey Smiley and the Wilkersons;
  someone was needed in the truck bed
to hold the fourth leg of Kathey's chair
  so Robby Wilkerson could drive to the hospital.
Naturally we thought the story had gone with us,
  but then we got back to the house in Grayton Beach,
we found the story was still there
  and had been all along.

All the lights in the house were on;
  the house was so brightly lit
that it looked as though it were on fire.
  And everyone was walking around outside,
either crying or vomiting. One of the guys,
  Bob Fisher, had been drinking all day long
and had begun to lie down in front of cars
  as they bounced along the little beach road.
He'd pretend he was an accident victim,
  and when the drivers got out to see if they could help,
he'd cackle and lurch off into the bushes.
  In fact, we called him Lurch after the character
on *The Addams Family,* since he was big
  and ungainly and had a low voice.

As the Wilkersons and I took Kathey
  to the hospital, some of the other guys
decided to follow us, so they filed into
  Greg Cangelosi's jeep and took off.
Lurch, who was quite drunk by now,
  ran down the road a little bit, hid in the bushes,
and flopped down in front of the jeep;
  in all of the excitement, Greg didn't see him
and, in fact, didn't even know he'd run over him
  until one of the guys looked back

and saw Lurch lying there with his legs broken
    and his chest crushed.
And that's the scene we came back to
    after we'd taken Kathey to the hospital.

That's the problem with the story of Lurch,
    because it's the last thing I remember:
the unnatural light that streamed out of the house,
    and everybody outside, crying or vomiting.
Obviously the police were brought in,
    and Lurch's body was taken somewhere,
probably to the hospital where Kathey was lying,
    coming in and out of consciousness
and thinking during her wakeful moments
    that the story was still there with her.
And Lurch's parents must have been notified,
    and surely somebody led a prayer at the beach,
and there must have been a funeral
    when we got back to Baton Rouge again.

But all I remember is the chaos
    and the bright, hazy pain
that streamed from the windows
    of the house in Grayton Beach
and then nothing; the next thing I knew,
    I was sitting in class again,
trying to make sense of what my teachers were saying
    and wondering whether I should keep going out
with the girl I'd been dating.
    She was really pretty, but she was getting
more and more sarcastic all the time,
    so I was thinking of asking out a girl
I sat next to in The Eighteenth-Century Novel
    who was plainer but had a better disposition.

So, on the one hand, it was as though
    nothing had happened. On the other,
the worst thing that could have happened did.

I'm still not sure where the story of Lurch begins.
All I'm sure of is the bright, painful middle,
   the house, with that horrible light coming out of it,
and everybody out front, sobbing and throwing up.
   And it's obvious that the story can't end there,
sans dénouement, as it were. But if I'm not sure
   where the story of Lurch begins,
maybe it doesn't have to have an ending.
   Or maybe some stories simply don't end.
Certainly the story of Lurch never ends;
   it just stops being told.

Peaches and Plums

The father took the children for long walks on Sundays because he imagined they shared his enthusiasm for the flat fields of the Beauce in summer, with the light clouds drifting across a pale sun, the hawthorn hedges flecked with fragile white flowers, and the edges of the wheat stained with red poppies. But the two girls did not share his enthusiasm for the flat fields of the Beauce, or even the sight of an occasional rabbit darting for cover, or the floppy brown ears of the pointer reappearing in the wheat. It was convenient for the father to imagine the girls shared his enthusiasms, but the truth was, all they shared was their name, Trubetskoi, which was embarrassingly difficult to pronounce, and the houses they lived in with their mother, and the Scottish nanny, and the cook from the Gold Coast. They lived in the winter in a house on a blind street in Paris, and in the summer in a villa on the side of a cliff in Italy, and then in the old stone mill in an unexpected declivity in the Beauce.

When the two girls lagged behind on the muddy fields, their father would wait impatiently for them to catch up and talk as he strode onward in an effort to entertain them. "The first time I met Pamela," he would say with a little tremolo in his voice, his eyes misty, speaking of their mother as though they had no connection with her, "she was standing at the door in the sunlight in the Parioli with a Panama hat in her hand. She looked like that Gainsborough—or is it a Reynolds portrait of Lady Hamilton? You know the one I mean, where she holds a straw hat in her hand, with that flush in the cheeks and that russet hair tumbling down her back and the soft laughing mouth and that air of rushing in or out somewhere. She was Enrico's girl then, of course. You remember the Italian, don't you?—the one who was the papal guard. He'd taken me to see her, this girl he had found, who came from some wild country and, he said, had *tante di quelle miniere di diamanti,*" and the father would imitate Enrico—

whom the children had never heard of before—speaking Italian and shaking out his long slim fingers to indicate the gold mines or the gold or money, anyway, the children understood, falling from his fingers like leaves from a tree. The father would stare down at the girls expectantly, apparently waiting for some sort of response, a laugh, perhaps, but he seemed not to be seeing them, his two girls, Sarah and Anne, with their limp pigtails, their gray slanting eyes, and their cold pink knees, exposed in the kilts brought back from Edinburgh by the nanny and let down from the waist, so that they never seemed to grow out of them. The father seemed to be seeing imaginary children, boys, perhaps—their father had always wanted boys—red-cheeked, rambunctious boys who would run around the fields and chase rabbits, not pale-faced, frail girls who were frightened of big dogs and bored by these long monotonous walks and preferred to lie in their warm beds and eat chocolates and read books or sit by the fire and listen to their mother tell stories.

Their father spoke in cadences that seemed strange to the girls, full of unfamiliar idioms, unlike their mother's or even their nanny's clipped formal English where the sentences were ordered and precise, with the adjectives and the adverbs in place. He did not seem to realize how odd he sounded, or how strange he looked to the girls. Everything about their father seemed embarrassingly excessive: he had a large arched nose, a big mouth, and thick dark hair on his chest. He was very tall. He had long legs, long arms, a wide stride, and he swung his head from side to side like a metronome as he walked. They had to crane their necks to see his face, and when they saw it, which was not often that summer, he would appear suddenly on a Sunday morning sometimes, scuttering the pebbles of the driveway as he charged up to the house in his Porsche—he never looked the way they had imagined him. Nor did he correspond to their mother's description of him, which was handsome. Even the Scottish nanny, who obviously did not approve of their father, said he had a *certain presence*. Nor did he resemble his photographs, which their mother kept in prominent places, such as the piano in the drawing room. In the photographs, he was always wearing a wide-brimmed hat and grinning broadly, and he looked very pleased with himself; he rarely looked that way that summer. On the contrary, he seemed solemn and anxious, as though he were about to tell the girls something, but just not right away.

As for their mother, she tiptoed around the house silently in their father's presence like a shadow and hovered near the telephone in the hall in his absence, as though it were a volcano that might erupt at any moment. The traces of their mother's presence when he was there were always apologetic. She kept her voice low, and her clothes pale and soft. She lost weight, and even her lovely thick red hair seemed thinner and less red. All these changes told Sarah, the elder of the children, that her father was rather as frightening to her mother as he was to her.

Sarah believed her father did not care for his children particularly. This was not of great consequence, as they did not depend on their father in any practical way. Their mother provided for their well-being. She was a melancholy but steady presence. That summer she wept rather too copiously over *Little Women*. She seemed to the girls a failure as an adult.

Sarah could remember summers when the sun had seemed warmer and the old mill less damp and cold. This summer was so cold and damp that both girls wore their flannel shirts and their Shetland sweaters, although the wool pricked their necks. Despite the three years' difference in age, the girls were always dressed identically. They wore their long woolen socks, their heavy lace-up shoes, and their short kilts. As they tramped across the wet fields, thick mud clung to their shoes. Wind stung their knees. Their hands were bluish with cold. The sky was low, the clouds heavy as stones. They dragged their feet with difficulty, toiling along behind their father listlessly. The wheat was not as high as it should have been for that time of year, and if it rained again before the harvest, the farmer told them, the crops would be ruined.

Then the weather changed: the sun blazed fiercely in a white sky, and the leaves of the chestnut tree on the edge of the fields hung down heavily like ripe fruit. White dust blew up in their faces as they descended the narrow road that went past the local mansion with its high iron fence and slow swans reflected in dark still water. The mansion seemed smaller than Sarah remembered it. The garden had gone wild, the paths were overgrown. Sarah watched pink petals fall slowly to the ground.

"Apparently Mlle de Marcy has eloped with a Spaniard and left for Spain," their father told them, speaking of the owner of the mansion, as they pressed against the iron bars of the gate.

"What's eloped?" Sarah wanted to know.

"You know, run off, gone away, beat it," the father replied impatiently. He was always telling Sarah she asked questions to which she knew the answers, but it seemed to Sarah that there was always some piece of information that did not fit. It was a puzzle that she was unable to fit together.

"Why would she want to run off with a Spaniard?" Sarah asked, because she remembered Mlle de Marcy as an elderly lady with hair that stuck out like little gray wings on either side of her pale face. She wore a gray pleated skirt and a cardigan and pearls and had once come for tea with Sarah's mother and smoked a cigarette and tried to sell her mother a field.

"For God's sake, child, at your age, don't you know why women run off with men?" her father exclaimed.

Sarah did not believe babies were brought by the stork or found under cabbage leaves. Nor did she believe the magazine she had once read with pictures of men with whips and women in short leather skirts and no tops, their legs spread apart, draped in chains. She looked up at her father and tried to think of something appropriate to say, but he had already moved on, was striding down the road under the tall leaning elms, so that he seemed suddenly small and alone, even lonely. She wanted to call out something to him, but she was not sure how to call him back, or whether to call him Father, which sounded strange, or Michael, as her mother did, or even Mr. Trubetskoi, which everyone else in the house called him.

Sarah became aware of a monotonous, aggravating noise at her side. She looked up and saw her sister, who had left the road and was sitting on a log, kicking her shoes against the wood and wailing, "I'm tired of walking. I want to go home to Mummy." Her mouth looked large and red and ugly.

"Well, go home to Mummy, then, if you're going to be such a baby," Sarah said. Anne kept sucking her thumb.

"Go on, go home. I'll catch you up in a minute," Sarah said, though she was not at all sure her sister could find the way home. Nor did she intend to catch her up. She watched Anne walk alone down the road, aware that the trees had darkened, and the sky was swept clean of cloud. It was that time of day when the French sky turned brilliantly clear for a moment before the fall of night. Sarah felt the eyes of unseen animals, hares, squirrels, foxes, a lone wolf watching her from the woods, as her sister walked off uncertainly, her head bowed, wiping her cheeks with the back of her hand.

Sarah looked up at the mansion and saw a light glimmering in an upper window and imagined Mlle de Marcy and her dark-skinned Spaniard lying entwined in one another's arms on the floor. She shivered and then without a glance over her shoulder ran along the road under the leaning elms. She ran up the hill, her heart pounding, the glare of the setting sun in her eyes. She ran on toward her father. At first she thought he had disappeared, but she found him standing in the gloaming, gazing blankly at the dark roses climbing up the stone wall.

"Where's Anne?" he asked Sarah.

"Gone home," Sarah replied. Her father found this explanation satisfactory. She slipped her hand into his, and he looked down at her, as though he had just noticed her. He asked her to remind him just how old she was now, and was it not ten or eleven, a big girl in any case, and did she not know a thing or two? They walked on in silence while Sarah wondered what to respond to such a question. As night fell, her father told Sarah what she had already guessed. Anne, Sarah was certain, had fallen into a ditch in the dark by then. When Sarah asked him for some sort of additional information, her father thought for a moment and said, "You know, it's rather like having a plum and a peach on your plate, and not being sure which one you want to eat."

Sarah tried to imagine whether her mother was the plum or the peach, but neither fruit resembled her mother's slim, pale shape. Sarah walked along the dust path in the dark, concentrating. What came to mind was the unknown woman. Sarah imagined her quite unlike Sarah's mother, quite unlike Sarah herself. She saw her as a woman who was courageous, who would never have deserted her little sister in the dark, or wept over *Little Women,* a woman with lustrous dark hair and flashing black eyes, big bosoms, and a plum-shaped behind, a woman who danced with a high comb in her hair, a woman called Candella, like that Spanish girl at school, who smoked cigarettes through a cigarette holder, and swilled red wine that stained the dark hair of her upper lip, and sat with her knees apart. Sarah imagined the woman with her father's baby, a plump, red-cheeked boy, slipping across bright satin on her rounded hip.

The moonless night was now dark. Above the great flat French fields, there were only a few pale stars. Sarah stumbled blindly along the dust road beside her father, her hand burning in his.

JOHN LOUGHLIN

Heritage

He could appreciate all
The explosion accomplished,
The tools they handed him, the manifold tools
And their manifold applications.
As I was starting to say—the explosion . . .
A pungent lawlessness in the air,
Like sheep ablaze.
He found the barrenness
Quite attractive, and said so,
So that everyone heard, could hear,
But not in the terms you or I could
Hope to attach sentiment to. The scope was greater,
Taking in the jumble of the constellations
And whatever comets happened by.
Blood was no factor in the explosion's program,
Though a fluid akin to blood
Was reported and many raised squeaky voices
Of righteous opprobrium. Nor were any
Women assaulted, some even recovering
Their books and blowing the dust off.
In fact, it wasn't damaging
In our sense of the word, though admittedly,
Windows were rattled, some shattered
For good, and this was a good thing.
It meant a freedom; it meant
We didn't have to stand in
The wooden shoes of our forefathers,
X's over our foreheads and genitals.
No one had ever seen blue
Quite that way.
Many scratched their bald pates,
Preferring succotash with their breakfast

And frowning on pheromones.
But isn't freedom a subtler constraint?
He had the tools and was grateful,
A rising sense of dawn
And glad ankles.
Standing on the jetty, his eagle eye scans
The blue-green groovy seas.

Inside the Chinese Room

—suggested by John Searle's thought experiment

My one bulb may cast
more shadows than light (the corners
are always lost) but it proliferates
in the red and black lips of my four
thousand six hundred twenty-three
lacquered trays, and I can see

well enough to do my job.
The room is compact. I can reach
any word within seconds. My swivel chair
is beautifully oiled, and by now I know
every address. When the buzzer sounds,
I snatch my orders and ricochet

swiftly, rhythmically, from tray to tray,
compiling the proper sequence.
The code is not my business.
My contract clearly stipulates:
No questions. And I can understand
the need for a neutral middleman,

a semantic buffer. The goal
of the project, whatever it is,
is safe with me. I am privy
to nothing. Nevertheless,
I cannot suppress speculations,
and recurring combinations

are teasing me into belief.
My nerves have built up theories.
Over the years, my chair has found

favorite paths, and my hand
reaches out now of its own accord
for "the ramshackle house" to set beside

"the pond with the single carp."
Which they are not, I know.
But maybe they are, and since the truth
might well turn out to be
unbearably ugly or dull,
or entirely reference-free—

ink blots, or random doodles
concealing no message at all beyond
some elaborate math—I tell myself
that the stories I generate
are as good as any others,
and certainly better than none.

As long as the work gets done,
my methods are my own affair.
The gate clicks and delivers
assembly instructions; I follow the rules
as best I can, and the words
(or whatever they are) seem to play along, to rush

into my hands, and the unmarked scroll
unrolls to receive my brush,
and I transcribe. With each dark motion,
I tangle the blankness. Each mark reveals
fealties, plots, A vs. B, bone and muscle
under the skin, a welter of conjunction, lush

with structure. But in what feels
like only a moment, the gate
clicks up and demands the product.
Then, while the ink is still fresh
on my lips, there is sometimes time
between jobs to unfold my fan,

beat a few leisurely strokes
with the painted bird, lean back
and listen to the words rustle.
Ceiling to floor, on all four walls, they shiver and wait
for their next concatenation.
The gate is small and it opens

and shuts in an instant.
The outlines of the larger door
are almost gone, the cracks filled in
with paper dust, maybe, and the sticky
residue of incense smoke.
I may once have been outside,

but I cannot remember. In any case, confinement
is a relative concept: I picture
an ocean naked and swaying,
constantly rearranged,
my papers drifting, soggy, starting to melt,
and myself thrashing slowly after them, all weight, my
    mouth

filling, overflowing, with cold salt.
My room glows like the core
of an old coal, faded black,
breathing red, exhaling
motes of gold. They flash through the narrow
passage and blow away. Recently, I received

an assignment that seemed to ask
whether I wanted the key.
I followed instructions and felt relieved
when the answer I constructed
included "the empty cherry tree,"
my personal figure for "no."

Paths, Crossing

for Gary Holthaus

Seven geese, southwest,
and seven flat-black ships, converging
in the Colorado sky, before

the pale haze of early winter,
bright and bronze and empty,
on a Sunday just approaching noon.

I count the birds again: seven.
And the helicopters: seven, in a line
northeast, their rotors blurred

and sounding faint percussion, high
above the freeway hum. Seven of each kind,
too perfect, almost every way, for trust,

the numbers, parallels and vectors,
sheer coincidence: the ancient memory of the geese,
a war game on the seventh day.

The two flights cross and pass, I count again.
Exact. Their flight paths make a great ghost *X*, flat
and horizontal, signaling *unknown*.

And, true, I know near nothing of the geese
except that they are alive, and nothing of the ships
except they carry unknown men,

uniformed and practicing
for a presumed event, a hard, black presence
fuming in burnt air above the towns,

the teeming highway, muddy farms,
and ponds where geese still winter, in a world
where men have taken on black shells
and learned to fly.

near Longmont, Colorado

LIAM RECTOR

Our Own Ones

I will be coming up the hill from school in an hour...

Lena stretches to the clothesline as Carl
Is coming slowly back over from the barn...
Between them the field dips deep and the field

Slopes long and half the day, already, is done.
She pushes a wooden pin onto a cotton skirt
And the wind competes for dominance here.

He'll live until his sixties; Lena into her nineties...
The fields will reside when they're gone
And the farm, as farms do when the property is not

Owned, will change hands, change families.
I will make a living somewhere else
Making lines I remember from the life

I saw here, using forms from what held us
While in the hold of this place, but for now
I will be coming up the hill from school in an hour...

    My mother got caught and put
    In the penitentiary. My father
    Could not afford me or did not

    Want me (both struck me
    As true), so I was sent out
    To the country while he worked

A failing business in the city.
In the 1950's, after the war,
People from the country,

Along with people from other
Countries, made their way to
The American cities. The food

Was still grown in the country
(Where else could it be grown—
On roofs in the cities?),

But the real hurl of action turned
Towards the marketing of things
In "the major American cities."

Suburbs, full of people
Who did not know how to live
In them, soon formed

Around the cities, and I swore
I would do something
About this someday, but the day

My mother was sent up I got
A break from this mess for a moment—
I was sent out to live with them,

With Carl and Lena in the country.

Carl moves towards the lunch of pork which Lena
Has left on the table. He will eat, crap, sit while
He's able, and be back over to the barn in an hour.

Lena will come in, feed herself, phone on the party line
The woman down the hill, and they will wade
Through their loneliness as late afternoon goes over.

I will be coming up the hill from school in an hour.

Built cheap, built to sell quickly, thrown up
To house men back from the killing, women
Going back to the home from the factories

Where they had worked to support The War Effort,
And children about to be born and form the single
Largest generation in American time, the "boomers,"

The suburbs in the postwar era were built around
The car: carports, forts isolating each family,
Each adolescence for the children spent without

Any real place to gather other than the mall,
The market, or the woods (and adolescence is
Nothing if not a strenuous effort to come in

Out of the woods), and meanwhile in the cities
The old houses torn down to put up housing
"Projects" for the poor: hanging schizophrenia

In mid-air, bad buildings, wrong turnings,
And much of it dynamited down by the 1980's . . .
Just before those my age took the helm in the 1990's.

They were kind to me. They were glad to have me.
At first they thought they were too old, really,
To tend to me, but I tried to be a good boy for them

—I spent much of my time alone in the woods anyway—
And soon they were glad to have me. I would fetch
Things for them and unlike their other ones, gone

To the city, I was enchanted by the country;
I didn't yet have to make any money.
I was their grandson come to live with them then

Late in their lives with their children raised
And the love all but gone from their marriage.
They took me in and they loved me then

And without them there would have been no rudder...
I got older, they died, the farm got sold out from under
Everyone, and again I took on the fate of the cities.

With Carl and Lena gone that was pretty much the end
Of any of us getting together as an "extended family."
The American family changed, and though many tried to

Will the old family back (such will is cruel;
Such cruelty expressed itself politically),
Most took up forming the different family.

I now have a daughter, I'm divorced, and I make a living
As an architect in Cincinnati—forming windows, arcs,
    lanes...
And though I know there is no going back I try to bring back

Something of the nineteenth century to the American city.

We Should Not Let Munich Slip Away

There was rain which soon turned
To snow and no place we had in mind
We wanted to go so we stayed in bed

And made love all afternoon...
As the lamps lit the street
We got up from each other

Because there was money to be made
Because we did not grow our own food,
Because someone else owned that place;

So we got dressed for the club where
We went to play the music, where the people
From the offices spilled in from their day,

And you said we should go to Munich soon,
That we should not let Munich slip away—
That the work, the money, was better there,

That things were not getting better for us here,
And that you had some money, some money
You'd not told me about—money squirreled away.

All my life it's been a question:
Whether to go or to stay.
I woke up violent with fear one morning,

I woke up violent with hope one morning,
I picked up this horn one morning,
And it played me until I was away.

Uncle Snort

My aunt was upset by lesbians:
Her sister, her sister's lover, in particular.
She imagined them, I think, giving each other

Head over and over, though from what I knew
—And I knew plenty—that couple made love
With roughly the same frequency

As did Auntie and Uncle Snort. They
All had plenty to worry about, though since
The minds of the Snorts were bent

Around projecting their demons wildly
Onto others, introspection—and the following
Quiet and responsibility comes there—was lost

On the Snorts, which worked out pretty well
For them most of the time, except theirs were
Unexamined Lives, stupid beyond belief,

And they were hell to pay come election time.

G. TRAVIS REGIER

The Taxidermist

April

Owen shows up at my flat around midnight. He doesn't knock, but I spot him waiting in lurk beyond the screen door. Outside, the rain jumps like pixies on the floodlit blacktop. His hair is soaked and his boots are muddy.

"Come on in," I say, and he does, slowly. His eyes have that look they get when the cauldron inside his head boils. I wrap a towel around his head and clear some junk off the couch. Owen glances around and smiles, amused as always by the mess I live in. His own place is so clean and bare.

"It's weird at home," he says. "There's somebody there. I had to get out of the house."

I want to hold him then, but that doesn't help. First I need to know what's going on. "Think a minute, Owen. Is there really somebody there? Or is it a ghost?"

"I don't believe in ghosts, Randi."

"But you see them sometimes."

Owen smiles a little. "It's a real person. A girl." He floats a hand out, winds the front tails of my flannel shirt into his fist. His thumb knuckle presses into my navel, and his fingers brush against my snakeskin belt—the one he made for me, three years ago.

"No," I tell him. He lets go. I sit in the chair. Owen and I are lovers sometimes, when he's thinking straight. He's not a hunk, but his hands are slow as warm butter, and his mouth is like no one else's. "So then, you want to talk about it?"

"Her name's Melissa. She's sleeping."

"Maybe. Maybe she's loading your VCR in her car." I fix our coffee. He likes lots of cream. "Do you like her?"

He shrugs. "I just—" he swallows hard. "I woke up and got scared. You know. I looked at her..."

I don't ask whose face he saw. Mine, maybe. One of the ex-

142

wives. So many others, I don't want to know. In the old days he would call me by other women's names. I played along; I thought it was a game, and back then I thought games were cool. I didn't know then about Owen: the drugs, the jails, the dark and bloody maze of his childhood. I didn't know about the ghosts.

Owen's confused but he's trying hard, he sweats and blinks, and I put my hand on his. "She's been there a couple days," he says. "I thought maybe you could tell—if she's bad for me. Or what."

Owen used to trick me into running off his bimbos, then call me a jealous bitch. We'd both cry, and he'd promise to be straight with me. I've learned what to say:

"I don't want to meet her."

One hot July midnight four years ago, when I was still in my twenties, Owen sat beside me on somebody's boat dock and showed me the scars on his arms. He had done them with cigarettes, he said, after his ex-wife left him. (Later I found out how he really got them, pouring iron for brake shoes at the Rayco plant in Oklahoma.) I told him about my own divorce, all that boring carnage that still seemed so unique to me then. We passed a bottle back and forth, trailing our bare feet in the moon-smeared water and watching skyrockets smash into green and gold fire above Bull Shoals Lake.

We knew some of the same people, and they had paired us up at a rockabilly club. He was my type: leathery skin, square, cal-loused hands, gray in his black hair. Something was wrong with his right eye; it didn't track like the left one, but sat stonily fixed. "Randy," he said. "That's a boy's name." He squeezed my plastic lighter between his fists, then sparked it as he spread his hands. For an instant, flame swirled in his open palm.

We danced and sweated under those jagged lights for hours, then went for a ride. At some point it became easy to just let him talk, to lie back into the blur of his voice and let the words go. At some point it was easy to pull up my skirt and show him the tat-too on my hip, my green and scarlet feathered serpent.

"Quezalcoatl," he said. "Aztec god of death."

"It's my sign," I told him. "My coat of arms."

Some people from the bar drove up then, and Owen got to rapping with a black guy who said he owned a leopard.

"She's retching and bleeding," the guy said. "She might could die."

"I ain't a vet, Joel. I'm a taxidermist."

"You told me you went to vet school two years."

"Yeah?" Owen smiled just a little. I didn't know what that meant then. "Did I tell you that?"

They drank some more whiskey, then started off, as if I weren't there. People forget me that way, because I'm small and quiet. "Hey," I called. "Can I come with?"

Owen grinned at my Yankee talk. "Yeah," he drawled. "You can come with."

I think I passed out in the truck, but then we were at the fairgrounds, and there were rows of tractor trailers, and the sweet stench of manure and hay, and a tableful of roustabouts playing poker under moth-swarmed light bulbs. In a cage by herself, the leopard paced and let out her devil whines. My eyes caught on the slink of her tail.

"She don't act sick," Owen said. "Something's hurt her." He pawed through a kit Joel brought him, dropping worn-out instruments to the ground in disgust. Eventually they knocked her out with a long hypodermic, and Owen pried her jaws apart and probed around inside with his finger.

"She's caught a needle in her pharynx," Owen said. He cut it out with a scalpel, then stitched the wound. The blood and pus on his hands made me dizzy, and the next thing I remember was lying in the dark on a futon. Owen was beside me, eating something, watching TV with the sound off.

"Where's your stereo?"

"I don't like just music." He thumbed a cool strawberry into my mouth. "I took your dress off," he said, "so it wouldn't get wrinkled."

"Did we do anything?"

"Not yet."

I kissed him. "That was wild with the cat."

"I had two years of med school," he said. He started massaging me, down my back and up my legs, rubbing me till his hands felt like part of my body, like my body was made of light. I let my eyes close and open, open and close.

"I can see through you," he said. "Like stained glass. I feel like I know you."

"You're so full of shit," I said. "Take off my panties."

Owen and I saw each other a lot. I liked hanging out in his shop, watching him work on a deer's head till the antlers shone and the brown eyes came alive. We went dancing, or drove out by the airbase and spread a blanket on a grassy hill, to drink a thermos of martinis and watch the C-130's come in. But most of the time it wasn't worth it. He wanted to swing with other couples, and sulked when I said no. He wouldn't show up for a date, and the next day I'd hear he was at a party with some chippie. We were hot together, but he wasn't my boyfriend. I couldn't trust him.

When I got sober he was part of my old life, and I didn't see him. This year he started coming around again.

In the night I hear Owen walking around. I go to him, pulling jeans on first and making lots of noise so I don't startle him. He stands at the window, backlit by the streetlight, watching the rain. His back is gnarled with tension and molten with sweat. When I say his name he doesn't answer, just lifts his fist and starts hitting the glass slowly, a long breath between each blow.

"Stop it, Owen. Stop it."

He stops then. Carefully I slip one arm around his shoulder. Then I notice what's in it: the handgun I bought a year ago, when I got my own place. Owen had helped me pick it out, and he knew where I kept it.

I take the gun carefully from his hand, check it out. It isn't loaded. I slip it in a drawer, under some linens.

"Do you know where you are?"

He dares a glance over one shoulder, then looks back at the rain. "Your place? But it don't look right."

"You're thinking of the old place, the trailer. This is my new place."

"Okay."

"You want to sleep some more?"

145

"Okay."

I help him back to the couch. He tries to touch me, and I'm glad I put on my pants. He's not sure who I am. I don't want him that way.

He tells me about his dream. "We were napping and you were teasing me. Then you took off your pants and there was no vagina, only smooth flesh. *See,* you said. *I told you.*"

"It's just a dream."

"I love you, Randi. You know that?"

"Don't use the L-word, Owen."

"I just wish..." He cups my chin, turns my face to catch the light from outside. "I wish that I could treat you better," he says. "That you were mine."

"It can't be that way," I say.

He says, "I know."

In the morning Owen cracks eggs one-handed into my iron skillet. I brush my hair in the living-room mirror. He cuts toast, squeezes oranges: everything appears with magical quickness. I sit to my basted eggs. The news drones on my countertop TV, sharp and clear instead of its usual muddy picture. Owen's done something to it.

"So," he says. "You want to go out next week?"

"Aren't you dating someone?"

He just grins.

I take him home on my way to work. He likes my convertible. We play a game, his arms around me to steer and shift while I work the pedals.

"...so I dream I'm on TV, playing Death Jeopardy. The host puts the knife by my ear and asks, *When is New Zealand?*"

I clutch, he shifts. "It's Zen Jeopardy," I say. "None of the answers have questions."

"I was on it once, the real one. I won a thousand bucks."

"Yeah?" But I don't believe it. He has that look he gets when he's telling stories. Then he puts his head back into the wind and sings. When he was my age he sang with rock bands in Memphis and New Orleans, and under the whiskey blur you can hear the good voice still:

Kept on looking for a sign in the middle of the night
But I couldn't get it right, couldn't get it right
Kept on looking for a way to make it through the night
But I couldn't get it right

Owen's hillside house and workshop look the same as they always do: peeling boards, sheet metal roof, plastic he hasn't bothered to rip from the windows. The same wheelbarrow and cement mixer still hulk in the gravel drive, the satellite dish in the backyard tracks its invisible god. As Owen gets out, his new girl opens the front door and stands there scowling. She's just a kid. She's wearing one of his shirts, and her hair is tousled, but she has on makeup. Owen glances at her and then back at me, his lips showing just the edge of a smile. He can't help but like his games, though they hurt him so badly.

"Bye now." I let out the clutch faster than I mean to; gravel skitters behind my tires. Out on the highway I try to figure out why I started shaking when I saw her. Then I know: she had good legs, but she wasn't really pretty. She could at least be pretty.

August

I'm an airline ticket agent, one of those efficient and courteous voices who answer those 800 numbers. It's harder work than you think. One's eyes get tired of staring at ragged numbers on a video screen, and one's flawless courtesy wears thin. You can't let up for a second, because the bosses spot-check you with their wiretaps. It's a long day, and when I get home I want to drink. Instead, I go to meetings, and listen to more talk.

Tonight, for a change, I do some talking myself. I talk about Owen. After me, a woman named Sue says, "I've been listening to what our sister here says, trying to get the logic of it. And while I don't claim to know what's right for her, I know a few things that have worked for me and for others in the fellowship. When you're trying to stay sober, you have to move away from anything that threatens your sobriety. You have to change your playground and your playmates." People around the room nod amen. It sounds so cold to me, and I'm getting pissed off, so I push back from the table and get some more coffee. She just goes on talking. "As for your friend, well, you know him, I don't. All I know about him is what I know about everybody, and that's that he's got to find his own way."

Finally she shuts up. Then this guy, one of the old farts with lots of sobriety, says, "My name's Jorge and I'm an alcoholic."

"Hi, Jorge," everyone says.

"I've got a personal rule that works for me," he says. "Never sleep with anyone who's crazier than you are." Everyone laughs. My fingers knot around the coffee cup, squeezing the ceramic till they hurt. But I keep quiet.

When I get home the phone is ringing. I let the machine answer it.

"My name is Melissa, and I'm staying with Owen Rigdon. I'd like it if you called me. Please."

What the hell. I pick up. "Hello. What's wrong with Owen?"

"He's acting kind of crazy." She has a kid's voice, cuddle-boppy. Just what he likes. "I wondered if maybe we could have lunch or something."

"No. We can't."

"He told me a lot about you."

"Of course."

"Maybe you could give me some advice or something."

"I don't think so."

"You care about him, don't you?"

"That's not your business."

"I know. I'm just worried about Owen."

She sounds sincere, though how can you tell? And if she is, does that matter? Owen's sleight of hand usually leaves no trace.

I'm dressed to beat her, sexy but discreet, like a lady lawyer. Nail polish, heels, a black dress that's back in style. She's tried to dress up, but doesn't know how. Her skirt's too short and her makeup too gaudy.

I like her, though. She doesn't fool around with small talk. We get our salads, and she starts in telling her story. The cops come around, and Owen won't tell her why. He stays up for days, then sleeps twenty-four hours. He says he hears voices.

"How old are you, honey?"

"I'm eighteen. But I'm old inside. I've been through a lot."

I tell her about the meetings. She looks puzzled. "Owen's not an alcoholic."

"Oh, he isn't?"

"He gets wasted sometimes. But that's not the problem."

"Okay."

"The problem is he's crazy."

"Well, duh."

"Excuse me?"

"Sorry. But yeah, I know Owen's crazy. Do you know how many shrinks he's gone through?"

"Owen went to a shrink?"

"He's been inside. Detox, shock treatments. And he was in prison, you know, before that. Armed robbery."

"He never told me about that," she says slowly.

I realize I'm staring at the wine list, so I close it firmly. "Don't you get it, honey? He wants *me* to tell you. He wants *us* to worry about him."

"Owen doesn't know I called you."

"I'll bet he does. Anyway, I'm not going to play this game. I can tell you one thing, though. You should leave."

"I don't want to."

Everybody has to find their own way. But God, it's hard to watch. "Then there's one other thing I can tell you."

"What is it?"

"Nine-one-one."

"You mean the emergency number?"

"You get it. Nine-one-one."

October

Each day I get stronger. I don't need to go to meetings any-more—all they do is talk and talk. I go to work at six and get off in the middle of the afternoon. At home, I sit on the porch swing and drink ice tea from a mason jar. This is a good place, I've decided, this small town in Missouri I never thought to spend more than a month in. Now it's been five years. This is where I belong, maybe. This is where I got sober.

Before I see it come over the hill, I recognize the deep hum of Owen's truck. It's a Chevy from the sixties, but he keeps it tuned like a race car. As he climbs down, I try to size up his mood, like I used to in the old days. What I can see looks okay. There's nothing weird in his smile, or the glint in his eye.

"Sit it down here, you dog."

"You're looking good. Healthy."

He means it, and it's true. I hold my shoulders straighter now, and my skin has a ruddy color. My blood pressure is normal. Each day I get stronger.

"So then, how's that sweet girlfriend of yours?"

"Drifted on. She wants to be a rock star."

That sounds like a story, but I don't ask. "Do you miss her?"

"I dunno. I've been dating. But it's all gone flat, y'know?"

"Maybe you want something else now, Owen."

"I'm not as spiritually advanced as you are, darling. I always want something else."

He's fencing with me, challenging me to lay a recovery spiel on him, so he can turn sulky and defiant. I don't want to play that game. We sit side by side on the porch swing, pushing off lightly with our feet, listening to the creak of the swing chain. We don't talk, and it feels good. For months I've been talking, pumping the poison up out of my soul; I've been listening to people talk about their own struggles, as a way of finding a key to my own. But sometimes you need someone you don't have to talk to.

At the 7-Eleven, Owen hangs on my arm while I read the labels on condoms. "*Nyet,*" he whispers as he tongues my ear. "I want my bare dick inside you. You should take the pill."

"Grow up, Owen. People are dying."

He sighs. "This ain't much like the old days."

"I didn't like the old days."

November

Owen likes to walk through the rooms of his house naked. He likes stepping barefoot from plank floor to terry-cloth rug, and he likes the feel of air-conditioning on his body. Some nights he works naked in the shop: not when he's cutting molds on the band saw, or curing hides, but sometimes when he's shaping the heads, packing the ears and nostrils with clay, airbrushing a trout with rainbow colors. He has a big, flat table he keeps sanded smooth as my inner thigh, and a walk-in freezer, with the fish he's working with stacked on one side and his food stored on the other. He buys glass eyes by the barrel.

"Look at this." He's working on a bearskin rug. "They cut the throat to drain the blood, thinking they were helping me. Now I've got to stitch it, and it's going to look like shit."

"Did you ever hunt bear?"

"Sure, in Alaska." I check his eye but there's no gleam; this is a true story. "You can salvage about three-fourths of a bear, and the meat is sweet and greasy. After a while even the dogs won't eat it."

Up in the loft, stacked behind other old junk, are the last canvases he started before he quit painting. He studied at art schools, and exhibited in galleries. The Ancient Days, he calls them. But then somehow he lost that, and he hasn't painted since before I knew him.

"Come down from there."

"You should finish this," I say, staring at a half-done portrait of a nude woman. Her head is thrown back in ecstasy, her throat flushed. A layer of dust darkens the colors.

Later, in his big claw-footed tub, Owen's hand-feathers the edge of a barber's razor along my thigh, carefully scraping away the hair-flecked lather. Its touch stings less than a bee, but makes me shudder. He dots a finger to the nicks and raises it to my lips. The blood tastes sweet.

Owen smiles. But he doesn't like this game; it's mine. I put one finger in the blood, then to his lips, but he doesn't want it.

"What were we like, Randi—in the old days?"

"You were crazy. I was a drunken whore."

"And we were in love."

"You're talking about sex, Owen. Not love."

"Same thing."

"Tell me about love."

"Love is a blind worm that lives inside you." He eyes the razor, turns it through slow angles. Light walks along the blade. "When it feeds, it thrashes in its excitement, and it gnaws at your guts, makes them open and bleed."

"And if you don't feed it?"

He shrugs. "It dies. You die."

I put my mouth on his shoulder. "Love isn't pain, my love."

"Love is pain."

The next time I get on top. His hands rub my ass as I bear down.

He's different from most guys; they let you on top but it makes them nervous. Owen likes to be the woman. I don't mean like a fag. Just that he likes to lie there, and be fucked.

December

I haven't been home in three days. After work it's closer to go to Owen's, and after Owen it's easier to stay the night. I keep some clothes there, and my makeup and blow dryer and things I keep in a carry-on in my car. Owen's been staying home, staying out of trouble; we make love and cook food and watch the million channels on his giant TV. We don't use the L-word, but when he comes in me, he whispers, "I want to keep you." And I hold his bottom more tightly and murmur, "I want to stay with you."

In the night, his mouth on my stomach wakes me. He takes up a flashlight and examines my body with it inch by inch, ending with the pearl of blood that is my clitoris.

"Oh baby," I whisper. "O my detective."

March

"We should go to the new club Gary told me about. The Locker Room."

"It's a strip bar."

"Is it?"

"You're so full of shit, Owen."

He takes a slug of beer. We've started getting wasted together again, but we only drink beer: our fantasy of control. "Hell, Randi, we're so straight nowadays. A little excitement never hurt nobody."

"So go. But I don't want to hear about it."

We watch TV a while, flipping channels. Then he says, "You sure you don't want to go? There might be somebody working there we used to know. We could hang around with her."

"Who is she, Owen?"

"I don't know," he said. But I catch what he's trying to hide, that bit of a smile.

"Okay, Owen. Tell me what the game is."

"I don't know..."

"Yes you do know, Owen, goddamn you! You do know!"

Without any warning at all I'm shaking with rage. I dump the popcorn over his head. The metal bowl clangs on the floor. Then the lamp, the phone, bottles, anything within reach.

But then I stop. It's no good. Owen is grinning.

"Shit, girl," he says. "You going to spit on the floor now?"

"Just tell me the truth, Owen. Do you *want* to be with me? If you don't, then stay the fuck out of my life."

"That's not what I want." He's starting to cry now. Tears flow from his unblinking eyes. "I try to tell you things. I just get scared." He takes a breath deep enough to make him tremble. "If you know what I'm like—what I'm thinking—then you won't want me around."

"Oh, Owen."

So then we go. You're going to say I knew better. And yeah, I did know. But I wasn't ready to see it. I hadn't hurt enough yet.

Lights. Music. Action. The barkeep calls out the girl's pseudonym, then starts a CD at deafening volume. I order O.J. Owen gets mad that I won't drink with him, then forgets it, as one girl after another slowly strips off her sequins and spreads herself open before his eyes. After his second beer, he switches to whiskey with a splash of Coke.

After her dance, each girl comes around in her panties, holding a carafe for tips. Some guys look away. For the ones who dig deep, she sits beside them on the bar stool, laughing at their jokes, letting them touch her throat and thighs. There are booths in the back for private shows; the girl is nude and nobody asks what happens. Guys hand over their credit cards and go back there, then come out three songs later buckling their belts and grinning, while their buddies halloo and pound them on the back.

Lap dancing is ten bucks, and the girls smile like robots through their makeup as they writhe and push against the lumps in the men's jeans. The men touch them all over, but are supposed to stay out of their pants; it's the law. But one guy gets hold of a girls' throat and bends her back against the bar, then very deliberately pulls her panties down her hips. Two bouncers start toward him, but the crowd gets in the way. The guy blinks with drunken concentration, staring down at his own hand as he pushes it around inside her. I can see it all too clearly: his fingers rubbing her clitoris, pressing into and out of her vagina. Her head is bowed back against the cold wood of the bar, and her eyes glisten with tears.

Then I see Owen's face. His eyes are locked on her eyes. I've never seen a look quite like that.

Desire.

Rapture.

The bouncers break it up. The manager pats the girl on the shoulder, and I hear him telling her to get dressed for her next dance.

"I'm outta here," I say.

"Stay here." Owen grabs my arm; I try to shake it off, but he's too strong. "Cut it out," he says. "You can't go out there alone. Some creep'll rape you."

"Those girls are getting raped."

"They're getting paid."

He trails me out to the parking lot, and grabs me before I can get in my car. He shoves his face into mine and yells, but I can't make out the words. His breath stinks. I spit on the ground. Then the security comes up behind us and says up-against-the-wall. Owen wants to swing on him, but he's not too wasted to assess the piece in the man's hand. The guard pats him down, then suddenly knees him in the kidneys. Owen goes down, his cigarette sparkling along the gravel.

"It's okay," I say. "Leave him alone."

He slips a fold of bills into his shirt pocket, then tosses the wallet at Owen's feet. "You two get off the property."

"Give him back his money!"

"You're drunk, sister. I don't know what you're talking about."

I get Owen to the car. He leans over the hood and throws up, while I wait behind the wheel.

For years alcohol was good to me, and then for years more it was pain in a bottle. All through both those lifetimes, it had a glamor I couldn't resist, a sparkle more ruthless and keen than any gem. Now it's none of those things; it's just this waste, this shame, this man with an empty wallet vomiting on dirty gravel. Now it's boring.

At Denny's, we fall in with a companionable table of drunks. We all order lots of food and then put our cigarettes out in it. Somebody has cards and Owen does tricks with them, pulling four jacks off a burning house. Owen makes up a story about the bruises on his face. The girls like him, but their dates are uneasy.

"You want to go, then?" I say to Owen. He fixes his crooked eye on me.

The fourth time we have sex I black out, just for a few seconds, I think. He's different tonight. He stays inside me so long, makes me come so many times. I'm used to him making love to me all night with his hands and tongue. But he's never *fucked* me this much before.

I know why.

"You don't want *me*," I say when he wakes me up for another round. "You want that girl."

"Come on, baby." He's as hard as the first time. His fingers are inside me, nibbling my favorite spots, but I'm turning to ice inside. The mind is its own body. I don't want him.

"Can you see me, Owen?" I shove my face against his. "Who am I? Who do you see? Besides, we can't. We don't have any more condoms."

He reaches for his pants. "The all-night store..."

"No," I say. "Don't leave, Owen. I don't want to be alone. Just hold me."

His hand cradles my stomach, and we sleep together like spoons. But in the night I feel him pressing against me again.

"No, Owen. Dammit."

"Just let me..." Owen's never rough with me—but suddenly he is. He wedges my hips against the mattress, grinds my face into the pillow. I try to yell but my mouth is fouled with lace. He ignores my nails digging into his shoulders, so I use my fists, but they feel like nothing, like air, against his hard muscles. I raise my right foot, take a breath, and kick him hard in the side of the head.

It's a mistake. I can see his face in the moonlight, and it's not the face of anyone I know. His lips snarl, and his fists and elbows come down on me, over and over. Finally I just let him do it, lying there cold while he puts it in and out. I don't want him, but the motion makes me wet, and his dick is bigger than it ever gets; I can feel it touching a spot down in there that he never reaches. When he comes I push my hips down, but part of the slime goes in.

He rolls away, starts snoring. I dry my tears, try to wipe away what he put inside me. The toilet paper sticks to me, and my hands are shaking so I can't get it right.

At home, I stand under the shower for two hours, trying to wash him off me. I can't. The bruises on my ribs and hips are big as saucers, and my swollen eyes are turning purple. I load my gun, and keep it in my hand as I pour all the beer down the sink and fling the bottles into the trash. Then I call Mary from AA. She says she'll come right over.

April
"I want to make it all right."
"You can't."
"Will you just see me?"
"Stay away from me, Owen."
"Just tell me what the game is."
"Here's the game: If you come around here, I'll kill you."

June
Each day I get stronger. Each night I'm able to go to sleep easier, think about Owen a little less. I even go out on a date once, but when he calls me again I tell him no, I'm not ready. Then one day a call comes from Darleen at the sherrif's office, telling me I should come and get my stuff.

"I don't understand."

"Well, Owen broke the lease, y'know...He left all his stuff, and it'll end up sold at auction. There's a trunk in the living room with your name on it. Figured you'd want it."

"Owen left town?"

"Sorry, honey. Thought you knew. I heard he went out to California, just threw some stuff in his truck and hit the road. Told people he was going to live in the woods and get sober."

"I wish I could believe that. But you know Owen. He's such a liar."

"You never know."

After work I'm going to drive out there, but halfway to his place I get scared and go back home. But then I can't sleep, and around two in the morning I go back. The power's off, but I shine a flashlight around and find the key under the brick. All his furniture is there, and his video gear and tapes and books. It looks like he left everything but his clothes and tools. The trunk is in the bedroom. There's some clothes I left here—sex clothes, mostly, the kind I don't wear anymore—and kitchen things like a sandwich maker.

So then I step into the shop, throwing my light into the black room: and my heart stops.

Head of a goat, but the body is a collie dog. The stubby horns gleam, and the blunt, black claws. For a second, terror grips me, as I half expect it to move. But of course it stays still; it's no space mutant, just something Owen has made, using his skill to fasten one animal part to another. Very slowly I walk about the room, looking at them all, at this museum of freaks he's made. There's a racoon's face in an owl's skull, and a young gator with a cat's head and shoulders. Sleek black fur bristles where it overlaps mottled yellow-green scales.

He's arranged them carefully, some crouching behind a table, others raising their claws. Track lights are positioned to light them, so I throw the main breaker and switch them on. In the sculpture of light and shadow, they loom like mythological creatures: centaurs and basilisks, or the beast-headed gods of Egypt. Pride of place goes to the feathered serpent: eagle head and torso trailing the heavy grace of a diamondback rattler. Beside it, stuck in the plank wall with a switchblade knife, is a piece of paper.

Randi,

Has he gone crazy again, or regained his Art? Who knows? These images of resurrection, I make in your honor. It's been a lot of years since I tried to live like a human being, tried to do more good than harm. I think it's time I tried again.

Be of good cheer, Randi, and know how I'm thinking of you, how I miss you, how much I'll always love you. There's a chance that some night years from now, in your cozy house somewhere, you'll open your door and let me in. I'll bring in my bags, and you'll make me a bed on the couch, and we'll brew hot tea. We'll take off our shoes, and we'll talk until the night's blue shades to gray.

And we'll hold hands like we used to—but it won't be the way it used to. It'll be the way it should have been.

Love Always, Owen

Reading the note again, I notice its literary side, its edge of play. It's just more Owen-theater, maybe, just another story. But it's a better, cleaner story. I hope he keeps telling it to himself. I read it one more time, then sit down and begin looking at the animals, at the strange life Owen has crafted into their faces. The goat-dog looks menacing, the bird-snake bold and sly. The owl-racoon looks troubled but like he's trying.

How long I sit and study them, I don't know. But when I look up, night is rubbing at the windows, and the dust in the beams of the track lights is a swarm of golden bees. I realize that he's gone. I look inside myself for the hollow place, and find it.

Be of good cheer, Owen, and make a life for yourself. I don't expect to see you again in this one. But I can see you now in my mind's eye, somewhere west of here, driving with your arm hung out the window and the ball of your right foot warm on the gas pedal. You top another hill, start down into a long valley. The day is clear and you can see everything before you.

DAVID RIVARD

Welcome, Fear

For one thing I'm glad
the goal of enlightenment means being so utterly stupid
as to actually slip out the door
every morning & live. With no second-guessings,
no poses, just this leaning & slouching
the experts term hope. Because people like me aren't guilty
of laughing at the passing streets. I mean I believe
we better be better than those grins
you see plastered to the sides of every bus,
a couple of thousand smiles claiming power
for a single pair of basketball shoes.
But what do I do, what am I supposed to
do when I want someone
to hold me? How easy it is, & inevitable
and paramount & sweet, to recall
how you would dress before the mirror—
in those minutes before a blouse
started to button itself on, when
sunlight from the window
might rest briefly on your back, & I would begin
by tipping my mouth to your skin
the way the first imagined oar dipped
into an unimaginable sea. Now nothing seems right

between us, neither finished nor
unfinishable. Whatever I once wrote to you fills me,
torn into many small pieces. Sometimes
it seems as if that mirror I mentioned before
has been lost, perhaps stolen, but by men I'd hired myself,
mistakenly. I am my own
bad influence. Many
things have gone wrong. And I will never be what you

wanted me to be. You will always lean toward the mirror,
putting on lipstick, kissing the air,
but since the mirror has been revoked
the kiss collects in the shape of space attempting
to kiss itself. Well
the tragic can go fuck itself. Even if, once,
in the middle of the night, I woke
because a smoke detector went off, signaling
its batteries were dying. Even if it's like that. Fear,
like that: walking naked
through a cold house, moving from alarm
to alarm, unable to find the right one. Even if it's like that.

The Shy

We even breathed shyly, all the while
envying everybody
their courage & finesse.
But either our nerve
gave out, or we were much too patient,
always over-rehearsed, like those old men, the frowners
who spend hours fly casting
in the park, practicing, each flick of their wrists
erasing the memory of streams
and flame-spotted trout.
So everybody else's
boldness tasted
inebriating. And we would have asked
for risks but blushed at our clumsiness, our imperfections
like lamps of oil
lit just beneath the skin. Shamefaced. Rosy. Reddened.
Look, look. There must have been
many hours like coal mines,
very dark & confusing, dripping & quiet & cold,
which required
that light. So we outfitted ourselves
with modesty & doubt. Secretly
we were delighted
to be mispronouncing our words, to be mangling them
in front of any audience our
anxiously glad egos could get.
Whole days would be lived
as if standing beneath an elm
in a light rain, caught
where the sidewalk remains dry
reliving some humiliation, some disgrace simple
as absent-mindedness. Chagrined.
Bashful. Flushed. Because what
would shyness have been

without shyness? Without it
there might have been calm.
The green of the elm no longer
ruffling leaves. The street
quiet, the motorbikes & cars having vanished
with the sudden grace of dolphins,
and the rain ending, a lull, like
the one in which a mouse might pause,
about to devour
a live cat, having played with it
for a while.

DAVID ROMTVEDT

Who Owes Us

No one owes us anything.
We claim it's mother and father.

How can you live in this place?
The floors are so dirty and it stinks.

I sit waiting for the mailman. There's a package
he's bringing. Why isn't he here yet?

The worm is alive. The apple tree, the coyote, the walnut,
the beggar, the oilman, the stone and the dust and the sky.

If a man or woman finds nothing in work, it is time to retire.
Or find something new. Surely God is not tired of his job.

It is so pleasant to look into the empty bucket, the velvety
dark space. If you have to, cut a hole in the metal bottom.

I am a lecturer in the university. My students sleep
through my talks but wake up in time for the tests.

Glory

The autumn aster, those lavender ones,
and the dark-blooming sedum
are beginning to bloom in the rainy earth
with the remote intensity of a dream. These things
take over. I am a glorifier, not very high up
on the vocational chart, and I glorify everything I see,
everything I can think of. I want ordinary men and women,
brushing their teeth, to feel the ocean in their mouth.
I am going to glorify the sink with toothpaste spat in it.
I am going to say it's a stretch of beach where the foam
rolls back and leaves little shells. Ordinary people
with fear of worldly things, illness, pain, accidents,
poverty, of dark, of being alone, of misfortune.
The fears of everyday life. People who quietly and secretly
bear their dread, who do not speak freely of it to others.
People who have difficulty separating themselves
from the world around them, like a spider hanging
off the spike of a spider mum, in an inland autumn,
away from the sea, away from that most unfortunate nation
where people are butterballs dying of meat and drink.
I want to glorify the even tinier spiders in the belly of the spider
and in the closed knot of the mum's corolla, so this is likely
to go on into winter. Didn't I say we were speaking of autumn
with the remote intensity of a dream? The deckle edge of a cloud:
blood seeping through a bandage. Three bleached beech leaves
hanging on a twig. A pair of ruined mushrooms. The incumbent
snow. The very air. The imported light. All autumn struggling
to be gay, as people do in the midst of their woe.
I met a psychic who told me my position in the universe
but could not find the candy she hid from her grandkids.
The ordinary fear of losing one's mind. You rinse the sink,
walk out into the October sunshine, and look for it

by beginning to think. That's when I saw the autumn aster,
the sedum blooming in a purple field. The psychic said
I must see the word *glory* emblazoned on my chest. Secretly
I was hoping for a better word. I would have chosen for myself
an ordinary one like *orchid* or *paw.*
Something that would have no meaning in the astral realm.
One doesn't want to glorify everything. What might I *actually say*
when confronted with the view from K2? I'm not sure
I would say anything. What's your opinion?
You're a man with a corona in your mouth,
a woman with a cotton ball in her purse,
what's your conception of the world?

The Death of Shelley

A punt, a water keg and some bottles
washed up on the beach at Viareggio.
Eight days passed before they found
the body. The face and hands were
fleshless, and everybody knows Keats's
poems were in his breast pocket,
though what pierces me the most
is how the book was *doubled back*
as if the reader in the act of reading
had hastily thrust it away.
Back in the never-reached Lerici
he'd decorated the margins of his work
with sketches of yacht rigging. It appears
he was capable of two things at once
and often distracted.
Was he so lost in his reading
he failed to notice the blackening
clouds, the wind flipping the pages?
It is possible reading killed him, though
that's putting it bluntly. What is life
that we read about it as if it were
an antique curiosity?
How does the sky recede to an indifferent
shade?
Once I thought Shelley pulled out the poems
after the storm had started,
as if they were a manual
on how to abandon ship.
He might even have thrust the book away
over some irksome image that galled him
and sat reading the clouds instead—
how they flowed like ink from a new nib
building themselves to a fret that seemed significant
for a while—

I often see his eyes tracking and doubling
back, and then the sudden clearing
to which they were unaccustomed
and have to look away.

Rising Bodies

On July 14, 1954, Frida Kahlo, who had swallowed the world
whole, sat up in the crematorium cart and spit it out,
her hair blazing like an aureole, her face smiling
in the center of a sunflower before she disintegrated along
with her seeds. The phenomenon of heat causing a body to rise
has been much discussed. God pushes the rose mallows up
in the swale, he causeth the neat white stitches of snow
to fall, the pinky white steam to pry open the clam, the arrows
ascending to return to the dirt. On September 11, 1958,
I sat up in my math class and looked at the world.
One of the ceiling squares was beginning to rise, slowly
at first, into the swart and empty space behind it.
Doubtless my mouth made an O because the world was full
of wonderwork, as no one could explain it so I could understand.
I have been looking at the paintings of Miss Kahlo along with
those of an earlier age. Some people have had a sad term
on earth. The Blessed Virgin, having wept three days and nights
for her son, began to rise, a little shaky at first, but soon
in a steadier way. A carnation relaxing her edgy chiffon,
she rose in a blush-colored vapor crenately formed of air.
She too had something around her head. I think it was the heat
of the moment, the heat of knowing you're on the ground
and knowing if there is a swart or empty space over or in
your head, you can fill it by thinking and it will be gone,
the way *dissolve* wanes into *solve*, then waxes back.
Having not been there myself I cannot explain it in sadder
terms: for the moment, it is merely a problem of mine.

PETER JAY SHIPPY

Where Everything Is When

The June humid stars
puff above the living
giving our street the delicate
shade of a sad mirror
given to dark compulsion.

How strange everything is
when everything is so simple.

The people of our street
pace the spotlit sidewalks,
they so not speak,
they wait like patients wait
for loved ones gone, gone.

We break out sighing
perhaps morning will arrive.

Some among us suddenly
become aware of the earth's
ecstatic motions,
they fall to all fours
stunned by heavy memories.

How strange everything is—
perhaps morning will arrive.

The street grows red, pleasant,
and vague as in fever,
pollen pins our eyelids shut as

if at the bottom of an ocean; we
wait for one last ascent.

When everything is so simple—
we break out sighing.

Creepy About Being

I'm hanging out and on, on a froggy Saturday
with my friends Tragedy, Ecstasy, Doom,
and So On, stimulisting in the O room,
motivated by the jukebox of haunted songs.

Here, when it gets dark, it gets very late
and as cold as the sibyled voice invented
by insomnia, in the pseudonymous syntax
used by one just breathing to one just dead.

When the moon stops buzzing, its silence
insufferably confirms a crash in the air
below the night's crest, bright as a nest
of eye-whites or snow-starts or last kisses.

There's nothing left but the last recourse—
so I deftly open my chest to the off
position and peel away petals of wet skin
(the way springs de-wing swaddled buds)

then Aztec-like I remove my black box,
which is the keeper of pre-crash waxes, clues.
My machine looks like a bashed-on Walkman—
prolix, if not profound, singing if not sung.

My stethophone plugs into the static sea;
I listen, listen on the idiot frequencies
for impulsions, for the ineffable ersatz
answers to the questions I ask myself...

I only hear a voice whisper, "Dummy,
everything will begin again tomorrow."
And that cool effluvium, that small spell
puts the world, for this day, together.

Crèche

Would you know a saint if you saw one?
Say you're on the delivery table, legs drawn up
For each agonizing push, while everyone else is poised
To welcome forth your frightened protégée—
When, instead, a smiling light slowly issues out
From your dark interior, assembling itself
Like a mirage hovering above the linoleum floor—
And into the room spills a luminescent silence,
as if all human breath had awaited this dazzle:
You've borne a child, half angel, half star.
What then? How to go on living?

Or say you've thrown a party until three a.m.,
And all your guests have gone home, except you
Think there's someone drunkenly hiding in your closet,
So you creak it open, but instead of a man asleep with
His nose buried in overcoats, you find a little boy
With ebony hair levitating above your hiking boots.
How do you know he's not hallucinating you up like
A magician pulling a rabbit out of his top hat?
How do you know anything at all anymore?

Or perhaps you're vacationing in Mexico, instead
Of stringing up mistletoe—it's winter again—and
You're in the womb-warm waters off the peninsula.
Say you have a new girlfriend and she's as passionate
As they get, and you think it's she who's lapping now
Against your leg in the turquoise Sea of Cortés, but
Now you see that it's a long wreath of seaweed, and she's
Turned into a mermaid who's handing out lobsters
To the hungry urchins huddled around her on shore.
Do you forget your neatly worded proposal?

Do you pinch her scaly rump to check for barnacles?
Do you sing a dirge to Neptune? To anyone?

Of course, you'll never know among whom you walk,
Nor how each known and unknown face is taunted or graced
By something everyone wants but can't quite muster—
How in varying degrees each of us starts to believe
In miracles when faced with the world's luster.

The Work

for my father

1. Today

Today, this moment, speechlessly in pain,
He fights the terror of being poured out,
The fall into darkness unquenchably long
So that even as he hurtles he keeps holding

Back like a dam the flood overtops—but nothing now
Can stop that surge, already he swirls
To the source of Voices, the many throats inside the one
Throat, each swallowing the unstoppable flood...

And as if that, all along, were what he'd wanted,
He hears the Voices begin to die down
The way a marsh in spring pulsing and shrilling
Sunup to sundown falls gradually still

—Unappeasable, the silence that will follow
When his every last drop has been poured out.

2. Countdown

In your hospital bed, the plastic mask across
Your face siphoning air into your lungs,
You lie helpless as an astronaut
Blasting into space: Eyes oblivious

To ours, your body's fevered presence
Shimmers like the phantom heat that will trail
Up the pipe of the crematory oven:
How distant we will seem after

Such intensity... We drift in your stare
Like the dust stirred by the cow your parents
Gave you as a boy to teach responsibility.

Already you are space immeasurable
By your slide rule, your graphs that plotted
Payload, lift-off, escape velocity.

3. Prayer

In the house of the dead I pace the halls:
The walls, collapsing, stretch away in desert
Or flatten into horizonless ocean.
I step outside, the door clicking shut

Comforting in its finality...
Now I see the house as if I looked down
From far off mountains, and saw you crouching in
The sun-scoured yard, eyes keenly focused,

Pupils narrowing to a cat's green slits:
I can't look you in the face, you see only
The openness of sky rising above mountains.

(Only after the world has emptied
You and filled you with its openness
Will I feel the love I pray to feel?)

4. The God

A Dream

A warming pulsing flood like blood surging through
Veins, and now the god stirs in my hands
Dull as stone in this gravity-less Nowhere.
Sensation shivering through me, deliberate and sure,

I cradle you, I sponge you clean
As if you were *my* son, the emptiness you
Drink like heavy black milk erasing
Your wrinkles and gouged lines of pain.

The god bends me to the work, my fingers driven
By the god, blinded by the god's
Neutrality, until I pull apart the threads
In this place the god commands:

Face wholly unwoven, without heart, mind, you
Are nothing in my hands but my hands moving.

5. His Stare

Absently there in a moment of pure being
He sits in his chair, eyes locked, staring:
The air's transparence gains solidity
From his looking; while his emaciated features,

The way his flesh sags from sharpening cheekbones,
Make the summer air weigh like marble on the harsh green
Of the trees he is too weak to prune.
And yet the contemplative distance he is sealed in

Projects with ferocious purpose the will of his body
To withdraw into this eerily removed contemplation
Like one who has heard a tuning fork ringing
And enters and becomes each spectral vibration;

So utterly absorbed that love is a distraction; even
The world, its barest colors, bleeding away before that stare.

6. The Current

The numbing current of the Demerol
Sweeps him out to sea where the secret night

He lives in slowly begins to darken,
His daytime routine of watching his blood cycle

Through the tubes of a machine shadowed by blackness
Blinding as an underwater cave. Already
He filters the dark water through gills aligned
To strain that element he more and more resembles:

Like walls of water held in miraculous
Suspension, the moment of his death looms impartially
Above him, my hand holding his tightening
Its grip even as his hand loosens...

As if my hand could lead him past that undulating
Weight towering above us out of sight.

7. The Rehearsal

I lead you back, your Orpheus, until you
Stand inhaling, on the topmost stair,
The rank rich air of breathing flesh—
But like fumes rising from earth's molten core

The voices of the dead reach out to you,
Your whispering parents, dead for forty years,
Entreating me to turn—and so I
Turn, as must you: Your footsteps die,

You dwindle, blur into unfillable
Space echoing like the dark of a cathedral...
But there is no dark, no stair, no Orpheus

—Only this voice rehearsing breath
By breath in words you'll never read these
Lines stolen from your death.

The Souls

Poised in the garden just before dawn
Souls hover in a trance before the window
Or fly slanting and darting through the trees.

And down on the plain where the sun
Has yet to rise but whose heat roils
Upward and turns the night to silver vapor,

Souls swarm across the stubbled fields.
Now, as if the molten core of earth began to speak
The sun boils up, sulfurous, shimmering,

Warning the souls to seek refuge from the world
Before the world wakes and claims them;
So that one becomes a hummingbird,

One a bat huddling in the darkness of the eaves...
But the more curious remain, astonished
By the vigils that human souls must keep!

—His soul too, which still watches as he sleeps,
Hovering over his bruised, diffusing flesh;
Yet restless in its care, anticipating its own delight,

Finally knowing itself free to depart:
Lingering a moment even as its wings begin to beat,
His soul's eyes peer into his face.

PRISCILLA SNEFF

Chance Become My Science

Though I've lived a life and I have lived amongst men and I have
Loved this life as an experiment—an act of science
And an act of ruth—I've kept for this city my last half heart
(I lost the other to the chance of art.) And so, stirred of a
      loud silence,
Slow snow as the city falls into place neath the beautiful
Face of a clock; it is a lifetime; it is something, finally, to know:
The dark white moon, the scarfed knobs of some passersby, the
      fact
Of death; but O to give the grave a rest, a demigoddess
Of the demimonde; she is walking her body home; they all
Are walking their bodies through the dismal streets: wraith,
      wraith, wraith;
I've loved you well; it's been an act of dada and an act
Of faith, but still the world refrains... *Shsha'n't,* a sigh
As the heart chills in the broken autoclave of the breast.
I shall give up earthly loves and earthly things. I'll sing like
Oxygen, like monks in their cells sing, until that singing
Becomes me whom it is silencing; already silence
Walks my body, loosing with soft skilled fingers my knot of veins.

179

Dreamobile Joseph Cornell

Showered in ghosts his trees sing forked over by wind
each inherits a musical gift but the fever's got by subscription
revelry abounds on wet cobblestones of the commuter moon
the moon's new zoo's main attractions being card-boxed turmoil
(say the mobile mind breaks down on its own Utopia Parkway)
by Joseph Cornell and softly copious comets rambling
through the ears of squinching rabid dogs wanton with gizzards
as your wings fail you your destination does not
you fall into a miniature box inhabited by sharp-creased tourists
wielding dull rubbery objects each carries a satchel
full of postcards depicting off-season French coastal resorts
with the jitter of your sleep you ring the bell
extended like a prayer on the counters of these
nightly there white walls of a fortress of clouds encases you
by morning you remove and place them in the black water of a
    machine
they float there disassembled forming strategy for coming night
some rub off in troughs of the forehead in trails snails favor
your sleep gathers itself by the glass fountain of a square
where invisible notices are impossibly posted like a dreamer
mute and illiterate before the language of the dream
as the flutterby's go on burbling like a spring
chattery and awake in a nave wet with walls of tongues
their panoramas are prisons for the eyes
on those long circus days before catch and release

Dreamobile Francis Bacon I

With your brother nepenthe you fell through ashen snow
his eyes colored a deep caged absolve lifted you spirits
green pigeons clawed your lone pant leg intent to fly
sexless and regenerative wind in your ear a meditative gait
in its black rubber room three laughing figures liplessly drain
an impotent effigy of its sombre stomach feathers
you find her feet are doctored scales of a classical terror
all daylorn lost her bride shorn off in a subfusc light

Hot

He eats in silence as frost plumes
at the panes and stars tighten,
teeth marks on the freezing sky.
His boots stand in snow water,
melting by the wood stove that he burns
hot to husk his legs of cold.
The fire bumps, drops, cracks
in the stove. His wife and daughters'
talk goes louder then softer,
in and out of the raw, raw
of the chain saw still in his head
where he fells trees that moan
before they drop muted by the snow.
His legs hurt in the snow,
then his body heat loosens the ice
in his beard and as he prunes
the fallen trunks, he opens the zippers
his wife sewed into his pants
across the thigh, behind the knee,
like the slits in a pie. The trees
don't bleed in winter.
Sap pulls back to the core.
He rises, shudders a crowbar
through the slender iron doorway
to the red flare inside.

Glass

for R. Voisine

His father, two brothers, and me, we turned off our saws
for a rest of water and cake. Thirsty, he stopped, walked over
and the loader's back gate yawned and slipped its
catch, threw him down onto a fresh stump, still
that pink-white wet. I scooped him up. Blood
fell on the path, my arms. He asked to walk by himself,
and I let him, my hands tried not to slip on his shoulders.
When we got to camp, he said
Still, I'm thirsty, and the cook and foreman, they ran
for water. He took it carefully so he wouldn't drop
and break it. He drank what they gave him. The water poured
out the bottom of his jaw and struck his chest
while the saws stopped in the woods.

True Stories

Already pregnant, she
writes her name and his,
Lou and Mike, over
the cloudy pictures in *True Stories*.
Black-and-white pictures
of a leggy woman (Lou) draped,
the arching stem of her throat
almost tears from her head,
so thrown back with pounds
of hair and a dark man's
(Mike's) kisses. Done eating,

Mike scrubs the wishbone
from supper and dries it
in the wind on the porch
with Lou and her ancient parents.
All digest and watch cars
go by, what happens every night
when it's warmer. Mike gives Lou
a leg of the ashy bone. They break it
as the light falls and all
color goes away. The parents

hoot *Who won? Who won?*
and Mike takes her shorter piece,
says *This is the man.*
He waves the other part
that kept the joint, says
This is the shovel, and delicate,
he, in his palm, buries
the man with the shovel.

Neglect

The muscular hollows: eye, lung, heart,
stomach, hand. The parts that you
enliven: lips, hair, spine.
The necessary and cleansing wastes—
sweat, blood, urine, stool, and sperm.

But certain places of my body
are not specified or named
until reached by the first
unexpected drop of rain,
or the careless, accidental
touch of your fingernail.

(And the name varies
with the kind of touch:
area, temperature, duration.)

The Off Season

"Zip's getting married," Chase tells Marianne, coming into the bedroom and shutting the door behind him.

"Oh. Who's the woman?"

"Her name is Flora Ritchie."

"And when is the baby due?"

He narrows his eyes at her. "December." He pulls his shirt off. "But it was still a bitchy thing to say."

"Sorry." She watches him throw the shirt onto a chair. She is already in bed, propped up on a pillow against the rough wooden wall. She closes her book, keeping her index finger in to hold the place. "So, who is she?"

"Some girl he met in the schools. She's a traveling music teacher, I guess."

"I wonder what she's like."

"She's coming here tomorrow. You'll find out then." He lets his jeans slip to the floor and leaves them there.

"Does Zip seem upset?"

Chase shrugs.

"But you are."

"It's a half-assed way to get married."

"You think all ways of getting married are half-assed."

"Oh, Jesus, Marianne."

She gets out of bed and picks up his jeans, and folds them. "Were they serious, before she got pregnant? I mean, would they have gotten married anyway?"

"I didn't ask," Chase says, going into the bathroom and shutting the door.

The sportswriters call Chase Savoie the wise man of basketball. One year, early in his career, they tried referring to him as "Savvy" Savoie, but it wasn't a nickname that stuck. Mostly they content themselves with what they can do with his first name. "The Thrill of the Chase," said the *Sports Illustrated* cover. The story in *Newsweek,* when the team was on the verge of winning the championship for the third out of four years, was called "Chasing Glory," and there was a separate little story, at the end of the big one, that compared him to Walt Frazier, Bill Russell, and Larry Bird. Then as he got older and kept playing, the stories had titles like, "Is the Chase Winding Down?" and "Chasing Thirty-Five." Chase has framed the clippings and hung them by the bed, so Marianne sees them first thing every morning and last thing at night.

She met him at a beauty contest fourteen years ago. She was Miss Oregon and he was one of the judges. He had seemed gloomy and depressed when he interviewed her, so she invited him out for a hamburger. It was unethical, but she didn't care; she wasn't going to win anyway. The contest was full of real killers: girls who owned dozens of beauty titles already, at the age of seventeen; girls who had moved hundreds of miles away from their families so they could train with professional coaches in baton twirling or ventriloquism. The contest billed itself as a "scholarship pageant," and Chase, at twenty-two, was foolish enough to almost believe it; he rolled his eyes and told Marianne over a beer that he had half expected to see young ladies parading before him, solemnly reciting Wordsworth.

Where have you been? she asked.

On a basketball court, he told her, whenever I wasn't holed up in one of the Yale libraries.

Oh. She had never heard of him before—he had just finished his first year in the pros—but she knew enough to be impressed. She had never met anyone as smart, as big, as sternly handsome. He asked her what she was doing in the pageant, and she told him she wanted to be an actress.

Don't be a jerk, he said. Go to college.

He seemed so pleased with the idea of setting her straight that she didn't have the heart to tell him she was planning to go to college anyway. She went to bed with him in his motel room, and at the end of the week she collected her thousand-dollar check (she finished fourth) and followed him up to Maine, where he lived during the off-season.

The entourage then was pretty much what it is now. There was a secretary, a cook, and Chase's agent, darting in and out. Chase's brothers, Danny, Zip, and Doug, ranged in age then from fifteen down to nine, and there was a guy known as "the tutor," who took care of them, overseeing their swimming and sailing and tennis. When Chase was around, he coached them in basketball for a couple of hours every afternoon. Chase's mother, Mimi, wandered around murmuring about finishing her dissertation on learning disabilities in the inner city schools (which she still hasn't finished). Chase's father had already been dead for six years when Marianne came. He'd been a doctor from a Boston family otherwise made up of bankers, so the infusion of Chase's basketball money didn't appear to Marianne to be throwing his family for a loop. They were already comfortable and discreet; Chase's astronomical salary only seemed to make them more so.

She settled in as Chase's girlfriend, but before long she'd taken on another role, as a kind of emotional business manager for the boys. Chase took care of them all financially, and Mimi provided a sort of vague spiritual guidance; she built a special pavilion, solely for the purpose of meditation and reflection, at the lakeside Maine tourist camp Chase had bought for them all to summer in. But it was Marianne who became the real parent in the family.

When Danny was thrown out of prep school for drugs, Marianne went around New England with him looking for another school that would take him, and she helped him write college application essays about how his expulsion, which was a big blot on his already mediocre record, had helped him grow as a person. When Dougie flunked seventh grade and got held back, and Chase raged and threatened to stop his allowance, she took Doug to Boston and got him tested and diagnosed as dyslexic, and then she hired a teacher to come to the house every day after school to work with him. When Danny, at nineteen, was found by the police on the middle of a railroad bridge one night, holding a gun, screaming that he had to stay right there, at the very center, or the world would end, she bailed him out of jail (Chase was out on the West Coast for a series of away games) and got him to a good mental hospital, where the doctors told her it was definitely drugs and possibly manic depression. Mimi brought a bonsai tree for his bedside table and read to him from *Zen in the Art of*

Archery. Marianne brought Zip and Doug in for counseling, and the doctor told her to watch out, she was going to have big problems with both of them.

In the beginning, she assumed she and Chase would get married. He never brought it up, and whenever she did, he told her that getting married wouldn't make her any more a part of the family than she was already.

What about children? Marianne asked him.

We've got children, he said.

Not your brothers, children of our own.

We're still young. We've got plenty of time.

Now Chase is thirty-six and has one more season before he retires, and Marianne is thirty-one and telling herself that it still might happen. She's made her peace with the fact that his stardom—a whole world of people a foot shorter than he is think he's perfect—has given him a kind of arrogance and also an undeniable power. He calls the shots in this household.

He has bought Danny a chain of sporting goods stores, helped Zip set up a basketball clinic which tours to schools, and gotten Dougie an entry-level TV sportscaster job. Mimi has her own money, inherited from both her father and her husband, but it is Chase's money that funds her more extravagant projects: the meditation pavilion, the Savoie Shelter for the Homeless, the grant to the animal protection league to buy cat and dog food for strays who would otherwise be put to sleep.

Marianne's dependence on Chase is absolute. She's never held a paying job in her life, never had her name on a lease or a mortgage, never had to worry about money. You could look at it another way and say that the Savoies depend on her, that without her, Chase would have been lonely, and the boys' tangles with drugs and depression would have been far more disastrous. She doesn't mind their dependence, considering it a mark of truly familial love. Still, she would like to be married. She would like to feel more officially entrenched. And she would like Chase to declare, before a multitude, that she is utterly necessary to him, his next of kin.

For the most part, she manages not to think about it anymore. Chase is right: it doesn't make any difference. But occasionally, to

Marianne's own surprise, barbs slip out. The night Chase tells her about Zip and Flora, everything that comes out of her mouth is sharp and dangerous.

Marianne's first impression of Flora is that she looks like a girl off the wrapper of a chocolate bar. She has on a white blouse with puffy short sleeves, an olive-green dirndl skirt, and a darker green chamois vest that laces in zigzags over her chest. Her cheeks are washed with pink (the glow of pregnancy?), her red hair is worn in a braid down her back. She smiles at Marianne when she climbs down from Zip's old Jeep, a bit tensely, unsure of her reception. Zip, beside her, is slow and reassuring, cupping her shoulders as he makes the introductions, and then rocking her gently, absently back and forth as they stand talking by the vegetable garden, where Marianne has been picking lettuce for lunch. Marianne is intrigued by Zip's air of sleepy confidence: the sleepiness is habitual, but the confidence she has never seen before—except when Zip is doing something with a small child or animal. She thinks, watching him with Flora, of the day when Chase saw a skunk run under their bed, and Zip managed to coax it into his hands and carry it out of the house without getting sprayed.

"I'll take her luggage around to the Bullfrog," Zip says. "Maybe you guys want to get to know each other."

"Sure," Marianne says, trying to sound comforting, picking up the look of panic that crosses Flora's face. Zip gives Flora a long slow kiss before he goes (Marianne looks away; it's like being in the first row at the movies), and then, surprisingly, he hugs Marianne. His body is damp and fruity-smelling beneath his blue T-shirt, which has YES, I REALLY AM HIS BROTHER printed on it.

"Well," Marianne says as soon as he goes. "How are you feeling?" She has decided that the best way to put Flora at ease is to acknowledge the pregnancy right off, but in a gentle, taking-it-for-granted way.

"Okay."

"No morning sickness, or anything?" They begin to walk toward the main house, where the family gathers for meals. Mimi has built her own house down by the lake, and the boys each have a cabin, with Pullman kitchens for morning coffee, but the biggest kitchen and dining room are in the main house, where Chase and Marianne live.

"I did in the first couple of months, but not anymore."

"That's right, you're pretty far along, aren't you?"

"Five months."

"You really don't look pregnant."

"I know. I was beginning to worry it meant a small baby, but the doctor said it's normal. A lot of people don't show at all till six months. You can see it without clothes, though." She stops walking to pull up her shirt and push down the elastic waistband of her skirt. Her belly swells white and round below the bulging navel, and there is a red crinkled line left by the elastic on her skin. "You want to feel?" she asks.

"Oh, no thanks."

"It's hard," Flora says, putting her own hand there. "I always thought it would be soft, but it's like a rock."

"Can you feel the baby moving?" Marianne asks, walking again toward the house.

"Not all the time, but sometimes." She smiles. "I was going to have an abortion, but now I'm glad I didn't." Her voice, even when she is talking about her own happiness, is cool and flat.

"Zip must be really excited about the baby."

"He's great with kids," Flora says. "That's how I first met him. He was running one of his basketball clinics, at a school where I was teaching." She looks at Marianne. "You and Chase don't have children, do you?"

"We're not married," Marianne tells her.

"Oh," she says. "Oh. I thought you were. Zip always says 'Chase and Marianne,' and I guess I just thought—"

"That's okay." She is beginning to find Flora's lack of artifice a little exhausting. Is it really possible that she could have reached the age of—what? twenty-four? twenty-five?—and have so little finesse or protective covering of any kind? But then, Zip doesn't have much protective covering, either. The two of them, she thinks, are going to get creamed.

"This really is a wonderful place," Flora says, gazing around at the old tourist cabins scattered among the trees.

"We love it," Marianne says.

"It feels so real, I mean, like real people live here."

"Gee," Marianne drawls, "how 'bout that?"

Flora blushes. Even her bare legs turn rosy above her galumphy little Heidi boots. "You know what I mean. The way Zip talks about Chase, I wasn't sure what to expect."

Her embarrassment is cut short by Mimi, appearing at the edge of the woods in a bathing suit and a big straw hat. She waves and trots over to them, her bare feet toughly oblivious of pebbles and pine cones. She holds out her hands to Flora. "It's so lovely to meet you!" she says warmly, and then she swoops in and embraces her. "We're just delighted about you and Zip. Really. And of course, the little one."

"Thank you." Flora swallows, looking immensely relieved.

Mimi turns to Marianne and hooks an arm in hers. "I've just had the most wonderful idea."

"What."

Mimi holds out her other arm to Flora and then begins to stroll, pulling them both along. "I think we should plant an asparagus bed. Right on that flat place, below the strawberries. The drainage is excellent, it's sheltered." She turns to Flora. "Don't you think it'll be marvelous—asparagus from our own garden?"

At lunch, Mimi interrupts the general conversation to say, "Oh, and Chase, there's that trunk of linens in the attic."

They all look at her: What? Zip has been telling Flora the story of the tourist camp, how Chase bought it from a woman who had inherited it from her mother, who had run it as a summer retreat for Jehovah's Witnesses.

"You know," Mimi continues, looking at Chase a bit impatiently, as if she doesn't understand why his mind isn't running along the same lines as hers. "That stuff from your father's mother. Four sets of everything, for when you children get married." She turns to Flora. "We'll go up after lunch, and you can pick out what you want."

Marianne trails up the attic stairs after them, knowing it's masochism. The trunk is almost directly over the bedroom she shares with Chase. Inside the lid is a list, taped there so long ago that the paper makes a cracking sound when Mimi pulls at it, and it comes off leaving a frame of brown tape behind.

"Fingerbowl doilies," Mimi reads. "Well, some of this stuff is ridiculous. But let's have a look."

Marianne reaches out and helps Flora, carefully, to unfold the layers of white tissue paper. They lift out stacks of napkins, damask and linen, lace-edged and plain. "There are eight sets of twelve," Mimi says, looking at her list and calculating, "so Flora, you can choose two."

"How beautiful," Flora breathes, fingering lace.

Mimi picks up a stack wrapped in cellophane and pushes her reading glasses up to squint at a tiny white label. "Do you know, I don't believe these were ever used? Ireland. My guess is that Zip's grandmother bought these the year before she died. Ireland was one of her last trips."

"What was she like?" Flora asks, sitting back on her heels.

Marianne, despite herself, also hopes for anecdotes. All she knows is that everyone was tall; in all the old brown pictures that show them standing next to friends, servants, college teammates, the Savoies tower above everyone else, as though they belong to a different race or species. Chase doesn't seem to know or care much about his family's history, and Mimi is too vague to be much of a storyteller. Maybe the trunk of linen will cast some sort of spell on her, loosen her tongue or her memory.

But Mimi says, "Oh, not very interesting, I don't think. Bigoted. Stuffy. Dogs and horses. She always scared me to death."

Flora chooses, out of all the napkins, two sets with wide lace borders. Good, Marianne thinks, preferring the plainer ones.

They go through more layers of napkins, then linen towels, table runners, place mats cross-stitched in beige wool on colored canvases ("Zip's grandmother did those," Mimi sniffs. "Her only hobby"). Thirty-two linen pillowcases. Everything is neatly organized into layers, in multiples of four, ready to be divided.

Mimi seems unaware of any awkwardness in the three of them engaging in this task together. But Marianne notices that as they make their way down through the trunk and the riches accumulate, Flora seems to grow more and more embarrassed, shrinking among the towering piles of white. "Oh, boy, what'll I ever do with all this?" she finally says, placing six bureau scarves on top of one of the stacks. "Really, Mimi, this seems like plenty."

But Mimi is digging out tablecloths, lace after lace after lace. Finally a few plain ones, damask and linen cutwork.

Flora shoots a quick look at Marianne. "Oh," she hesitates, and then puts her hand on the two plainest. "This is fine, I guess, and this." Forgoing the frills she is naturally drawn to, leaving behind some of what she guesses Marianne may want, too.

"Oh—" Marianne says, before she can stop herself.

Mimi and Flora both look at her, when that little sound of disappointment escapes.

"Well," Mimi murmurs finally, lightly stroking Flora's pink forearm, "you must be tired. Maybe that is enough for one day."

Zip and Flora decide they want a big wedding, two weeks from Saturday, on the lawn in front of the main house. They want to ask everyone they know, everyone the family has ever known. They look defiant and proud, announcing this. They decide there's not enough time to fool around with printed invitations, they'll just call people. Chase lends them Trudy, his secretary, to help with the calls and the arrangements. They get hold of the minister who christened Zip; he's retired now, and living on Long Island, but he agrees to drive up to perform the ceremony. Zip calls a childhood friend whose rock band is struggling to make it in L.A., and offers to fly the whole band east if they'll play for the wedding. Mimi drives down to Boston to get her own wedding dress out of storage and altered to fit Flora's swollen abdomen. Even Danny and Doug, who go through cyclic drunk/stoned and sober periods, and who at the moment are both perpetually bombed, pitch in with the planning, volunteering to pick up liquor, dry cleaning, people at the airport.

Through it all, Flora sits on the sidelines, watching the Savoies tossing the wedding together, apparently having no preferences, no desires, no family of her own.

"Oh, sure, she's got a mother and father," Chase says, looking surprised, when Marianne asks him. He's gone out of his way to spend time with Flora since she arrived, sitting with her in the living room after dinner, driving her into town one afternoon when she wanted to mail a letter. Interviewing her, Marianne thinks. Becoming, surprisingly, her partisan.

"Isn't it usual for the bride's family to plan the wedding?" Marianne has to be careful, make herself sound neutral, not bitter. She's been sitting on the sidelines, too, as the wedding plans rumble along, and she's not sure if she's sitting there because she chooses to or because her position really has grown more awkward, now that a true wife and daughter-in-law is coming into the family.

"She tells me her parents are a bit overwhelmed by the whole situation," Chase says.

"By the baby, or by the idea of you?"

"Both, I guess. Anyway, they'll come to the wedding, but they don't want any more involvement than that."

They don't want it, Marianne wonders, or they're too frightened to ask for it? Her own parents have faded from her life. She's never asked them to visit and they've never asked to come. Every couple of years, she flies home, alone, with a shopping bag full of extravagant presents, to stay for a week. They've met Chase a few times, when his team was in Portland playing the Trail Blazers. They thought he was very nice, but she knows they find him intimidating. They never phone her; when they have something special to tell her about, like a sister's engagement or the death of her high school boyfriend, her mother writes a letter, and Marianne calls them.

"She's the best thing that ever happened to Zip," Chase says.

"Mmm," says Marianne.

"Don't you think he seems calmer than you've ever seen him? And happier?"

He does, but Marianne finds Chase's enthusiasm irritating. Since when is he so pro-marriage?

"Now that he has Flora, and the baby, he's got a reason to be responsible. Don't you think?"

Marianne doesn't answer. She is remembering what a psychiatrist once told her and Chase. It was the time Zip OD'd, and they hadn't known whether it was accidental or on purpose. The shrink watched them sympathetically but, she thought, judgmentally, and talked about how Zip was convinced that nothing he did would ever be good enough.

We know that, Chase said impatiently.

Knowing it is one thing. Navigating it is something else. You have to make it possible for Zip to come to you with problems before they blow up like this.

He can come to me if he wants.

Well, let him know that. But don't give him all the answers. What I would do, if I were you, is just open the door and play dumb.

"I think you're right," Marianne tells Chase now, slinging an arm around his waist, which is level with her shoulders. "He really has pulled himself together."

She comes upon Mimi and Flora on the lawn.

"I thought the altar there," she hears Mimi say. "Not a real altar, of course, just that narrow table from my library, with a cloth over it. A white cloth, do you think, or should we go for a spot of color?"

Then Mimi sees her coming, and stops talking. They actually jump apart a little, guiltily, so that Marianne feels she's stumbled upon a tryst.

"I think a colored cloth would be nicer," Marianne offers. "I have some fabrics Chase and I bought in Provence last year, which I've never done anything with. Would you like to look at those?"

Sure, they say, exchanging glances, as though they've just unexpectedly gotten away with something.

That's when Marianne decides to go, just for a few days. She worries, because of the way they've begun tiptoeing around her, that everyone will think she's fleeing in a huff, but she can't help that. And as it turns out, Chase doesn't even seem to notice that she's going. "Boston?" he says. "Are you sure you don't want to wait till after the wedding? I'd come down with you, then, for a few days."

"No, there are some things I'd like to take care of this week. Get my hair done, buy a dress for the wedding. And you and Mimi seem to have the planning pretty much under control."

"Well, let's go away together after this whole thing is over." He kisses the top of her head. "We'll do one of those fjord cruises, or that bird-watching thing in Alaska. Think about it."

"I will," she promises.

She stays in Cambridge, at a plain-looking, expensive hotel in Harvard Square. She constructs for herself the kind of cultivated, sanitized life she imagines she might have now without Chase— museums, bookstores, modest restaurants. Her tastes, after more than a decade with Chase, have inevitably been shaped by him: she spurns Newbury Street and the department stores that would have so attracted her during her beauty contest days, and takes instead the ferry that runs out to the harbor islands, where she spends an afternoon wandering around a deserted civil war fort. The fort is supposed to be haunted, according to the guidebook, by a woman who was executed for trying to help her imprisoned husband escape.

She does go to Filene's Basement one afternoon, where she has a momentary flirtation over a table of men's shirts. "What size are you looking for?" asks a man in a tweed jacket standing next to her.

"I couldn't begin to tell you," she says, smiling back at him. She heads down to the dress racks, where she finds a turquoise silk from a fancy store, one she often shops in, reduced to a quarter of its original price. Marianne buys it, feeling it proves somehow that she could survive without Chase. She could get a job, find a little apartment, and shop in Filene's Basement. It would take a little extra cunning, but she could do it.

The rehearsal dinner, at Mimi's, is big, warm, and jolly: the nicest event Marianne has ever seen in the Savoie family. A strange collection of people: friends of Zip's in thrift-shop funk, hair bleached and spiky. Flora's sisters and their husbands, the sisters with blue eyeliner and charm bracelets and frosted, blow-dried Princess Di hair, the husbands bricklayers and electricians with careful table manners. Some of Chase's teammates, at a different level from the rest of the guests, like mountaintops poking through the clouds, heartily egalitarian, gods leaning down to converse with mortals. Chase, beaming. Mimi, flitting through, murmuring nervously, "I think we should start getting people into the dining room, don't you?" And Zip, calm and happy, in a navy blazer and the new mustache he's grown over the past two weeks, hovering around Flora, refilling her orange juice, bringing her crackers and cheese.

Flora, to Marianne's surprise, hasn't dressed up at all; she's wearing the olive-green dirndl skirt with a man's shirt tucked into it, and she looks uncomfortably bunchy around the waist. She has on knee socks and a scuffed pair of clogs. Her face is so grim and miserable-looking that Marianne feels sorry for her, and strolls over to talk. "How are you doing? Are you going nuts with all this wedding stuff?"

"Not really," Flora says, not smiling. "I have been. But now I feel like the whole thing's finally in motion, so all we can do is just relax and go with it."

Mimi puts a light hand on each of their backs. "I think we'd better get people into the dining room."

In Mimi's dining room, with its wide windows overlooking the lake, six tables for eight have been beautifully set. But it doesn't feel at all formal. Loud talk, and every few minutes, ping-ping-ping: a knife tapped on a water glass, someone giving a toast. People tell stories about Zip as a child, as a teenager. "To Zip and Flora," they end, and everyone drinks. Chase tells about Zip and the skunk. Someone tells about the basketball clinic, and how Zip paid for real hoops when he found some kids in a playground using a garbage can to shoot baskets. Chase gets up again and talks about how in the fifteen years since the family started summering in this place, there have been some wonderful parties here, like the one the first year the team won the championship (applause), and the one the second year they won (applause), and especially the one the third year (applause and cheers), but that this is the best party of them all. Dougie gets up unsteadily and says how happy he is to have a new sister-in-law, and a new niece or nephew. Embarrassed laughter, and everybody drinks. Zip stands up and thanks everyone for being there, and proposes a toast to Flora's parents. Then Flora's father stands up, short and dark and pale, and he holds up his glass and looks straight at Zip and says, "Take care of my girl." A momentary silence.

Danny gets up, the court jester, and defuses things by telling a long unintelligible joke which has "shit" in the punchline. People laugh uncertainly when it's over, and Danny raises his glass silently and then sits down. Chase stands up again, and talks about how happy he is.

After the dinner, Chase takes a couple of his teammates down to the lake for a swim, and Marianne stays to help Mimi oversee the cleanup. Mimi says, "Well, I hope we have a groom tomorrow."

"What do you mean?"

Mimi shakes her head. "There's been a psychiatrist in and out of here all week. Let's just pray he knows what he's doing."

Marianne presses, but all Mimi will say is that Zip has been having some problems.

Marianne walks slowly back to the main house. All the lights are on tonight in the tourist camp, in all the cabins that are usually empty: the Whippoorwill, the Cathy-O, Faraway, Gone. This is how the camp must have been in long-ago summers: lamplight reaching out to meet other lamplight, radios playing softly, muffled voices from behind the cabin walls, distant shouts and splashing from the lake. Climbing the last stretch of path up from the lake, she smells the sweet, unmistakable scent of marijuana. For some reason, she doesn't just ignore it and keep walking.

"Who is it?" she asks.

After a moment, Zip's voice. "Me."

"Oh, Zip, don't." For Zip, a joint is never just a joint.

He doesn't say anything.

She takes a few blind steps off the path and makes out his tall silhouette in the darkness, standing still among the trees. "Come on. Put it out."

"I should have let her have the abortion," he says. "She was all set to do it, but I talked her out of it. I was the one who wanted to get married."

"Well, so what's wrong with that?"

"I shouldn't have made her believe she could depend on me."

"Why not?"

Zip starts to cry. He cries for a while, and Marianne holds him. Then he says, "Maybe I could stay with you and Chase tonight?"

She tightens her arms around him and then pulls away. "Go

stay with Flora," she tells him.

She won't tell Chase, she decides, getting undressed. If things have been this bad all week, then Chase already knows what's going on. She wonders why they haven't canceled.

Chase and Marianne are still in bed when the door of their room opens and Flora walks in. "Zip's gone," she announces.

They sit up. "What?"

"He kept me up all night saying, 'Tell me again why you want to marry me? Tell me again?' and finally I said, 'I'll tell you once more: I love you and I want to marry you. And that's it. No more.' He looked at me and walked out."

Chase throws back the covers. "I'll go find him."

"No," says Flora.

"No," says Marianne.

They both look at her. "He has to come back because he wants to, not because you drag him."

"The hell with that," Chase says, getting out of bed and walking naked over to his bureau. "There are going to be two hundred people standing on our lawn in a couple of hours, and he damn well better be here to face them." He pulls on his clothes and goes out.

"I'm going back to Zip's cabin," Flora says grimly. "And I'm going to stay there until he comes and tells me he loves me."

Marianne pulls on jeans and a shirt and heads over to Mimi's house. Mimi is already dressed for the wedding, in bright blue linen. "I know," she says. "Chase stopped by. What should we do, do you think?"

"Well, it's too late to cancel. People are already on their way."

"Oh, well, canceling. I don't think it's a question of that," Mimi says, frowning. "I'm sure Zip will come around."

Marianne nods.

"But it's so hard on Flora. I'll go to her now, I think, don't you?" Mimi strides off toward Zip's cabin.

Danny and Doug are sitting on Mimi's front porch, tipping their chairs back, smoking. They're both wearing green sports coats and Ray-Bans; they look like employees of some hip, slightly sinister airline. Dougie has his arm in a sling.

"What happened to you?" Marianne asks.

"Fight," he says.

Last night at the party, he was fine. She opens her mouth to ask, then closes it.

"Anything we can do?" Danny asks.

She looks at her watch. "Show the guests into the garden, I guess. And act like nothing's wrong."

"Sure thing," says Doug.

In the garden, two hundred people mill around. Zip's old green rowboat is up on pilings, filled with ice and liquor. A yellow tent, its poles wrapped with vines, is filled with flowers and balloons. Danny and Doug, lilies of the valley in their lapels, stand on either side of an archway made of two blossoming cherry trees in pots, bent toward each other so that their branches intertwine. "Come on through," they say jauntily to Marianne, and she wonders for a moment if they know who she is.

"Is Zip back?" she whispers to Doug.

"Nope."

"Marianne, how are you?" someone asks, and she is sucked into the party. People say things to her.

"You look wonderful."

"Isn't this the perfect spot for a wedding?"

"Chase must be so thrilled."

She looks at her watch: just after ten-thirty. The wedding is scheduled for eleven.

"Such a beautiful dress. I love the color."

"So Chase is planning to retire after next season? Can't you talk him out of it?"

"What about the bride? What's she like?"

"Where is Chase, anyway?"

"And Zip—where's Zip?" It's ten past when someone finally asks this: Gloria Rangeley, married to Carl Rangeley from the team. Marianne has always liked Gloria, who has her own line of mail-order cosmetics for black women. Mail-order so I don't get totally killed if he gets traded, Gloria says. I move, but the fulfillment house stays in the same place. It's just good business. When are you going to line something up for yourself, to make sure you don't get totally killed? "Is anything wrong?" Gloria asks now, in a lower voice.

Marianne peers back into her kind face, glowing beneath a fuchsia straw hat. "Oh, no, no, just a little delay."

"I heard a rumor that the groom hasn't showed up," another voice at her elbow.

"Oh, I'm sure that's not true," Marianne says.

A quarter of twelve. Chase comes out onto the lawn, in a checked shirt and jeans. Holds up his hands. "Thank you all for coming, but I'm afraid there isn't going to be a wedding here today. Please stay, and eat and drink. Thank you again." He puts his head down and ducks back into the house before anyone can talk to him. Murmur, murmur, murmur. A fat lady in a monogrammed sweater is crying. A huge hand wraps around Marianne's upper arm. "Hey, man, tell Chase I'm really sorry, okay?" She hears from someone that the minister is angry: he drove all the way up from Long Island and he's damned if he's going to drive all the way home without his lunch. She hears screaming from the living room, a man's voice, furious. Zip must be in there, and some man is giving him hell. But no, Danny reports, when she sends him in to check, it's a retired stockbroker, an old friend of Mimi's, telling a Wall Street joke. People cut into the Brie, rummage around in the rowboat for beer.

"It was the minister's fault," Marianne overhears someone saying. "He said something to Flora right before the ceremony was supposed to start, and she took off."

"No, it was Zip who took off," someone else says.

Marianne looks up at the shaded windows of her bedroom, wondering if Chase is up there. How can he stand it, listening to this party going on? She wants to go up to him, comfort him, ask about Zip—does anyone know where he is?—but she's become, in the absence of Chase and Mimi, the hostess of the party, and she keeps saying thank you to people who tell her how sorry they are.

Finally, Chase comes back out, and holds up his hands. "Thank you very much for coming. I've closed the bar now. Thank you for coming." The guests begin to move at once, seven-footers ducking under the cherry-tree archway. "Please take your presents back with you," Chase says, his eyes full of water. It's the kind of crying no one acknowledges and neither does he; people are having quiet farewell conversations with him as though it's not happening.

Mimi is out on the lawn now, too, an old Shetland sweater thrown over the shoulders of her party dress. She is crying in a sniffly, brittle way that makes people not dare to approach her. She flutters around looking very busy, doing nothing, talking to no one. Every now and then as people pass by her, discreetly looking away, she recognizes friends and she snatches at them, crying, "You're not *leaving*?" Yes, yes, we have to get back, work, traffic, they mumble, and she lets go of them.

"Where's Flora?" Marianne murmurs to Doug, not wanting to intrude on Mimi; but he, oblivious, calls out, "Hey, Mom, do you know where Flora is?"

"Her father's with her," Mimi says, coming over to them. "They're taking her home with them." She catches sight of the rowboat, still half-full of bottles. "Oh, no," she cries, her voice carrying over the lawn. "Oh, Chase, Chase! What are we going to do about the liquor?"

He sprints over to her, not wanting to conduct this conversation in shouts. "The Ritchies paid for it, so we can't exactly keep it."

"Is Zip back?" Marianne asks him. It's the first chance she's had to ask.

"He's in the woods," Chase says flatly. "He's sitting on the rocks down by that little waterfall. He wouldn't come."

"What about a charity ball?" Mimi asks, sniffing. "Could we donate it, do you think?"

"I don't know of any," Chase says.

She takes out a handkerchief and wipes her eyes. "Well, then, maybe the best course is to return it to a liquor store, and send Flora's family a check."

"But most of it's been opened," Chase points out. "All the foil is off the champagne."

Marianne walks away from them. Danny is folding up the wooden chairs that were set up under the trees, for older people who might not be able to stand through the whole ceremony.

Dougie watches him, grinning; he can't help because of his hurt arm. "How did you hurt it, anyway?" Marianne asks, standing right in front of him.

"In a bar. This guy said I was sitting too close to him, and I said it was public property, and he hit me."

"Like this?" she asks, punching his hurt arm. "Or was it more like this?" Punching harder.

He stares at her, not even moving to protect himself.

"I don't know what goes on in this family," says a voice behind them, and Marianne turns to face Flora's mother, pale and red-eyed in her shiny gray mother-of-the-bride dress. "But it's sick. And it's got to stop."

She waits for someone to answer her. Over her spangled shoulder, Marianne sees Chase trying to catch her eye, shifting from foot to foot. "Excuse me," Marianne says, and goes over to him.

He puts an arm around her and bends his head to speak into her ear. "Zip's back. He's upstairs, waiting. I'm going to take him to the hospital."

She nods.

"Will you be here when I get back?" The anxiety in his voice is new.

"Sure," she tells him, and then she goes back to help Danny finish folding the chairs. Doug is trying to help now, too, using his good arm to stack the chairs on the grass. He makes the stacks too high; at one point, the top chairs start to slide off, but Marianne catches them and settles them uneasily back into place.

ROSEMARY WILLEY

The House We Pass Through

It is just a family. I am just a girl
posing at the mirror in a flowered
cotton shift, combing back my short hair,
deciding whether I'm beautiful. I know
the creak in the floor by heart and the hiss
of the door behind me, drawing itself shut.
When I cross the room, my brothers and sisters
don't care, their faces turn to the TV set.
From under the basement stairwell I see
my mother lifting laundry from the dryer,
my oldest brother behind her, white as a sheet.
The *slosh, slosh* of the washer muffles my mother's
words. *Buck up, buck up,* I hear her warning.
The next of us is about to be born.

Love

An insane bald homeless white man on a children's bicycle
rode over to where my girlfriend and I were walking and he said,
"Couldn't find a real woman?"
My girlfriend is black.

Okay, tell me—what does one do in this situation?
The man must have been at least sixty, but he was very muscular,
wearing no shirt, and carrying a hammer on his belt—
in other words, potentially dangerous.

Me, I'm a children's book editor.
I stand 5´ 4˝ and weigh in at 120 lbs.,
and I look about thirteen years old.
My hobbies include playing the penny whistle.

The thing is: I wanted to kill the guy.
So, as a compromise, I told him I thought he was disgusting.
Which caused him to circle back and say
"I wouldn't stick my dick in that."

At this point I pictured myself
taking his slippery bald head in my hands
and bashing it against a nearby apartment building
till I'd rendered his bloody skull of its obscene contents.

But instead, I only cursed him
then went with my girlfriend to a diner
where, over french fries, we had an exasperating conversation
about racial issues, and the best way to deal with them.

She thought I should have ignored this man,
just like I should have ignored the black man who spit on us

in the park, or all the black people who made rude remarks
as we walked down the street hand in hand.

We are no longer together.
Now I watch a lot of baseball,
ride the bus at night a lot
and stare at black women.

We Are Not Like Other People
& Do Not Need Them

There is a danger in living;
it is why we file our nails
instead of our wrists;
it is why we label things away.
It's why when we think of mass
transit we think of concentration
camps, we think of people packed
like oysters in the little shells
we're allowed, the brine & hope
of forgiveness like fortified shorelines
or western ideas of what it means
to be forsaken.

I often think of your dark beauty,
the waves like a forbidden song
against the planks of a pier
no one thinks about: the face
in the yearbook, the scuttled boat
& its peer, the sigh
announcing him/her.
Blinded by the whole light
we reach for the insouciant
moon to pull it back.
The whole damn thing
can go off course
but memory is bold.
We hold on for
dear life
& row.

Sunglasses & Hats

When we thought of the future
it was wonderful & well-lit.
The sky could hold anything.

He chants about Beelzebub, Black Arnie & his
mismatched angels, about supplicants
& warblers that always tag along:
a talisman against the learning
the church leaves out.
He is on one leg & braced, a shout
that ignores its cure, tossing dice
on a straw stage.
One hand raised in succor, the other
for supper he tumbles into the churning,
a victory medal to the masses
who huddle under banners that proclaim
us sensible & proud, living in an age
that could have bewildered.

For sunglasses & hats, worn in the
proper shades to provide full
figured relief from the
sun & its increasingly sullen
glare at our skin,
can deter if not repair
the churliest of rays.
We plunge into the sea,
scrubbing from our backs the
misery of growths we cannot see.

Therefore, do not believe.

BOOKSHELF

Recommended Books · Winter 1994–95

THE BLUE HOUR *A novel by Elizabeth Evans. Algonquin Books, $17.95 cloth. Reviewed by Janet Desaulniers.*

In Elizabeth Evans's first novel, *The Blue Hour,* the narrator, Penny, recounts her teenaged years with both a child's twitchy, anticipatory dread of the future and an adult's sorrowful knowledge of the past. The book peels away the decorous lies of 1959 America, revealing people desperately caught up in the urge for upward mobility. Men throw everything they have into what they believe to be solid American concerns—meat, asphalt, doors—staking the financial and emotional lives of their families on bronze-colored Jaguars, sticks of furniture, skylights in the master bedroom. Penny's family teeters just on the cusp of this urge. Her father, cursed with the gambler's logic that only extreme risk brings extreme payoff, finds the percolating fears of his wife and two daughters such a terrible distraction that he insists on only happy words and pretty songs, as if the women were parakeets.

Penny, all eyes and ears, charts the strain. She hears the catch in her father's voice as he proclaims faith in his shady business partner, and she notices each step of her older sister's movement away from the family and into the relief of her own secrets with boys and drugs. Most wrenching, though, is Penny's witness of her mother, Dotty, a woman who gave up the dream of a career in medicine to find herself cleaning out the drain at the bottom of the refrigerator. Increasingly exhausted by the strict limits of her life and by the required devotion to her hapless husband, Dotty becomes a picture of barely swallowed hysteria.

Ten-year-old Penny doesn't make that mistake. She knows that love exists in this family, and she knows, too, that either the free or squandered expression of that love will be her legacy. "That's not nice! Be nice to Mom, Dad!" Penny shouts in the middle of one of her parents' quarrels. When her father, startled, says, "I think I know how to be nice to your mother," Penny cries out,

"Just kiss her!" The triumph of this book is that adult consciousness returns sorrowfully, gently, to the past, where it translates for us Penny's terrible need, the need of every child: If only we would be happy, then they could be happy, too.

Janet Desaulniers's short stories have appeared in Ploughshares, The New Yorker, *and other magazines. Her first collection is forthcoming from Knopf.*

THE GREAT FIRES: POEMS 1982–1992 *Poems by Jack Gilbert. Knopf, $20.00 cloth. Reviewed by David Daniel.*

One of the joys of reading Jack Gilbert's *The Great Fires* is how stubbornly it celebrates the courage and beauty found in the most habitual, commonly shared moments of our lives. This will come as news to no one who is a Gilbert reader. Take "The Abnormal Is Not Courage," the most famous poem from his 1962 Yale Series winner *Views of Jeopardy,* which gives this definition of courage: "The marriage, / Not the month's rapture. Not the exception. The beauty / That is of many days. Steady and clear. / It is the normal excellence, of long accomplishment." The same theme is developed as well, if somewhat more personally and provocatively, in 1982's *Monolithos,* but *The Great Fires* represents a culmination. It is Gilbert's best and most consistent book, and is easily among the best collections of the year. While it charts familiar territory, sometimes even in familiar ways, it nevertheless reaches greater, more satisfying depths.

Elegies for Gilbert's wife, Michiko Nogami, which run throughout the book, provide the background against which the other poems come to life. These spare elegies have a quality reminiscent of a classical ruin, equally remarkable for what it is as for what it is no longer. In "Married," one of the two poems here from Gilbert's very rare, limited edition, *Kochan,* the poet crawls around his apartment after his wife's funeral, searching for some of her hair: "For two months got them from the drain, / from the vacuum cleaner, under the refrigerator, / and off the clothes in the closet. / But after other Japanese women came, / there was no way to be sure which were / hers, and I stopped. A year later / repotting Michiko's avocado, I find / a long black hair tangled in the dirt." Later, in "Michiko Dead," the weight of her absence is no longer surprising, but, rather, it becomes familiar, something beautifully burdensome, "like somebody carrying a box / that is too heavy," which he shifts from one position to another "so that / he can go on without ever putting the box down."

The book's most powerful poems are not, however, the elegies, but the ones that accept ruined landscapes—of Pittsburgh or Greece, or of marriages failed or failing—and that begin to find new life there, free of nostalgia but born of the past's deep roots. In "The Forgotten Dialect of the Heart," discussing the inaccuracy of language, Gilbert dreams "of lost / vocabularies that might express some of what / we no longer can." Then, when thousands of mysterious Sumerian tablets appear to be merely business records, he wonders, "But what if they / are poems or psalms? My joy is the same as twelve / Ethiopian goats standing silent in the morning light. / O Lord, thou art slabs of salt and ingots of copper / / What we feel most has / no name but amber, archers, cinnamon, horses and birds." In this book, little by little, Gilbert deciphers the mysterious tablets of our lives, and what he imagines of them is—if not astonishing—alive, sad, funny, and, yes, courageous.

IGLOO AMONG PALMS *Stories by Rod Val Moore. Univ. of Iowa, $22.95 cloth. Reviewed by Don Lee.*

Selected by Joy Williams for the 1994 Iowa Short Fiction Award, Rod Val Moore's *Igloo Among Palms* proves to be a highly original and engaging collection. Set in dusty towns on both sides of the California-Mexico border, the seven stories are peopled by odd, refreshingly innocent characters who daydream of change, but feel doomed to inaction and inconsequence.

Tod, delivering dry ice to a supermarket, encounters a hitchhiker and a teenaged girl, both of whom end up having more romantic potential than Tod could ever imagine for himself. Tyrsa, a Mexican schoolteacher, impulsively sneaks across the border and accepts a job as a housekeeper, then tries to rescue the daughter of a door-to-door evangelist. Catalina's parents own a motel in Mexico, where her mother's hobby is découpage, pasting magazine cutouts onto plywood to make clocks, and where her father, a Peruvian weight lifter who insists on being called The Inca, drives around town with speakers on top of his car, broadcasting advertisements. Claudette and Tina decide to move in together, only to discover, after a bat drowns in their swimming pool, a basic incompatibility. Brad and Tyler, students at India Basin College, set out for Mexico on a marijuana-induced lark, but get stranded at a campground, where they are convinced to sell their plasma.

Not all of these stories are entirely successful as individual pieces, but collectively they build in power. Moore's language is lyrical and at times incantatory, and he has a true gift for the comic and bizarre, creating a primeval but beautiful desert landscape in which misperceptions lead to whims and a desperate desire not to squander opportunities, exemplified in *Igloo Among Palms*'s best story, "Grimshaw's Mexico."

Covering roughly twenty years, the story first shows Grimshaw, a police sergeant, driving his wife to a clinic in Baja for allergy treatments. Intent on exploring the town and taking in the culture, he instead falls asleep, and upon awakening, finds that his six-year-old son, Timothy, playing baseball with some Mexican kids, has miraculously learned to speak Spanish with near fluency. However, Timothy grows up to be an academic disappointment. Grimshaw encourages him to make a sheet-metal skeleton for a high school science fair and ultimately, pathetically, takes over the project. Later, after retiring from the police force, Grimshaw returns to Baja with his wife. Sitting in an outdoor café, he watches an old man with a battery demonstrating his ability to withstand the electricity fed into two rods he holds in his hands. Suddenly, Grimshaw stands up and grabs hold of the rods: "Here at last, he thought, squeezing the metal, here was the chance to do as Timothy had done, to play some Mexican baseball, to learn to speak Spanish in a moment, and he waited for the furious shock that would stand his hair on end, turn his body transparent, as in a cartoon, to show the glowing, aching skeleton underneath."

MERCY SEAT *Poems by Bruce Smith. Univ. of Chicago, $9.95 paper. Reviewed by David Rivard.*

In the epigraph to a poem called "Self-Portrait as Ornette Coleman," Bruce Smith quotes the legendary saxophonist as saying of Spike Jones's treatment of an old standard, "He'd take 'Stardust' and run a saw through it then come back with the melody." This might also describe Bruce Smith's method in his third—and best—book of poems, *Mercy Seat:* the tune that Smith riffs off of is the history of anyone "growing up white male North American" in the fifties and sixties, and the buzz saw he uses is a style of expressive disarrangement honed by a slyly formal sense of craft. *Wicked,* we used to say growing up, and that's the way I think of Bruce Smith's work.

The disturbed and disturbing energy of *Mercy Seat* comes in part from the tension between Smith's ear for American idiom and the orchestrations against which he casts that idiom. The off-kilter swervings through varied intonations, the humming into lyrical flight, the montaging of image and metaphor, all are held together by elemental concerns for song. The effect is akin to that of stride piano—the left hand laying down a kind of bass line while the right flies out on the melody, a melody made out of slurred notes and bent phrasings. One of Smith's favored formal devices is the rhymed couplet: "What was the question, the tune, the equation / of the new physics? What was the variation, / / the chord change, the rumor, the murmur / against the maker? / / We went to the funeral in 4/4 time / to the slow Napoleonic drums and the urge of Rome, / / but we returned in 2/4 to *Didn't He Ramble?* / to hold ourselves and scuffle and tremble" ("Against the Maker"). The result is both mournful and jubilant, like a second-line strut.

The source of Smith's expressiveness feels more cultural than personal, shaped by our times—our parents and family more or less as real in the inner-life as Vietnam, race riots, James Brown, the SALT talks, Quaker Oats, Attica, etc. There is a moment in "The Sandwiches," one of the book's many sonnets, where Smith makes a little secular theology out of eating at a football game while watching "the great Bednarik, MacDonald, and Jurgenson" and seeing "what our god was"—I confess to being thrilled by seeing Sonny Jurgenson and God inextricably linked. For Smith, "our faces come from movies, the dim business / of action lit and twisted." Not just movies, *Mercy Seat* makes clear, but from all the machinery of the age of information and entertainment. In one sense, the book is about the birth of this age.

The book is also about birth in the making and remaking of self-identity out of the weather of our times: "He would be either a standard of living or a cold war. / He would be either a peaceful ocean or, in the worst / version of their plan he would be a wall shadow and strontium / 90 falling from the unprotected heaven with the rain . . . ," Smith says in "Self-Portrait as Foreign Policy." In a poem called "In the City of Brotherly Love," he shows himself as one of two brothers listening in the dark to a radio, who "crossed the borders of oblivious / and white, then got back with the news of the Black Jesus / / and the *please, please, please* and the standard mama-jama / alto badness we received from WHAT in Philadelphia." And in the book's sweetest and most moving poem, "Mercy," he waits for the birth of his daughter "in the unscrubbed father room / with the Jamaican and Puerto Rican (What island / was I?)," his daughter about to be born in a hospital "across from the Audubon Ballroom where Malcolm X was shot," born into a country where "our paradise is our bondage is our paradise," where "what I must do is hold / you, nervous, then let you go, but not / yet, little white girl, my Moses."

Mercy Seat is filled with poems of consequence and intelligence, dark humor, and a vision as strange as the 1990's. Bruce Smith's voice is singular and true.

David Rivard's collection, Torque, *was published in the Pittsburgh Poetry Series. He teaches at Tufts University and Vermont College.*

COCONUTS FOR THE SAINT *A novel by Debra Spark. Faber and Faber, $22.95 cloth. Reviewed by Ann Harleman.*

Bright, wistful, and brash, Debra Spark's first novel, *Coconuts for the Saint,* snares the reader instantly. On the surface it is a mystery story: Who is Sandrofo Cordero Lucero, and what is he hiding? Beneath lies another mystery, *the* mystery, the one we all live out. "This is the world," says one of the novel's several narrators, "the one we're so desperate not to leave. Our attachment seemed beautiful, but an endless puzzle. Why? Why do we want to stay here?"

The question of Sandrofo's identity is first raised by Maria Elena, the woman to whom he has proposed marriage. Sensing that he is not what he claims to be, and unable to make him reveal himself, she turns to his three teenaged daughters from his previous marriage for help. Melone, Beatriz, and Tata—identical triplets with very different views on life—take turns, along with Maria Elena, in narrating the life-changing events that Maria Elena's quest sets in motion.

The deeper mystery, the mystery of our attachment to the world and to each other, is one which all of these characters, in their different ways, pursue. The novel's prologue shows Sandrofo bringing his five-year-old daughters from New York to Puerto Rico. It is a kind of exile: the girls' mother, who died in childbirth, grew up in San Juan, but neither they nor their father have ever been there before. They reopen a bakery owned by the dead woman's family and begin to weave themselves into the life of the town. Of course belonging cannot be constructed, but father and daughters seem—until the advent of Maria Elena—to have achieved a satisfactory illusion.

As for the world's worthiness of such efforts, Spark's language greets us from the first page with lavish gifts for the ear and eye— indeed, for all the senses. Her maximalist prose seems made of color and light, like Puerto Rico itself. It creates "a world too leafy to think of baldness," whose inhabitants enjoy pastries filled with guava jelly, chocolate sandwiches for breakfast, shortbread with hazelnut cream. The inhabitants themselves are beautifully revealed in the gestures they make. We see Rayovac, Melone's aspiring lover, "kneeling in a bag of flour and scooping his hands up under her apron, her flower print dress"; Beatriz swimming naked in the rain, her nipples "shriveled and tightened like old fruit"; the girls' grandmother scattering bread crumbs on her daughter-in-law's grave so that birds will come. In this heightened atmosphere, the gathering desires of Spark's characters envelop us like a gorgeous fever.

Not only the physical world but the world of the heart, as well, is bared and burnished by Spark's prose. The novel's structure, with its self-contained, story-like chapters and alternating narrators—though occasionally creating a centrifugal effect that undermines the plot—allows its characters to reveal themselves and to comment wryly on each other and on the novel's themes. Maria Elena's outrageous observations on love and sex, Tata's view of sisterhood, Sandrofo's version of fathering, Beatriz's wintry openness to grief—these are all great pleasures. Would we ever have thought of punctilious behavior as "emotional duct tape," or of lying as an attempt to "unravel the sweater of fate"?

The novel picks up speed in its last third; dramatic events and revelations, although they occur a bit too precipitously, nonetheless bring the plot to a satisfying resolution. The mystery of Sandrofo Cordero Lucero, whose alias includes the words for "heart" and "light," is solved; the mystery of our beautiful attachment to the world, happily deepened.

Ann Harleman's collection of short stories, Happiness, *won the 1993 University of Iowa John Simmons Award. She teaches fiction writing at the Rhode Island School of Design.*

LATE EMPIRE *Poems by David Wojahn. Pittsburgh Poetry Series, $10.95 paper. Reviewed by Diann Blakely Shoaf.*

"History has to live with what was here," wrote Lowell in one of his offhand but authoritative pronouncements. In an age emerging from the New Critical hegemonic concept of literary and historical tradition that Lowell was schooled on, David Wojahn, in his fourth collection, *Late Empire,* adds a necessary codicil: history must also live with what *is* here.

Hence, a poem like the book's title piece, which leaps from the eighteenth to the twentieth century then back again. The poem's subjects include the launch of the world's first hot air balloon near Versailles, the World War II bombing of Dresden, the stage antics of the post-punk Screaming Blue Messiahs in a London club, and an apocalyptic dream, in which "the terrible / incinerating light has come, the dead / / frozen black to the wheels of their cars." These fugal, associative moves between past and present, between history and autobiography, and between canonical and popular culture are made with virtuosic assurance throughout *Late Empire.* Some pieces, like "Human Form" and "Emanations," which along with the title poem are written in triadic stanzas and a rangy, expertly varied pentameter, use the musical structure of statement and counterstatement in the space of forty to sixty self-contained lines. Other impressive moments in the book come in sonnet sequences, a form Wojahn has made more disjunctively capacious since his collection *Mystery Train's* "rock and roll" series. "White Lanterns," a crown of sonnets detailing the death of

Wojahn's mother from cancer, and "Wartime Photos of My Father" comprise *Late Empire*'s second and third sections, these sequences striking for their technical mastery, their relentless self-questioning, and, ultimately, for their tough-minded empathy.

Wojahn's memories of childhood—beginning in the early 1960's with bomb shelters and duck-and-cover drills in classrooms—broaden and wheel through *Late Empire* like Yeats's widening gyres, their spirals containing films, popular music, and accounts of recent demagogues like Idi Amin and Khomeini. Interlaced are chronicles from other times, such as those left by seventeenth-century Dutch sailors, Pavlov, mid-century American pornographers, Ryszard Kapusinski, and an ecclesiastical commission investigating an occurrence of the stigmata.

Like Yeats, Wojahn writes with the shadowy thrill of the eschatological in his pulse, but *Late Empire*'s final poem, "Workmen Photographed Inside the Reactor," hints that such a thrill is to be resisted. Imagining himself as one of the space-suited technicians charged with cleaning up Chernobyl, Wojahn writes: "One last breath, last glance at the trees, / Down the staircase to the pit. Each thought—/ the pike before me, stabbing at the gloom." If Yeats often cast himself as the Oracle of Thoor Ballylee, drunk on séances and embodying the world's collapse in a slouching beast, and if Lowell's dynastic tyrants in *History* are uncomfortably similar to his nihilistic poet-heroes, gazing summits to rubble, Wojahn offers a less self-glorifying, if riskier, alternative. We are to let that summit gaze *us* nearly to rubble, to stab at that gloom only after we have descended into its terrors: the writer of *Late Empire* exists to be conquered by the world in which he lives, not to be a latter-day conquistador of its territories, literal or metaphoric. A danger, of course, exists always in such an enterprise. Not all countries recover from occupation, and not all voyagers into evil's frozen heart emerge. But if Aspley Cherry-Garrand, who perished with Scott in Antarctica, is one of the genii of Wojahn's *Late Empire*, a collection which can truly be called major, another is Dante, who emerged from a place far worse than Chernobyl to see the hopeful gleam of stars.

Diann Blakely Shoaf is a frequent reviewer for the "Bookshelf." Her collection of poems, Hurricane Walk, *was published by BOA Editions in 1992.*

EDITORS' SHELF *Books recommended by our advisory editors.* **Rosellen Brown** recommends *The Stone Diaries,* a novel by Carol Shields (Viking): "A marvelously written, poignant, and funny chronicle of a Canadian woman's life. This has the wit and authority of a nineteenth-century novel with a knowing contemporary slyness to it." **Philip Levine** recommends *The Dear Past & Other Poems,* a collection by Janet Lewis (Robert L. Barth): "These poems were written over a period of seventy-five years, from 1919 to 1994, and though they demonstrate a variety of strategies and structures, they are brought together by the extraordinary precision and clarity of Lewis's artistry, as well as by the poet's incredibly intense love of all that grows and lives and the landscapes that define us. Hardy would have loved these poems." **Joyce Peseroff** recommends *The Waters of Forgetting,* a poetry collection by Barry Seiler (Univ. of Akron): "Seiler brings together poems that spring from the tensions between memory and forgetting, past and present, the daily and the eternal. He connects public moments with personal history in lyrics that are bittersweet and fresh." **M. L. Rosenthal** recommends *Complete Poems,* a collection by Kenneth Fearing (National Poetry Foundation): "It's a special joy to have the work of this wry, sardonic, thoroughly alive Catullus of the American Depression once more in print. (Edward Dahlberg compared him with Corbière—and that was true, too.)" **Lloyd Schwartz** recommends *Offspring,* a novel by Jonathan Strong (Zoland): "Reading a novel by Jonathan Strong is like finding a secret treasure in a dark attic. 'Every unhappy family,' Tolstoy wrote, 'is unhappy in its own way.' *Offspring* is the tale of a peculiarly happy family that lives in an unhappy world which can't understand—or stand—their happiness. Disturbing, haunting, and very moving, this book kept me awake long after I finished it. I'd call it a masterpiece." **Maura Stanton** recommends *Crazy Woman,* a novel by Kate Horsley (Ballantine): "This first novel is an imaginative tour de force. By using the form of a 'captivity narrative,' Horsley incorporates surreal events successfully into a realistic narrative. The result is dazzling language and vivid characters."

EDITORS' CORNER *New books by our advisory editors.* **Donald Hall:** *Death to the Death of Poetry: Essays, Reviews, Notes, Interviews* (Univ. of Michigan), a collection of writings in defense of the vitality of contemporary American poetry. **Philip Levine:** *The Simple Truth* (Knopf), a collection of new poems, of which Harold Bloom says, "I wonder if *any* American poet since Walt Whitman himself has written elegies this consistently magnificent." **Tim O'Brien:** *In the Lake of the Woods* (Houghton Mifflin/Seymour Lawrence), a novel about a Minnesota politician who searches for his missing wife and confronts long-suppressed memories of My Lai. **Charles Simic:** *The Unemployed Fortune-Teller: Essays and Memoirs* (Univ. of Michigan), a collection of memoirs, essays, and journal entries that illuminate the origins of Simic's poetry. **Maura Stanton:** *Life Among the Trolls* (David R. Godine), a poetry collection that explores themes of love and hate. **Richard Tillinghast:** *The Stonecutter's Hand* (Godine), a collection of poems that extols the virtues and pleasures of travel. **Tobias Wolff:** *In Pharoah's Army: Memories of the Lost War* (Knopf), a memoir of Wolff's Vietnam years.

POSTSCRIPTS

ZACHARIS AWARD *Ploughshares* and Emerson College are proud to announce that Tony Hoagland has been named the 1994 recipient of the John C. Zacharis First Book Award for his collection of poems, *Sweet Ruin*. The $1,500 award—which is funded by Emerson College and named after the college's former president—honors the best debut book published by a *Ploughshares* writer, alternating annually between poetry and short fiction.

Tony Hoagland was born in 1953 in Fort Bragg, North Carolina. The son of an Army doctor, he grew up on bases in the South and around the world. After "barely surviving" his adolescence in southern Louisiana, he attended and dropped out of several colleges, picked apples and cherries in the Northwest, lived in communes, followed the Grateful Dead, and became a Buddhist. All the while, poetry was a passion for Hoagland, but he admits he was a late bloomer. "I was incredibly untalented," he says. "It took a long, long time for me just to get competent. When you're a student of poetry, you're lucky if you don't realize how untalented and ignorant you are until you get a little better. Otherwise, you would just stop."

Hoagland finally graduated with a bachelor's degree from the University of Iowa, then received his M.F.A. in creative writing from the University of Arizona. Subsequently, he worked in the poets-in-the-schools program, and has since made a livelihood teaching English composition at a dozen different institutions, from California to Kalamazoo.

He has published his poems and essays about poetry in *The American Poetry Review, Harper's, The Harvard Review, Parnassus,* and elsewhere, and his work has been anthologized in *New American Poets of the Nineties, The Best of Crazyhorse,* and *The Pushcart Prize*. In addition, he has received two fellowships from the National Endowment for the Arts, as well as one to the Provincetown Fine Arts Work Center.

Sweet Ruin won the 1992 Brittingham Prize in Poetry and was published by the University of Wisconsin Press. In reviewing the book for *Ploughshares,* poet Steven Cramer wrote about Hoagland's work: "His muscular, conversational lines sprint from narrative passages to metaphorical clusters to speculative meditations, and then loop back, fast-talking and digressing their way into the book's richly American interior.... Hoagland's is some of the most sheerly enjoyable writing I've encountered in a long time. With his 'foot upon the gas / between future and past,' he  dazzles and rants, praises and blames, and in his keen noticings and reflections, he 'accomplishes pleasure' on almost every leg of the journey. It's deeply gratifying to be along for the ride."

Hoagland currently lives in Waterville, Maine, and teaches part time at Colby College and at Warren Wilson's M.F.A. program in writing. He is halfway through a new collection, in which he is making a conscious effort to widen the scope of his poetry. "It's a real concern of mine to write about culture in a larger way, to try to make personal discourse merge with or be contextualized by cultural crises."

The Zacharis First Book Award was inaugurated in 1991, when David Wong Louie was the winner for his short story collection, *The Pangs of Love.* Allison Joseph was honored for her poetry collection, *What Keeps Us Here,* in 1992, and Jessica Treadway won the award for her story collection, *Absent Without Leave,* in 1993. The award is nominated by the advisory editors of *Ploughshares,* with executive director DeWitt Henry acting as the final judge. There is no formal application process; all writers who have been published in *Ploughshares* are eligible, and should simply direct two copies of their first book to our office.

LOUISA SOLANO We want to salute Louisa Solano, who is celebrating her twentieth year as the owner of the Grolier Poetry Book Shop in Harvard Square. Throughout that time, Solano has been an invaluable and supportive resource for poets and poetry readers alike, holding book signings, running a reading series, and administering the Grolier Poetry Prize. The Grolier, of course, has become an institution in itself. The small, one-room shop is the *only* all-poetry bookstore in North America. Too often, when people speak of contributions to the country's literary heritage, they point only to writers, critics, and publishers. But Louisa Solano, as a bookseller, has been singularly generous and influential in her quest to sustain the importance of poetry.

The Grolier Poetry Book Shop is located at 6 Plympton Street, Cambridge, MA 02138. The telephone number is (617) 547-4648. The Grolier also offers mail-order services, which may be retained by dialing (800) 234-POEM or by faxing (617) 547-4230.

ALL I WANNA DO Poet Wyn Cooper, who teaches writing at Marlboro College in Vermont, is listed as one of the co-songwriters of Sheryl Crow's hit single "All I Wanna Do," but the collaboration came about in the most unlikely, serendipitous manner possible. For a year, Crow and a group of musicians met every Tuesday at a studio in Pasadena, with the idea of composing a new song by the end of each evening. One night, Crow brought some music she liked, but she hated the lyrics she'd written. Looking for inspiration, her producer went across the street to a bookstore. He randomly selected ten books of poetry and bought them for Crow, who holed up in the bathroom with the books. She was drawn to Wyn Cooper's poem "Fun" in his collection, *The Country of Here Below,* which was published by Ahsahta Press in 1987. Crow changed some phrases, deleted a few lines, and added a refrain, and a song was born. "All I Wanna Do" became a number-one single, Crow's album went platinum, and Cooper began receiving royalty checks—unimaginable rewards for a poem he wrote ten years ago.

FIONA MCCRAE Fiona McCrae, the erstwhile editor at Faber and Faber, Inc., has been appointed Director of Graywolf Press. While at Faber, McCrae signed up an impressive list of writers, many of them from Boston and Cambridge, including Sven Birkerts, William Corbett, Askold Melnyczuk, and Debra Spark. We will miss McCrae's influential presence in New England, but we look forward to her tenure at Graywolf, which founder Scott Walker made into arguably the best small press in the country.

Ploughshares · Winter 1994–95

ALLY ACKER's first collection of poems, *Surviving Desire*, has just been released through Garden Street Press. She is also the author of *Reel Women: Pioneers of the Cinema* (Continuum), as well as the director of ten accompanying film documentaries. She lives in McLean, Virginia. CHRISTIANNE BALK's second book, *Desiring Flight*, won the 1994 Verna Emery Poetry Award. She has been the recipient of an Ingram Merrill Foundation grant, an Alaska Council on the Arts travel grant, and a degree with honors in biology from Grinnell College. She lives in Seattle, Washington, with her husband and daughter. BRUCE BENNETT, a member of the group of writers who founded *Ploughshares,* is the author of several poetry chapbooks and three volumes of poems, most recently *Taking Off* (Orchises, 1992). "Gertrude's Ear" is from his ongoing collection of fables, *Animal Rites.* He teaches English and directs creative writing at Wells College in Aurora, New York. ROBERT BRADLEY has published poetry and criticism in *The Gettysburg Review, Southern Poetry Review, Seneca Review, Poetry East, The Antioch Review, Plainsong,* and *Painted Bride Quarterly.* He lives near Nashville, Tennessee. WENDY BRENNER's story collection, tentatively titled *Large Animals in Everyday Life,* won the Flannery O'Connor Award and will be published by the University of Georgia Press in late 1995. She lives in Gainesville, Florida. BRUCE COHEN is Director of the Counseling Program for Intercollegiate Athletes at the University of Connecticut. Recent poems have appeared in *The Greensboro Review, The Ohio Review,* and *TriQuarterly.* He lives in Coventry, Connecticut, with his wife and three sons. MICHAEL DALEY's books include *The Straits, Angels,* and *Yes Five Poems.* He has work in recent issues of *Kansas Quarterly, Cumberland Review, Manoa, The Nebraska Review,* and *The Tampa Review.* He teaches philosophy and poetry classes at Mount Vernon High School in Washington State. STUART DISCHELL is the author of *Good Hope Road* (Viking Penguin). He was recently awarded with a Pushcart Prize. STEPHEN DOBYNS is the author of eight books of poetry and sixteen novels. His most recent book of poems is *Velocities: New and Selected Poems, 1966–1992* (Viking), and his latest novel is *Saratoga Backtalk* (Norton). He teaches at Syracuse University and in the M.F.A. program at Warren Wilson College. JAMES DUFFY was born in New York City in 1960. The recipient of an M.F.A. in writing from Vermont College in 1994, he has been employed as a gas station attendant, farm worker, foot messenger, and professional housecleaner, and now works as a mental health counselor in New Rochelle, New York. DENISE DUHAMEL's *The Woman with Two Vaginas,* a book of poetry based on Inuit folklore, is available from Salmon Run Publishers. She is also the author of *Smile!* (Warm Spring, 1993) and the forthcoming *Girl Soldier* (Garden Street,

1995). Her work can be seen in *The Best American Poetry 1994*. **ALICE B. FOGEL** is the author of two books of poetry, *Elemental* and the forthcoming *I Love This Dark World*. Her poems have appeared regularly in literary journals and anthologies, including *The Best American Poetry 1993*. She teaches writing at the University of New Hampshire. **IAN GANASSI**'s poetry has appeared in numerous periodicals, including *The Paris Review, The Yale Review,* and *Pequod,* and is forthcoming in *The Gettysburg Review*. He is seeking a publisher for his recently completed manuscript. He is a freelance writer, musician, and teacher, and lives in New Haven, Connecticut. **ELIZABETH GILBERT** had her first fiction publication last year in *Esquire,* and is now a contributing editor at *Spin* magazine. Currently at work on a novel, she lives in New York City. **MICHELE GLAZER** works in the Oregon Field Office of The Nature Conservancy. Her work has been published or is forthcoming in *College English, Delmar, Field, The Georgia Review, Ironwood, Ploughshares, Poetry Northwest,* and *Sonora Review*. She has completed one manuscript and is working on another. **H. L. HIX** was a winner of the 1994 Grolier Poetry Prize. His second philosophy book, *Spirits Hovering over the Ashes: Legacies of Postmodern Theory,* is forthcoming from SUNY Press. **TONY HOAGLAND**'s first collection, *Sweet Ruin,* won the Brittingham Prize in Poetry and was published by the University of Wisconsin Press in 1992. He teaches at Colby College and in the M.F.A. program at Warren Wilson College. **CHRISTINE HUME**'s work has appeared most recently in *Mudfish* and *The Indiana Review*. She recently relocated to Atlanta, Georgia, from New York City. **GISH JEN**'s short stories have appeared in *The New Yorker, The Atlantic Monthly, Best American Short Stories,* and numerous anthologies and journals. She has been the recipient of fellowships from the Bunting Institute, National Endowment for the Arts, Massachusetts Artists' Foundation, Copernicus Foundation, and Guggenheim Foundation. Her first novel, *Typical American,* was nominated for a National Book Critics' Circle Award. She lives in Massachusetts. **JESSE LEE KERCHEVAL**'s story collection, *The Dogeater,* won the Associated Writing Programs Award for Short Fiction in 1987. Her novel, *The Museum of Happiness,* was published by Faber and Faber last year. She teaches in the creative writing program at the University of Wisconsin. **DAVID KIRBY** is W. Guy McKenzie Professor of English at Florida State University. A recipient of grants from the National Endowment for the Arts and the Florida Arts Council, he is the author or editor of sixteen books, including *Saving the Young Men of Vienna,* which won the University of Wisconsin's Brittingham Prize in Poetry. **SHEILA KOHLER** has published a collection of short stories, *Miracles in America,* and two novels, *The Perfect Place* and, most recently, *The House on R. Street,* all with Knopf. Her story "The Mountain" appeared in *Prize Stories 1988: The O. Henry Awards*. **NORMAN LALIBERTÉ**'s paintings, banners, drawings, prints, sculptures, and murals have been exhibited in over three hundred galleries and museums throughout the world. His work is in the permanent collections of sixty museums, including the Smithsonian Institute's Renwick Gallery, the Detroit Institute of the Arts, and the Institute of Contemporary Art in Boston. Born in Massachusetts and raised in Montreal, Laliberté currently resides in Massachusetts. "Picture at an Exhibition" measures 5′ x 9′ and was created with oil stick on board in 1982. JOHN LOUGHLIN is a carpenter who teaches creative writing part time at Elgin Community College in Illinois. He has poems appearing in *Sonora Review* and *Colorado Review,* and is at work on his first collection. MELISSA MONROE lives and teaches in Boston, Massachusetts. She is working on a sequence, "Lives of the Robots," dealing with the mechanical replication of human activity throughout history. Other poems from this sequence have appeared in *The Kenyon Review.* C. L. RAWLINS has received a Stegner Fellowship and a Blanchan Memorial Award, as well as the Forest Service Primitive Skills Award for wilderness training. A recent prose book, *Sky's Witness: A Year in the Wind River Range* (Henry Holt, 1993), will be followed by *In Gravity National Park,* his second book of poems. LIAM RECTOR's book of poems, *American Prodigal,* was published recently by Story Line Press. He directs the graduate writing seminars at Bennington College. G. TRAVIS REGIER's stories and poems have appeared in a variety of publications, including *Harper's, The Atlantic Monthly, Amazing Stories, The American Scholar, Ploughshares,* and *Poetry.* He recently left his position teaching writing to study philosophy and literary theory at Ohio University. DAVID RIVARD is the author of *Tongue,* winner of the Starett Poetry Prize. He teaches at Tufts University and in the M.F.A. program at Vermont College. DAVID ROMTVEDT's books include *A Flower Whose Name I Do Not Know* (Copper Canyon, 1992), a National Poetry Series winner; *Crossing Wyoming* (White Pine, 1992), a historical novel; and *Yip: A Cowboy's Howl* (Holocene, 1991), a poetry collection of parody and homage. A new book of poems, *Certainty,* is forthcoming in 1995 from White Pine Press. He lives in Buffalo, Wyoming. MARY RUEFLE is the author of three books of poems, the latest of which is *The Adamant,* which co-won the Iowa Poetry Prize in 1989. She lives in Bennington, Vermont. PETER JAY SHIPPY teaches at Emerson College. His poems and reviews have appeared in *The Denver Quarterly, Epoch, Ploughshares,* and other magazines. MAURYA SIMON is the author of three volumes of poetry: *The Enchanted Room* (Copper Canyon, 1986), *Days of Awe* (Copper Canyon, 1990), and *Speaking in Tongues* (Gibbs Smith, 1991). She has two new books of poetry appearing in 1995: *The Golden Labyrinth* (Univ. of Missouri) and *Weavers* (Blackbird). She teaches creative writing at the University of California, Riverside. TOM SLEIGH is the author of three books of poetry: *After One* (Houghton Mifflin, 1983), *Waking,* and *The Chain* (Univ. of Chicago/Phoenix Poetry Series, 1990 and 1996, respectively). He currently holds a three-year Individual Writer's Award from the Lila Wallace–Reader's Digest Fund. PRISCILLA SNEFF has published poems in *The Yale Review, Sulfur, Partisan Review, The Southern Review,* and elsewhere. In 1994 she received an NEA fellowship in poetry. She teaches composition and poetry writing at Tufts University. PETER VIRGILIO's poems are from the manuscript-in-progress *Dreamobiles.* He lives in the North End in Boston. CONNIE VOISINE has held a variety of jobs, including migrant field worker, waitress, welder's assistant, and teacher. She has published her work in *The Threepenny Review, Phoebe, New York Quarterly,* and elsewhere. She is finishing a poetry manuscript about her upbringing on the French-Acadian border of Maine. **JASON WALDROP** lives on a ranch near Sacramento, California. His poems and stories have appeared in *New Letters, Poetry Northwest, The Plum Review, Sequoia,* and *Beloit Fiction Journal.* His works-in-progress include a full-length screenplay and a collection of poems. **JOAN WICKERSHAM**'s fiction has appeared in *The Hudson Review, Story, Best American Short Stories 1990,* and *The Graywolf Annual Eight.* Her first novel, *The Paper Anniversary,* was published by Viking last year. **ROSEMARY WILLEY**'s poems have appeared or are forthcoming in *Poetry, Crazyhorse, The Green Mountain Review, The Indiana Review,* and other journals. She is finishing her first manuscript, *Intended Place.* She lives in Evanston, Illinois. **JONAH WINTER**, a clarinet instructor, children's book author, used car salesman, horseman, and exotic male dancer, lives in a tin lean-to on the edge of San Francisco, where he is currently finishing his latest collection of poems, *Lyrical Ballads.* **RODNEY WITTWER**'s poems have been published in *The Antioch Review, Cream City Review, Hayden's Ferry Review, The Madison Review, Ploughshares,* and other journals. He lives in West Medford, Massachusetts, and is the Director of Operations for The Hub Group–Boston, a transportation logistics company.

INDEX TO VOLUME XX

Ploughshares · A Journal of New Writing · 1994

Last Name, First Name, Title, Volume/Issue/Page

INDIANA UNIVERSITY

55th annual

June 25-30

workshops featuring:

Bernard Cooper   **Martin Espada**

Thomas Gavin   **William Matthews**

Jean Thompson   **C. D. Wright**

Al   Young

**IU Writers' Conference * Indiana University * Ballantine Hall 464
Bloomington, IN   47405 * 812-855-1877**

WRITERS' CONFERENCE

New York University

Master of Arts Program in Creative Writing

PERMANENT FACULTY
E. L. Doctorow • Galway Kinnell • Sharon Olds

FACULTY FOR 1994-1995

POETRY

Robert Bly
Derek Mahon
Marilyn Nelson Waniek

FICTION

Wesley Brown	Jessica Hagedorn	Mona Simpson
Peter Carey	Susannah Moore	Michael Stephens
Debra Eisenberg	Agnes Rossi	Mario Susko

Fellowships and work-study grants are available.

Application deadline is January 4, 1995.
For more information about our program,
call **(212) 998-8816** or write

NEW YORK UNIVERSITY
A PRIVATE UNIVERSITY IN THE PUBLIC SERVICE

*New York University is an affirmative
action/equal opportunity institution.*

**New York University Graduate School of Arts
and Science,** Department of English, M.A. Program in Creative
Writing, 19 University Place, Room 200D,
New York, N.Y. 10003

Attention: Charity Hume, Director

1994 Lannan Literary Awards

Simon Armitage
POETRY

Eavan Boland
POETRY

Jack Gilbert
POETRY

Linda Hogan
POETRY

Richard Kenney
POETRY

Edward P. Jones
FICTION

Steven Millhauser
FICTION

Caryl Phillips
FICTION

Stephen Wright
FICTION

Jonathan Kozol
NONFICTION

Lannan Foundation honors writers of
distinctive literary merit with an award of $50,000 each.

THE NOBEL LAUREATES OF LITERATURE

APRIL 23-25, 1995
ATLANTA, GEORGIA

PANEL DISCUSSIONS, READINGS,
CONVOCATION DINNER

PRESENTED BY

 THE ATLANTA COMMITTEE
FOR THE OLYMPIC GAMES
CULTURAL OLYMPIAD

Atlanta 1996
TM © 1992 ACOG

FOR REGISTRATION INFORMATION, CALL 404-224-1835

Ploughshares

Submission Policies

Ploughshares is published three times a year: usually mixed issues of poetry and fiction in the Winter and Spring and a fiction issue in the Fall, with each guest-edited by a different writer. We welcome unsolicited manuscripts. Our reading period is from August 1 to March 31 (postmark dates). All submissions sent from April to July are returned unread. We adhere very strictly to the postmark restrictions. Since we operate on a first-sent, first-read basis, we cannot make exceptions or hold work.

In the past, guest editors often announced specific themes for issues, but we have recently revised our editorial policies, and we will no longer be restricting submissions to thematic topics. You may still submit for a specific guest editor, but since our backlog is unpredictable, and since staff editors ultimately have the responsibility of determining for which issue a work is most appropriate, we do not recommend delaying a submission in order to target a particular guest editor. In short, if you believe your work is in keeping with our general standards of literary quality and value, submit it at anytime during our reading period. If a manuscript is not suitable or timely for one issue, it will be considered for another.

Please send only one short story and/or up to five poems at a time (mail fiction and poetry separately). Stories should be typed double-spaced on one side of the page and be no longer than thirty pages. Novel excerpts are acceptable if they are self-contained. No nonfiction (personal essays, memoirs) will be considered during this reading period; unsolicited book reviews and criticism are never considered. Poems should be individually typed either single- or double-spaced on one side. (Sorry, but "Phone-a-Poem," 617-578-8754, is by invitation only.)

Please do not send multiple submissions of the same genre for different issues/editors, and do not send another manuscript until you hear about the first. Additional submissions will be returned unread. Mail your manuscript in a page-sized manila envelope, your full name and address written on the outside, to the Fiction or Poetry Editor. (Unsolicited work sent directly to a guest editor's home or office will be discarded.) All manuscripts and correspondence regarding submissions should be accompanied by a self-addressed, stamped envelope (S.A.S.E.) for a response.

Expect three to five months for a decision. Simultaneous submissions are amenable to us as long as they are indicated as such and we are notified immediately upon acceptance elsewhere. Please do not query us until five months have passed, and if you do, we prefer that you write to us, indicating the postmark date of submission, instead of calling. We cannot accommodate revisions, changes of return address, or forgotten S.A.S.E.'s after the fact. We do not reprint previously published work. Translations are welcome if permission has been granted. We cannot be responsible for delay, loss, or damage (usually postal-related). Never send originals or your only copy. Payment is upon publication: $10/printed page for prose, $20/page for poetry, $40 minimum per title, $200 maximum per author, with two copies of the issue and a one-year subscription.